Connected

Book Five of the Mike Romano Novels

Joe DeCicco

Internationally read award winning author of
Angel with a Gun

The author may be contacted directly by E-mail at romanonovels@yahoo.com

Printed in the United State of America Charleston, North Carolina for

 **Associates Publishing Co.**

Hampstead, N.C. 28443

Published: November 1, 2016

Library of Congress Control Number: 201590223

ISBN 10: 0-9897227-5-9
ISBM 13: 978-0-9897227-5-9

Other Mike Romano Novels

Angel with a Gun (2006)
Worms in the Apple (2010)
Dirty Baggs (2011)
Bulldog (2014)

For Mom who was so very proud of
my novels

Police Officers may drive black and white cars,
however what goes on in their job is a lot of gray.

Arik Matson…*Minnesota Police Officer*

CHAPTER ONE

Detective Mike Romano brought his car to a stop at the intersection of Bath Avenue and Bay 22nd Street in Brooklyn New York. Sitting diagonally on the northwest corner was the entrance to the 64th Precinct.

The building looked clean and neat with two granite bands around the red brick facade. He especially liked the dignified, granite portico that reminded him of ancient Rome. *Modern centurions in an Italian neighborhood; how fitting. Not at all like some of the sterile buildings in Manhattan. Crap, what is all that noise on the next block?*

One side of the street was lined with several double-parked cars. Many of them had "the look" of unmarked Department autos. Against the station house curb were marked and unmarked diagonally parked cars. *This place is jammed, where can I park? I'm sure not gonna walk for blocks.*

***

One block away, a schoolyard was jammed with about one hundred protesters, most of them minorities, a drama was about to unfold.

Separating the chanting group from the local residents was a line of uniformed police officers that stretched across most of the enclosure.

Facing the crowd, was a rotund black man dressed in a dark blue velour jogging suit, his jacket open proudly displaying a large gold medallion hung around his neck.

Several men attempting to assure his safety accompanied the round blue ball. He was shouting through a bullhorn agitating the crowd.

"This is another case of our brothers and sister being ignored by the racist New York City Police Department." The crowd roared.

He continued, "Just a few days ago, a young black man was murdered right here in this neighborhood; he was killed in broad daylight. He was murdered because of the color of his skin, beaten unmercifully, and shot. The police claim that they have not been able to make much progress in the investigation regarding the death of this young brother."

There was another roar from the crowd as they began swaying back and forth.

"Are we gonna stand by and wait until they are good and ready to do something about it? I say no! The establishment would like us to leave this area quietly. I say no! Our presence here will force them to take action. We are going to march in force."

The crowd cheered.

"We are going to the scene of the crime and show our presence until those do nothing, racist police arrest his killers. Are you with me?"

The speaker then moved to lead the group out of the schoolyard. The situation became volatile and there were lots of angry voices and pushing and shoving followed by an anguished cry.

***

In front of the station house was a uniformed police officer. Mike turned put his flashers on and turned off his engine. Then he exited the vehicle, and walked over with his shield in his hand.

Quickly glancing at the man's nametag, Mike spoke, "Hello Officer Ferguson, Detective Romano, I'm looking for a place to park. What's considered okay around here?"

"Detective, anywhere across the street is good. You can double park using your Command issued vehicle ID; but only if you can see another ID and know that you're blocking another cop's car and not a potentiality irate civilian. Down on the next corner is a catering hall with a wide sidewalk on the side street. The space can hold two cars and the owner likes cops and make sure your ID is on the dash. Double parking is only tolerated on Bath Avenue, not the side streets."

"Thank you."

Walking back to his car, Mike heard, rather than saw, what sounded like boisterous activity. He turned to face the direction of the sound and saw a school on the next street, Benson Avenue.

Seeing nothing, Romano returned to his car, ignoring the sound and climbed in and drove to the catering hall that the cop indicated.

The sidewalk was empty; slowly he drove over the curb and parked alongside the building.

Just before entering the station house, Mike asked, "Hey, Ferguson, just what could those kiddies be doing in the schoolyard at this time of the morning to make such a racket?"

"I don't know if you heard about the young black kid that was killed a few days back. That's what the noise is about. There is a gathering of some marchers and that crazy loudmouth, gold chain wearing community activist, Reverend Wallace. They're protesting the handling of the case by the Department."

"That fat shit stirring idiot?"

"Yeah, he's there with his followers and news media. There's been no arrest in the case yet and he's accusing the Department of racial bias. We have lots of men and cars lining the demonstration route from the school and five blocks to the scene."

"Sure sounds like a potential problem."

"Not to worry, we have lots of cops around. I'm sure they'll fill you in upstairs."

"Later, and thanks." Mike shook Ferguson's hand before he entered the building.

***

The interior of the ground floor of the Six-Four was typical of the older station houses; the walls painted with the City's typical pea soup green, report room on the right side of the building opposite the high old-fashioned oak desk. Mike thought it had some style to it.

The lone occupant was an old, seasoned, uniformed Lieutenant. Alongside the usual three flags, American, City, and NYPD, behind the Desk Officer, the observant detective was able to look into a small room. He could see a small desk and several shelves holding a variety of boxes and a plethora of manila and plastic envelopes.

Every command had a property room and Mike assumed that was it because the edge of the opened door was quite thick and sheathed in sheet metal. It looked high security with a pull handle and what appeared to be the type of lock usually found on a cell door.

Sharing the platform the desk sat upon was a smaller desk with a teletype and computer terminal. There was an officer sitting on ground level staffing the command's switchboard.

Mike approached and flashed his shield as he spoke, "Good morning Officer, Detective Romano here. Where would I find the Squad office?"

After a quick glance at Mike, the young cop said, "Take the stairway behind me; one flight up, you can't miss it. Squad is at the head of the stairs."

"Thanks he replied as he slowly climbed the stairs.

***

From the landing, he could see an old wooden placard over the closed door that announced, *Detective Squad*. On the upper half of the dark green door was a large pane of translucent pebbled glass, below it, in a redundant statement, large block letters, *PDU,* were stenciled in black, an acronym for Precinct Detective Unit. Multiple layers of paint gave the door the appearance of impregnable except for the glass panel.

Mike knuckled the door twice as a courtesy and walked in. He was pleased to find that the first room he entered was not drab: even though it was obviously a shop worn office, the walls were reasonably clean and painted a muted shade of cream or what designers call almond. Five windows on two walls filled the room with natural light in addition to the usual industrial fluorescent fixtures.

There was also a small dark oak bench just inside to the right of the door, *a public waiting area.*

Romano enjoyed the ambiance of the low-blistered barrier with a swinging gate, painted the deep color of NYPD green, that protected three desks from the general public. It was obvious to him that they too, were far from new, yet remained highly serviceable.

To the left of the room's entrance was a detention cage constructed of heavy gauge rippled wire with two slide bolt locks. The cage was painted the institutional pea green color he had come to dislike.

Seated behind the first and third desk were men typing reports; the second desk was unattended.

The occupant of the first desk looked up; the almost ebony color of his skin highlighted his big bright smile and impish eyes.

Rising out of his chair and extending his hand the detective spoke first, "Hey, you must be the new man we're expecting. Romano, isn't it? The Six-Four Squad welcomes you. I'm Charles Wilson, and I'm old school."

Boy, I like this guy already.

The man at the far desk looked like the stereotype of an Italian detective; overweight, jacket off with his shirt sleeves rolled back, suspenders, shoulder holster; tie loosened, collar unbuttoned, full head of jet-black hair. Making the picture complete, he wore a big red stoned pinky ring that glistened when he moved his right hand. He continued what he was doing without bothering to look up.

Wilson extended his hand, Mike grasped it and responded, "First name is Mike. You must be psychic and my last name is Romano."

"Nah, I saw it in the telephone message book. That guy back there is Frank Pigro."

At the mention of his name, Frank's head snapped up, "Hey Romano, nice to see another Italian here. We gotta stick together; after all, it is Bensonhurst." Without ceremony, he returned to his paperwork.

Mike thought, how appropriate, *pigro means pig in Italian. I don't know if I'll like this guy.*

Returning his attention to Wilson he asked, "Charlie, seems like there's a storm brewing around the corner. The uniform man on the corner says it's about a controversial case that's still open. What goes?"

"Yeah, we have the case; it's three days old and still hot as a Saturday night pistol. Frank is assigned to it along with a guy from Sixth Division Homicide over in Coney Island, but we all worked on it the first twenty four hours. We refer to it as the *Robinson Case* because of the victim's last name. It's coming along slowly."

"It must be a pain in the ass."

"Yeah, but it comes with the job."

"Well, is the boss in? I should introduce myself."

"Yeah, come on, I'll be your guide. Follow me."

Romano followed Charlie past Frank and into an open door located on the left rear wall of the room. Inside was a smaller office; on a long table against one wall was a single chair, a computer terminal and printer. Opposite that were a window, blocked by several filing cabinets; a television set and video player sat atop other cabinets in one corner leaving little free room.

Directly opposite the room's entrance was a closed door. Charlie knocked. "Sarge, the new man, Mike Romano is here", he shouted.

"Come in guys."

Charlie opened the door and stepped aside, allowing Mike to enter the room alone as he backed away and closed the door.

Inside were two desks, facing each other. The man occupying the desk to Mike's left, rose with his hand extended, as the door clicked shut.

Mike thought, *must be one of the two bosses.*

The man looked like he was chosen by a Hollywood director to play the part of a tough detective squad commander and looked more like a *wise guy* than a cop, but he exhibited a ready smile.

"It's an extreme pleasure to meet you Detective Romano and welcome to our office. I'm Sergeant Anthony Scala, Tony to most of the men in this office. Sergeant Timothy Fitzpatrick is the C.O. Right now, he's on vacation. He left the day after our latest homicide. You'll meet him when he returns."

"I think I'll be happy here. It's my pleasure."

Tony pointed to the empty chair alongside the other desk, "Grab a seat Mike, and let's chat awhile."

"Sure thing, thanks."

"You go first, any questions?"

"Yes. Have I been assigned to this working squad and what is the big thing going on down the block?"

The sergeant smiled as he spoke, "Direct aren't you?"

"Sorry"

"Well, you haven't been assigned to this or any other squad as your working team, not yet anyway. That will be Sergeant Fitz's choice when he gets back from vacation. Right now, the office is two men short; one is on medical leave and should return soon. You are to replace a man that just made Sergeant, Detective Benjamin Arcola. Benny's a good man, we're sorry to lose him. Today this team does their turn around tour, tomorrow they come in for a four by twelve."

"As to your second question, three days ago there was an unfortunate incident within the command. Three black kids were here to buy a car that they saw advertised in the classified ads of a Brooklyn paper. Out in front of a building where the car was parked some local boys, all white Italians or Latinos, were hanging out with some girls. One of the girls, a Latina, told her boyfriend, an Italian, that she didn't like the way one of the car buyers looked at her. Words were exchanged and it escalated into a big fistfight. By the time it was over, one of the boys, a kid named Lemar Robinson was dead. He was struck over the head with a baseball bat that was found at the scene."

"Holy crap, any arrests?"

"Not yet and that's the problem. That's the reason for all the noise on the next street. There's going to be a march to the scene of the incident demanding justice; it's being led by a pain in the ass, an ugly overweight, jaw flapping, community activist, Theodore Wallace. The man claims to be an ordained minister. Uniform is handling it all. Frank, who you probably met outside when you walked in, has the case along with a special group working out of Sixth Homicide."

"Are you expecting any trouble?"

"Outside of him polluting the air we breathe, I hope not. We usually have no racial strife in this command area even though it's mostly Italian but the locals are not happy about the demonstration at all."

"Okay. I got it. We stay put. When do I catch cases? How does that work?"

"There's a list on a clipboard outside. As the complaints come up to us for review, the senior man in the squad assigns the 61's by rotation and gives it a case number. That's all there is to it. You work your cases, do a DD-5 within two days, a follow up within fifteen days and another if necessary, explaining why it should be left open; thereafter, every fifteen days until a closing one. We like arrests whenever possible. Naturally, each time you go out on one of your cases or do any work on it, you must report what you did on a DD-5, even if it's less than fifteen days.

Do you have any questions?"

"No Sarge. Thanks. Guess I'll go back inside, take the empty desk and get started. I'm sure Charlie and Frank can answer any other questions for me."

As Mike rose, Tony also did and once again,

extended his hand, "Welcome Michael. I have a good feeling about you."

"Thank you, Sir, for the complement."

"Sarge or Tony will do Mike."

***

Charlie spoke first as Mike sat down at the vacant desk in front of Frank.

Sam turned and asked, "Well Mike, what did you think of Tony? Can you work with him?"

"Sure can; he looks like a tough guy from Brooklyn but he seems to be good people. Why, is there something I should know?"

"Not at all; I'm just interested in your opinion."

"Well Charlie, let's get to it. How do I catch a case?"

To his rear Mike, was aware that Frank pulled the assignment clipboard from the wall.

"Don't worry Romano. There's plenty of work here. You can start today. Soon as Charlie gives you a couple of 61's to work on (complaints referred to detectives), I'll put you on the sheet in proper order of catching."

At that point, Charlie rose up from his desk and went over to the office in basket that sat on a small file cabinet next to "The Cage."

After withdrawing complaint forms sent up to the Squad from the prior shift, and quickly counted them.

"We've got seven today. That's two each." Then, apparently without reading them, he separated them into three stacks. Taking the first two for himself, he dropped three on Mike's desk, "Sorry, counted wrong," and gave the remains to Frank.

Pigro spoke, "Okay guys, call out the numbers and the alleged crime. I'll log 'em in. Mike, you're first."

In turn, the cases were recorded.

Charlie quietly spoke to Mike, "Romano, the first DD-5 (follow up report) is a must within three days. The squad CO wants another in eight days, regulations require fifteen days after the first one. Fitz is a royal pain in the ass about the eight day 5's, don't miss it."

"No problem", was Romano's response.

Mike spread his three 61's out on his desk and began to read them. One was for Violation of Order of Protection that was referred to the squad because the violator wasn't present when the patrol officers took the report. The second was for Extortion, and the third was for Grand Larceny, the complainant stating that an employee stole merchandise but could not prove it. He chose the Extortion to begin his first official investigation in the Six- Four and scratched some notes onto a lined legal pad. He would come back to the others.

Romano had been in his new command only about twenty minutes. He had just poured himself a cup of black coffee in the break room and returned with it to his desk, ready to sit down to call the complainant when it happened.

The shrill sound of sirens screamed up from the streets followed by shouts and mayhem climbing their way up the stairway from the station house lobby.

Someone bellowed, "Take it easy. Keep the crowd outside and get this guy up to the squad. Put him into the cage."

The pounding of multiple persons trudging up the stairs, accompanied with more orders being barked escalated, as the turmoil got closer to the office.

Within seconds, in stomped a uniformed Lieutenant

and two uniformed officers, one of which was a small
female accompanied by two men in street clothes. The
group surrounded a tall, light haired, white male, that
was obviously handcuffed and moved forward like a
crippled spider.

Alerted by the ruckus, all three squad members
stood; ready to do battle if necessary.

Charlie, closest to the cage, was shouted at by the
Lieutenant, "Open the damn cage and put this shithead in."

The old school cop jumped to comply just as Sergeant
Scala raced into the room, "What the hell is going on out
here?"

The cuffed man was thrown into the cage, the door
closed and bolted, as two uniform officers assisted a very
large, extremely overweight black man into the office.

The grumbling man was wearing a Maroon velour
jogging suit over a white shirt. Around his neck was a very
large gold medallion, his signature jewelry. He was also
holding what looked like a towel against the left side of his
chest just below his shoulder and it was soaked with blood.

The highly animated maroon ball was the infamous
Reverend Theodore Wallace, known activist and racial
agitator, followed by two very large men from his entourage.
They never entered the office, instead each man silently
assumed a post on either side of the entrance doorway.

The lieutenant ordered, "Get this man into your
break room and make him comfortable, EMS is on the
way."

Charlie chuckled, "Someone finally tried to kill that
shit stirring asshole. He makes me ashamed to be Black."

As Wallace was hustled past the cage, he looked in
and stated, "That's the cracker mother fucker who tried to

kill me."

Drunk as he could be and still remain upright, the prisoner sat on the bolted down bench against the rear wall. He began to slump sideways looking dazed and confused.

Seconds later, an EMS team hurriedly entered the office and began attending to Wallace.

Sergeant Scala demanded, "Okay, okay, who's taking the collar and subsequent investigation?"

The uniform Lieutenant, pointed to the nametag on his chest and spoke authoritatively to Scala, spitting out the following; "My name is Lieutenant Schwartz and I'm the commanding officer on the scene. The Boro Command and One PP have been notified."

Putting his hand on the shoulder of the female cop, he snapped, "This officer made the actual arrest and recovered the knife. She is officially the apprehending officer and a detail from one PP will take the collar. The office of Deputy Commissioner of Public Information will handle all notifications. One of their detectives will catch the case. Understood?"

Tony Scala was not used to being spoken to in that tone and snapped back, "I'm not a rookie Loo, get a grip on yourself and calm down. This is my office and you're a guest here. In case you can't remember, the Detective Division is separate from Patrol. You have no authority here."

Mike thought, "*My kind of guy...Tell him Sarge.*"

Obviously embarrassed by Scala's response, the lieutenant went inside to check on Wallace and use the telephone on the spare desk.

Tony gathered his detectives to the rear at Frank's desk. "Listen guys don't interfere with this fiasco, just stand ready in case a fist fight breaks out. This could develop into a pile of shit."

Collectively, the men all nodded.

The office became a beehive of activity.

In walked a booted cop carrying a ton of equipment. Someone had called for a highway officer to administer a *"drunk test"* even though the perpetrator wasn't driving.

Scala and his men quickly agreed that the arrogant lieutenant was probably responsible.

Another idiot claiming to be "Press" was arguing with Wallace's gorillas at the door and attempting to get inside. Two uniform cops interceded and successfully turned him away.

Just as the room settled down a bit, the EMS personnel and Wallace came out of the break room. The senior Med Tech announced, "He's fine. The wound is not deep or life threatening; we put a dressing on it and are transporting him to the hospital to be checked out. Make way please."

As Wallace approached the office doorway, his two men stood aside allowing Wallace and the Med Techs easy egress.

Lieutenant Schwartz pointed to two uniform men, "You and you escort them; one of you in the ambulance, the other follows in a car. Allow no media people near Wallace. Call for backup if necessary once at the hospital. Go!"

The highway cop began to setup his equipment in the vacated room, a video camera on a tripod and a breathalyzer.

The lieutenant then turned to Scala, "I'm leaving a uniformed officer here to witness the video. You and your men keep everyone out of here until we're ready to move the perp. Is that understood?"

"Sure. Now get out we have work to do," was the

quick retort from Scala.

Once the office was relatively quiet, the highway cop began to act as if his equipment was giving him trouble. "Hey Sarge," he called. "Please try to get some coffee into this guy while I check out why my equipment is acting up. I need him to understand me when I speak to him. Something to eat would help too."

To no one in particular Scala ordered, "One of you make a fresh pot of coffee and someone go across the street and get this guy a ham and Swiss on a roll. It should help absorbed the alcohol."

Charlie grabbed the coffee pot and Mike scooted out to get the sandwich. Frank sat at his desk shuffling papers.

When Mike returned, he found Charlie attempting to get the perpetrator to drink some coffee. The guy was having trouble understanding him. Charlie gave up.

Before Mike could try to get the poor sap to take the sandwich, Charlie Wilson asked, "Hey, Highway, why a drunk test for this guy. It's obvious that he's soused to the gills."

"The lieutenant in charge asked for it. He must have figured that stabbing someone like Wallace would go bad for the guy and maybe proving how drunk he was would help in his defense. You know, like he didn't really know what he was doing and shit like that."

Charlie chuckled, "Maybe the nasty lieutenant ain't so bad after all. I don't like Wallace either. Hurry up with your test and video, we'll hold off on the food and coffee. You gotta finish before the suits get here from downtown. Mike and I will help you with him if necessary."

Just as the highway man was wrapping up his procedure, two suits from downtown walked in. The obviously senior man demanded, "Who is the man in charge here?"

Tony Scala heard the demand and exited his office. "Sergeant Anthony Scala here. Who are you?"

"Detectives Burton and Wiskinski; we're from the Deputy Commissioners Office. We're here to process the prisoner. Is he ready?"

"From our point of view he is. Ask the highway cop."

The highway officer, closely watching the exchange Answered, "Soon as he finishes his coffee and sandwich, you can transport him, but give him a few extra minutes. He's just realizing what he did."

"Fine, you have five minutes and then we take him no matter what."

Mike noted that exactly five minutes later, Burton took the remnants of the sandwich from the perp, now known as James Kelly, and handcuffed him.

As they exited the office, Charlie Wilson, who was standing next to the doorway, held Kelly's arm for a split second.

"Next time do us all a favor and use a bigger knife. Good black folks don't like that ass hole either."

Burton saw no humor in the remark.

Mike commented, "Hey Charlie, aren't you afraid the Puzzle Palace will hear what you just said?"

Fuck them too. He is bad for black people and I am a black man; in case you haven't noticed.

Scala ordered, "Okay, guys back to work. You all have cases to work on."

CHAPTER TWO

With the Wallace assailant gone, the office personnel attempted to return to their normal routine.

Sergeant Scala, knowing the shit was about to hit the fan, grabbed a portable radio and went to the Boro Office before he was summonsed.

While Frank and Charlie were handling their workload, Mike began to digest his first few cases in the new command. *Well, my first day here certainly began with a bang.*

Romano telephoned two of his complainants in an effort to gather more information. There was no response to either call. He then turned his attention to the extortion report, determined to work the case until he arrested the perpetrator. Just as he labeled a manila folder to officially open his investigation, he was interrupted.

Police Officer Jack Paterson hurriedly walked in escorting a pretty, raven-haired woman, in her early 30's; the look on her face was as if she had just seen a ghost. Charlie was in the break room and Mike's was the first occupied desk. Patterson settled the woman into the chair intended for complainants alongside Mike's desk and tried to reassure her.

Mike spoke first, "Hello, ma'am," and smiled at her. He looked at the cop's nametag. "Officer, Paterson, the lady appears to be in distress. How can I help?"

"This is Mrs. Rachael Gold. She claims that she was kidnapped just a short time ago. I did a complaint report and brought her right upstairs. Can you take her statement and open a case?"

Seeing her distress, Mike directed his answer to the distraught woman. "Sure can. Mrs. Gold, first, can I get you anything; coffee, water or a cold drink?"

With quivering lips, she answered, "First, please call me Rachael. Mrs. Gold is for my children; I teach a Fifth Grade elementary school class,.."

She finally stopped shaking. "No thank you. Just catch the bastard. I don't think that I'll ever be the same. I thought my life was over."

Pigro's antenna deployed when he heard, "Catch the bastard," coming from a female and looked up. Frank was a notoriety junkie and always wanted the high profile cases. Rachael Gold was also very pretty. He couldn't resist.

"What do you have, Romano?" he asked as he rose from his desk.

Mike's bulldog gene automatically activated. He responded curtly with, "Relax. If I can't handle it or have questions, I'll call you. Let me do my job."

Charlie heard the tone of Romano's voice and quickly slid into the room. "Are you good on this one Mike?"

"Thanks, I have it."

Officer Paterson, obviously not wanting to watch two detectives argue, quickly left without a word.

Frank, taken aback by Mike's answer, just quietly slithered back to his desk without a word. Unable to give his attention to his own work, he leaned back and watched.

Detective Romano slowly took a deep breath and began, "Mrs. Gold, excuse me Rachael; please tell me everything you remember. Do the best you can. If I need clarification, we can go over that particular point again. Are you still sure that I can't get you something?"

"Yes, please, coffee black, if you have it. Thank you."

Charlie heard her and replied, "Coming up little lady."

***

Coffee cup in hand, Rachael took a sip and began her story.

"About an hour ago, I stopped at my bank in the Caesars' Bay shopping area at the end of Bay Parkway along the service road of the highway for some cash." She paused and put her cup down on the desk before continuing.

"Because it was broad daylight and I parked close to the entrance, I felt safe. Returning to my car, I unlocked the driver's door and settled into the seat. Without looking to my left, I tried to close the door but couldn't. When I looked, I saw this wild looking man. He was holding it open with his body."

Rachael began shaking again and reached to pick up her coffee and take another sip to regain her composure.

Mike encouraged her, "You're doing fine. Take a break and all the time that you need if necessary."

After a loud, deep sigh, she continued, "The man was holding a small revolver. It was black. I thought my life was over. I froze and thought of my family."

She shed a small tear before continuing. He ordered, 'Don't move or I'll kill you' and opened the rear door. After getting in, he climbed over the back and into the front seat. He ordered me to start the car, saying he would direct me to where we were going." She abruptly stopped talking.

"Are you okay? Please go on, if you can."

"Yes. He said that he wanted to go to Staten Island and that he had something to do there. I was terrified and asked what he wanted from me."

Between sobs, Rachael continued, "He answered that he wanted me to drive him and said, 'Don't make me hurt you.' I told him that I had money in my purse and that he could have my car. He only said, 'I want you to drive me.'"

After more coffee, she continued, "I told him that I was sick and to take everything but let me go. That's when he showed me his release papers."

Mike was surprised, "Release papers. What do you mean?"

"From his jacket pocket, he drew out a folded paper and slapped it into my hand. 'Here lady, look at this, I did time for Homicide. I just got out today and I'm on parole.' I looked at the paper and gasped, 'Oh my God', and he just smiled at me. There in black and white, was the word Homicide near the top."

"What else do you remember?"

"His name, it was Frank something. I think the last name was Spanish."

"You're doing great. Are you sure?"

"Yes, I'm sure. I asked him to let me go again. He refused saying that maybe we could do something together when we got the Staten Island. I made a decision right then and there to survive no matter what."

"How did you get away from him?"

"That's when I told him that I didn't have enough gas to get there and we had to buy some. He agreed and I started the car. He ordered me to drive along the service road of the Belt Parkway and when we came to the overpass at Cropsey Avenue, I pulled into the big gas station there. There was one guy in the garage part and another standing near the office."

Mike was fascinated by the strong woman and urged, "Please go on."

"I told him, 'You know that you have to pay for the gas first,' so I took my purse and I got out to pay the attendant. That Frank guy stayed in the car with his door opened."

After another sip of coffee, she continued, "He called for me to come back to the car. He was partially out, with one foot on the ground. He told me to let the attendant put the gas in, that's what he got paid for. I waved for the man to come over. As he did I planned my escape."

She had begun talking fast and Mike asked her to "Please slow down."

"I told Frank that the gas tank was locked and I had to pull the keys out and go open the cap for the attendant. I reminded him that he was in a hurry. It worked. He said okay. Soon as I had my keys and moved near the gas tank, I ran to the two gas station guys shouting, 'Help, help. He has a gun,' and ran behind one of the guys."

Mike asked, "Did he come after you?"

"No, maybe he was afraid. The gas station man was real big, at least 6'-3" and very broad. I stood behind him peeked around and saw my abductor running away toward the highway. The two attendants hardly spoke English and understand what I was telling them, but they all know how to count money. Finally, they let me use their phone to call 911. That nice cop and his partner showed up and asked if I was robbed. You know the rest."

Frank asked, "Is that at all?"

At that point, Sergeant Scala approached, "Mike, I heard most of that from the doorway, please come into my office."

Turning his attention to the complainant, Romano rose from his chair and said, "Excuse us for a minute Mrs. Gold."

***

"First, let me say, that was a good interview. You have the case, and that's an order. Second, I get a feeling that there is something left to tell. Do you believe her?"

"Why not?"

"This isn't like narcotics. It's quite a story, man with a gun and all. Maybe she's cheating on her husband and is pregnant. Next, maybe she'll say that she was raped to cover it up."

"Thanks Sarge, but I believe her. We can have her go over it again after she calls her husband if she didn't already do it. We'll see if the story remains unchanged. Okay?"

"I'll sit in and you work it. Go."

Back with his complainant, "Mike asked, Rachael, anything that you haven't told us? Did you notify your husband yet?"

"No Detective, I covered it all. I would like to call my husband now and have him meet me here. Is that okay?"

"Sure. Use the phone on my desk. Is your car here?"

"Yes; why?"

"I would like the keys and your permission to look it over while we wait for your husband. Maybe there's something that he left behind, some kind of clue."

"Sure. It's the green Saab, right out front."

"Thank you. Detective Wilson will stay with you."

Mike returned to the office carrying a red bandana. "Mrs. Gold, does this belong to you or your family?"

"No, it's not ours. That man wore one just like it. Where did you find it?"

"It was stuck in the rear seat cushion of your car. I'll assume that it belonged to the perpetrator and will voucher it as evidence. Later, I may dust your car for prints too."

Tony Scala nodded in agreement. He too, was now a believer.

Rachael phoned her husband.

Frank Pigro, for a reason known only to him, left the office at that point.

Mike, with a quick look at Scala, was actually asking his boss for permission to continue. Scala nodded.

Romano waited while the now shaking complainant finished her conversation and put the phone down. After a few seconds, remarkably she regained her composure.

Mike asked, "Mrs. Gold, Rachael, how much time do we have before your husband arrives? I would like to run through the entire incident back at the crime scene as it happened. Do you think that you are up to it?"

Scala, pleased with his new detective said, I'm sure Mrs. Gold would be happy to assist in catching that man. Take Charlie with you."

Rachael quickly answered, "Yes, let's catch him quickly before he hurts someone. My husband is at work in Manhattan and said he'll be here in about an hour."

"Thank you. Charlie, let's go and do this. Mrs. Gold, are you ready?"

"Yes gentlemen. Let's do this."

It took roughly forty-five minutes for Mike and Charlie to reconstruct the crime, step by step and location by location to assure accuracy of the reporting of Rachael's story. At the service station, Mike attempted to get statements from the attendants. They were both Pakistani immigrants and not able to speak English well. Both detectives thought that their lack of understanding was due to immigration status. It wasn't pushed because they did corroborate the complainant's account of the incident on the gas station.

Mike and Charlie drove their complainant to the Six Seven Precinct to look at the photos in the Ident-a-quick office where mug shots of most perps from NYC were accessible for viewing. They were classified by age, race, and crime and also cross-referenced by gender. Rachael was tired after half an hour and wanted to see her husband. Romano called the squad office to check if he had arrived. He was there anxiously waiting for her. Mike put her on the phone.

Rachael, after assuring her husband Bill, that the two detectives she was with were perfect gentlemen and patient with her, handed the receiver to Mike who then spoke to Gold, promising to bring his wife back there in less than an hour.

For another thirty minutes, Rachael looked at hundreds of more photos with negative results and pleaded to be taken to her husband.

Back at the squad office, Rachael and her husband, Bill, embraced unashamedly before he introduced himself to the two detectives and thanked them. Then he added, "Please gentlemen, call us the minute that you have him identified or arrested. Rachael and I are available if you need us to identify and prosecute the guy."

"We will, and I'll just hold your keys for the rest of the day and bring them to you after I check your car for prints. Is that good with you folks?"

***

Romano threw his whole being into the case. First he contacted New York City's main jail, the *Riker's Island Correctional Facility* and requested that a listing of all prisoners released anywhere in the system within the last two days to be sent via fax to the Six-Four desk officer. He also requested One Police Plaza to send out a tristate alarm to every police department in the area. He was looking for a young male; possibly Hispanic, fitting the description given by Rachael Gold. Mike thought *no sense in not covering all bases* and then he even included Pennsylvania. *I'll wait.*

By the end of the workday, Mike had recovered several latent prints from Gold's car. He properly processed, and vouchered them for identification to aid in the case. Later brought the keys to the Gold household and brought Bill back to retrieve his car.

Later that night, while having a quiet moment with his wife, Lillian, she asked about his day; he happily attempted to give her a lenghty synopsis of what had transpired.

Lilly was surprised, "Wow. I thought Bensonhurst was relatively quiet. You got involved with the stabbing of that big loud mouth, media grabbing, Wallace guy and a kidnapping. What will you do tomorrow, find Jimmy Hoffa?"

Just as Lilly was getting ready to leave for work the following morning, the telephone rang. She answered it and called upstairs, "Mike, It's your Sergeant; he wants to speak to you. Come on down."

After kissing his bride, he took the phone from her. "Romano. What's up Sarge?"

"Mike, Tony Scala. Come on in now and you're on the clock as of this phone call. There's been an incident in Staten Island that may be related to your case. Hustle."

"Quick as I can Boss. I'm on my way."

"What's up Mike, they found Hoffa?"

"No Lil, there's was an incident on Staten Island that may be related to my case. Gotta run, have a good day." He slapped her backside and ran upstairs to get ready.

Once in his office, Romano quickly introduced himself to two detectives who were working the tour, a salt and pepper team, Richard Levy and Sam Battle respectively. They both wished him a happy stay in the command.

Sitting in Tony Scala's office, Mike leaned the reason he was there.

"At 2030 hours last night, a lone female was shot by a male Hispanic in the parking lot of the Staten Island Mall. The victim gave a similar description of her assailant and was initially confronted by him in the exact same manner as Rachael Gold."

"Damn. What happened next?"

"The poor woman wasn't as slick as your complainant and panicked. She lunged forward to jump out of her car and was shot in the leg. The perp, according to her, was more startled than she was, giving her a chance to run. As she departed with a running gait, he fired again, hitting her behind the ear and knocking her to the ground. She was lucky. Both rounds entered and exited without any serious damage. She may have blacked out for a second and never heard the shooter run from the scene which he probably did because her car was still there."

"How is she?"

"Her wounds were, according to the responding detectives, from a small caliber revolver. She described the gun as black, just like your woman did. The call came to us from a Detective, Brian Caroll. He had received a call from an informant who saw the incident reported in an early morning newspaper and claimed to know the shooter. His name is Frank Islas and that he, Islas, was to report to his parole Officer today."

"Thanks Sarge. You are coming with me to the One Two One?

"Sure, I am Mike and looking forward to it. Let's go."

Romano and his boss jumped into one of the squad's Chevy sedans and almost flew into Staten Island. They used the bubble light and siren when necessary and covered the distance, nine miles between Bensonhurst, Brooklyn to Dew Dorp, Staten Island, in just over ten minutes.

Upstairs at the squad office, they were met at the door by an overweight detective, who identified himself as Brian Caroll.

The Brooklyn detective stopped and looked inside, beyond his bulk.

The bull working area had a gated entryway, but it lacked the ambiance of the Six Four's old style. There were six desks, Detectives sat at four of them. The squad's main room was twice the size of the Six Four's. Mike could see the Commanders office in the far right corner.

In the left rear corner was an alcove with real jailhouse type bars for detention of prisoners. Near the entrance door, also on the left, were two closed doors, one of which was likely the entrance to a lineup viewing room.

Detective Caroll cleared his throat before speaking, "Okay guys, let's get this party stared."

Mike did not like him straight off; he was arrogant, displaying the attitude of an old seasoned veteran that knew it all and considered himself, better than the invention of pantyhose. Cops called men him a hair-bag, usually not a complementary term.

Fat slob! Wonder if he's always like that or is it sour grapes.

Caroll wasn't the case officer, just annoying. He led them to Detective Jack Clayton, the assigned lead officer.

The two Brooklyn cops sat with Clayton and when over the parameters of their respective complaints' reports. Tony Scala listened in and kept Caroll from interrupting the case officers.

Jack had previously placed a call to the New York State Parole Office on Broad Street in Stapleton.

"Frank Islas is scheduled to make his first visit to a Parole Officer Reilly, at 1:30 that afternoon. I'd like to get him there if possible, controlled environment and all, but I doubt he'll show up. He can't be that stupid after what he did yesterday. Reilly will fill us in when we get there."

Mike answered the comment; "He showed my complainant his release paper. He's not the sharpest knife In the drawer for sure."

Tony Scala agreed that Jack and Mike would attempt to be at the office by noon in the event that for some odd reason, Islas arrived early. They didn't want his PO to be alone and then attempt to detain him, especially if Pagan was pack'n heat, if he showed at all.

Islas arrived twenty minutes early; both detectives were disappointed that he wasn't armed and he was placed under arrest without incident and brought back to the One Two One.

Normally, a line-up was the next step, but Clayton's complainant was still in the hospital. It was now necessary to substitute a photo lineup in her hospital room. Before they left, Mike contacted his complainant and informed her to be at the Staten Island command by 3:00 p.m. to view a lineup.

Clayton photographed Islas and set up a photo array for his victim to view, and with luck, identify the subject as the man who shot her.

Jack handed off his prisoner to Caroll, who was happy to be involved.

"Hey Brian, lock him in the holding cell and don't let him talk to anyone, including you. I don't want you screwing up my case."

Tony Scala, took a chair and got comfortable as the two detectives left for Staten Island Hospital to see the victim.

***

Walking up to the admissions desk, Jack and Mike flashed their identification; Jack spoke, "Detectives. Please tell us what room is Jane Lansing in."

The attendant responded, "Mrs. Lansing was assigned to room 510 but it says here that she is scheduled to be released. She may even be gone and it's not on my computer."

"Thank you," Mike replied as he turned to catch up with Jack.

Exiting the fifth floor, the men hurried to room 510. The room was a hive of activity.

Her attending physician was giving instruction to

her and her husband regarding post release care. Mrs. Lansing was behind a curtain with two nurses who were assisting her into street clothes. Another person, probably an orderly was bringing in a wheel chair and a set of crutches.

Jack addressed the physician forcefully, yet politely, "Detectives Clayton and Romano. We're here to speak to Mrs. Lansing about the incident that sent her here. Soon as she's dressed, please give us a few minutes alone with her. Everyone will have to step out except Mr. Lansing but he can't interact with her or he will have to leave too."

As the curtain was pulled back and the nurses stepped out and one of them spoke; "Doctor, we'll be right outside when you're ready to send the patient downstairs"

Jane Lansing was in her street clothes and propped up on the bed. "Good afternoon Detectives. I heard what you said. Did you find the man who shot me?"

"Ma'am, first, allow us to say that we are happy to see that you weren't more seriously injured."

Mike felt compelled to say, "That goes double for me ma'am."

Jack returned to business. "As to the man who shot you, we're not quite sure that we have him. Detective Romano is here from Brooklyn because of a similar incident in his command. He believes that he found his man."

The complainant winced and asked, "Two, my God, was the other person shot too?"

Romano answered, No, she escaped unharmed."

Clayton continued, "We would like to show you some photos and see if you can pick out anyone as your assailant. Do you think that you can do that?"

"Yes, I can gentlemen; do I look through a bunch of photos? Do you have them with you now?"

"Yes ma'am." He responded and then turned to Mike.

"Detective Romano, please hand her the three folders to look at."

Jack continued to instruct the complainant, "There are eight photos in each folder set into two rows of four each. Please take your time. Thank you."

After looking at the folders twice, Mrs. Lansing handed them back to Romano saying, "Sorry Detectives, I think I saw him but I'm not sure. What happens now?"

The Staten Island detective answered, knowing what he was about to say according to the book but sometimes necessary to help a complainant relax, "Are you comfortable enough to point out a maybe?"

"No Detective. I would not want to accuse the wrong man."

Clayton responded with, "Mrs. Lansing, we have Detective Romano's complainant coming over to my office for a line up at 3:00 this afternoon. Do you think that you feel strong enough to view that line up too?"

"I don't know, I'm still in pain and somewhat uncomfortable with the bandages on my head. You know how vain women are. Is there somewhere where I can see him and he can't see me? I don't want that vile man seeing me on crutches and all bandaged up."

"Not to worry ma'am. We are set up just like on TV, one way glass and he can't see or hear you at all. Besides, the bandages make you look like a hero tough guy. I'm sure your husband is proud of you."

Only then did Richard Lansing finally speak. "Detectives, thank you for making this traumatic event easier on my wife. Yes, she is a hero, my hero and I love her even more for standing up to that criminal the way she did."

He gave her a peck on the cheek and continued, "If she can stand while getting into our car, she will be there. We know where the New Dorp station house is."

"Ok, Mike, we did all we can do here. Let's go back and meet your complainant."

The two detectives excused themselves and left for the One Two One.

***

Upstairs in the squad office, Rachael and Bill Gold were waiting. Frank Islas and five other similar looking men were in place and ready for viewing while a uniformed officer secured the staging area.

Michael and his fellow detectives walked into the squad office. Rachel ran over and gave him a welcoming hug.

"Detective, you certainly know how to get things done. I can't wait to see the bum. I understand that there is another victim who was shot, is she coming too?"

Due to the serious of the moment, he answered very officially. "Yes ma'am, we think so. It depends on how she can move around. She should be leaving the hospital about now. Since you're here, we can start. You will view the men we prepared first. Do you need anything?"

Rachael squeezed her husband's hand hard as she answered, "No, let's get this over with."

Mike turned towards Jack Clayton, "Well my friend, here we go. Please lead the way."

Jack then turned to Bill Gold, "We'll be only a few minutes Mr. Gold. Please wait here."

Rachael Gold was introduced to Sergeant Scala, along with the squad's supervisor, Lieutenant Syms and Detective Caroll as the entire group entered the darkened viewing room. The subject didn't *"lawyer up"* so there was no defense attorney in attendance.

Tony Scala, wanting his man to get the credit, spoke first. "Mrs. Gold, Detective Romano will explain the procedure to you before we begin."

His next statement was, "Okay, Romano it's all yours."

There was the beginning of an objection from Jack Clayton as he opened his mouth to speak, but it never became fully formed words.

Mike guided his complainant to the center of the window and began, "Mrs. Lansing, when I tap on the window in front of you, an officer inside will raise the shade. You will then see several men who are similar in appearance to the description of the man you gave me during the interview about your abduction."

The nervous complainant interrupted, "But, what happens if I don't see him. Did you get that Frank guy?"

"We'll discuss that if it happens. Now, I'll ask you to take your time and look at the men. If you want to have them say something, quietly tell me and I'll convey the request. The men all have numbers. If you recognize someone, tell me the number of that person and we go from there. Okay?"

"Yes Detective. I'm so nervous I can't stand it but let's do it."

Mike knocked on the glass and the shade went up.

Instantly, Rachel exclaimed in what she considered a whisper, "Oh my God, there's the man, number two. That's him," Forgetting herself, she waved her hands and hit Mike's shoulder in celebration.

"Very good; now Rachel, please tell me why and how you recognize that man."

"That's the man who jumped into my car at gunpoint

and wanted me to drive him to Staten Island. That's him."

Mike tapped on the glass and the shade lowered.

"Thank you. You may step out now."

He then pushed the intercom on the wall. "Thank you all. Please relax and remain available. Officer, please return number two back to his cell. We have a positive identification."

Outside in the squad room, Rachael excitedly threw her arms around Bills neck. "He's in there. They got him, they got him."

Romano approached Rachael, thanked her and explained that he would call her to guide her through explain the next step in the process.

"Detective Romano, can I wait for the other lady?" I would like to support her."

"Jack, is there someplace the Gold's can wait a few minutes?"

Detective Clayton knew exactly what Mike was doing by preventing the complainants from meeting and answered, "Yes Mike, they can wait down the hall in the clerical office. We'll let the ladies meet as soon as we can. One of the guys will show them where it is."

Without ceremony, another detective escorted the Golds out of the room.

Minutes later, everyone's attention turned the doorway as Jane Lansing was slowly entering the office using a pair of crutches and an assist by her husband.

The wounded complainant was wearing a grey, loose fitting pants suit with her hair tactfully arranged in an attempt to cover the bandage on her head. She appeared excited as she hobbled in with an occasional wince. It was obvious to all that she was still pain.

Detective Clayton and Lieutenant Syms hustled to her side.

Jack Clayton spoke first, "Thank you so much for coming. This will make it easier on our end. If you identify the right man in the lineup, there may not be any further appearances needed."

Syms, slick as a campaigning politician said, "Here at the One Two One, we are so pleased that you didn't suffer any further injuries and we thank you for your dogged determination to help us bring your assailant to justice."

Tony Scala just shook his head at was what he thought was ingratiating remarks and smiled.

As Clayton and his boss explained the lineup procedure, Mike and Tony quietly watched, remaining silent.

Only when the group was about to enter the viewing room did Sergeant Scala speak to Clayton. "Detective, I'm sure that your lieutenant would not be upset if we witnessed your lineup. We'd like to come inside too. If you get a positive identification it will enhance our case."

Syms, waved his hand in a gesture of acceptance, "Quid Quo Pro, be our guest."

The then ordered another squad to collect the suspect and bring him into the lineup room.

Once the group, sans Mr. Lansing, was inside the darkened viewing room, the previous procedure began.

As the shade was lifted, Jane Lansing was so traumatized that she almost fainted. Jack Clayton caught her as she started to fall.

"Mrs. Lansing, are you okay? Is there something we can do for you?"

Syms ordered, "Someone get a chair and snap to it."

Once seated, without prompting, Lansing stated, "That's him, number five."

Clayton then ran through the questions; why, and what did the man do?

Jane answered every question put to her as clearly as Rachael Gold did.

Jack thanked her as Syms pushed the intercom, "ID positive, put that piece of crap back in his cage."

Brian Caroll, expecting positive results, had already brought the Golds in while Rachael Lansing was still viewing the lineup. They were in quiet conversation with Bill Gold as the group re-entered the squad office.

Rachael jumped up and ran to Jane Gold as soon as she saw her. "Oh my God, I'm so happy that you're well enough to view the lineup. I got my man, number two. Did you pick him?

Responding to her answer, she asked, "Oh, they're different men. My shooter is number five. Are you sure?"

Mike was the first detective to respond, "Easy ladies, you both picked the same man. We moved his position because it's protocol. You both did well. Thank you both again."

Several minutes later, the investigating detectives were sitting with Frank Islas in an interrogation room.

***

Jack Clayton began the questioning. "Frank, where were you the day before yesterday and that same night?"

Nervous, Islas shuffled his right foot as he began to answer, "On my way home to see my mother. Wh?,."

Mike pushed, "Why were you going home to her? Don't you have your own place?"

"No. I was just released from jail and haven't seen my mother in years. I just wanted to see her."

"Where did you get released from?"

"They moved me from Fishkill then down to Rikers, but you already know that or I wouldn't be here.

What are you trying to pin on me?"

Quickly, Romano moved closer to the subject, invading his space. Ignoring an impulse to bitch slap the man, he asked, "What did you do in Brooklyn?"

He smiled and snapped, "Nothing, because I wasn't there."

Clayton spit out his words like a rifle shot, "Were you on Staten Island the same night?"

"No."

The two detectives took turns trying to get some kind of admission from the subject for two hours with negative results.

They were about to give up when Brian Caroll interrupted. "Romano, your command called, some guy named Charlie, says to call right away."

Tony Scala said, "You guys keep at it, I'll make the call."

For the five minutes that Scala was gone, they were getting nowhere with Islas until Scala announced, "Well, Detective Romano, we have received results on the finger prints that you recovered from that green Saab two days ago."

"Terrific, who do they belong to Sarge?"

"The car's owner and I think Islas knows who belongs to the other set."

The felon's brow began to show beads of perspiration, bringing a graphic explanation of the term, *sweating the suspect*. "I only hitched a ride from the lady. I didn't do anything."

Mike leaned in towards prisoner again. "Really Frank, where did you sit?"

Islas was startled at the question and answered "Next to her, of course."

"Well, I took the prints from around both the front and back doors. Try again."

"I want my lawyer."

Jack responded with, "Sure thing you dumb shit." To nobody in particular he continued, "Quick, get him away from me before I beat the crap out of him."

***

Before Mike and Tony Staten Island and returned to Brooklyn, they learned from Parole Officer Reilly the circumstances of Islas' release.

Frank Islas had done eight years for the assault of an unarmed security guard at Staten Island Hospital. He was only 18 years old at the time when he jumped into the driver's side of a car being driven by a female nurse, pushing her aside, as she was about to leave work after her shift. She screamed for help. The hapless security guard had responded in an effort to intimidate Islas and the poor man was struck with the car as Islas fled and he was hospitalized at the time. Police picked Islas up several miles away with the nurse who was still an emotional mess but unharmed.

For those initial crimes, Islas was charged with Kidnapping and Assault. Due to his age at the time, he had pled guilty to the charges at arraignment receiving Youthful Offender Status and sentenced to eight years inside.

The guard died two days later and subsequently charged with Felony Murder.

Back in court again, Frank Islas again pled guilty, and received twenty-five to life.

Frank had a good attorney at the time even though he was a public defender and because of his Y.O. status, he actually served only eight years and with life parole. That meant if convicted of another crime during his entire lifetime; he would be back inside to complete his original sentence plus whatever penalties his new transgression would entail.

Immediately after his release, two days ago through the Brooklyn House of Detention, Frank Islas began his current crime spree. This time he would be returning to the system as an adult.

After digesting the news, Mike heard the voice of the Saint Michael in his head congratulating him on the successful conclusion of his first case in his new command.

Thank you. I'm gonna like it here. These first couple of days has certainly been interesting.

On the ride back to Brooklyn, Romano and Scala discussed how the court system operates and agreed that sometimes, it sucks.

CHAPTER THREE

It was Sunday, not one of his favorite workdays; the Italian cop always disliked working weekends, especially since marrying Lillian.

It was 0745 hrs. when Mike exchanged greetings with Charlie and Frank as he entered the office for the beginning of his third set of tours with the Six-Four Squad. He had been in the squad for almost three weeks. After signing the command log, he intended to say good morning to Tony Scala.

Sergeant Scala called out to him, "I hear you Romano, come into my office please."

Mike's heart skipped a beat, *Oh shit. Did I screw up already?* Dismissing negative thoughts, he answered, "Sure Sarge."

He relaxed as he saw the smile on Tony Scala's face. Tony pointed to an empty chair and said, "Michael Romano, the Bulldog. That's what they called you in narcotics, isn't it?"

"Huh, yes, Sarge. How did you know?"

"First, you deserve a well done regarding the extortion case. I read your closing DD-5. It must have taken some probing to get the complainant to 'find' the missing property and drop the charges. Closing it 'Exceptional Clearance' was the correct designation."

"Thanks Sarge."

"Now, the real reason for asking you to step in;

after the exemplary work you've exhibited since your arrival, I decided to call your old boss, Lieutenant Lou Tazzara and ask if you're always so tenacious or you're just trying to make an impression. He said something interesting, 'If you want someone caught, just unleash that bulldog and say fetch.' Was he right?"

Mike, hiding how proud he was regarding the nickname that he was given when serving as a narcotics investigator, he responded, "I can't really say. I always sink my teeth in when working a case. Guess I'm lucky he feels that way."

"Well, we had a nice conversation and based on what I learned, I'm giving you a case that just came to us last night. It wasn't your turn to catch it, but due to its odd nature I want you to work it. It's now yours, here."

Tony smiled as he handed the complaint to Mike.

Mike took the pink report sheet and quickly read it, trying to retain what he saw.

"Sarge, this says that a bride and groom were held up after their wedding. They got married right next door, across the street at Colonnade Catering on the corner! I thought this goes over to robbery."

"It occurred in our command so we get first crack at it. If we can't make headway, we, you in this case, with me signing off on it, can close it out as 'referred to Central Robbery.' Do you doubt your own expertise Mike?"

"No way. I'm gonna get these guys and not give the case away. Thanks for the confidence. I'm on it."

Mike went directly to the office coffee pot, poured himself a cup of steaming black java and returned to his desk. With his left hand, he placed it on the windowsill then he carefully read the entire *61*.

After celebrating their marriage, Doug and Janet Rossi had left the hall just after midnight.

Connected

They were passengers in a car owned by their cousins, John and Kim Segar. The newlyweds rode in the rear seat of the Segar's car. John, the couple's best man, drove.

The group had traveled five blocks to the intersection of Bay 17th Street and Rutherford Place, where they halted their car at a stop sign on the corner. The intersection was the beginning of a small residential extension of Benson Avenue and was not very well lit at night.

It was at that very moment that a black Chevy barreled past them, cut them off and screeched to a stop. Four men instantly jumped out waving handguns before the celebrants had a chance to react. The wedding party froze in fear.

One of them shouted, "Turn the car off, Muther Fucker!"

Next, the two couples were ordered out of the car. Once outside, the Groom and Best Man were punched by one of the men, knocking them to the ground. While down, they were kicked and forced to face the car.

Janet Rossi pleaded, "Don't hurt us, we just got married."

Each time the men on the ground protested, one of the robbers would threaten, "Yeah, we know. Quiet or we take the women and hurt them."

The bride, Janet, had reported that one of the men then leaned into their car and removed the Bridle Bag, known as, *La Borsa,* in proper Italian; *La Busta* in Mike's old world family dialect and the women's personal purses. He then took the ignition keys from the car and threw them across the street.

Before they fled, almost as an afterthought, one of the men demanded the men's wallets also. None of the victims could say which of the robbers stopped to take the wallets.

In their initial statements as recorded on the complaint, all four victims agreed that of the four men one man was black. They all agreed that the white men had foreign accents but they were unable to say what kind.

Romano made some notes and dialed the number listed for the bride and groom. It was now 8:30. As soon as someone answered it, Romano introduced himself, apologizing for the early call. The man who answered identified himself as Doug Rossi.

"Are you and your bride okay Mr. Rossi?"

Without waiting for an answer, he continued, "I have been assigned to your case and would like to speak to you and Mrs. Rossi while the incident is still fresh in your mind; if you can see your way clear to come to my office. "

Rossi responded as expected, "Detective, my wife and I are more than willing to come over now if necessary. Should we bring our cousins too?"

Romano thanked them and knowing it might get too confusing, told him the second couple would be interviewed later.

***

At 9:30, Mike received a call from downstairs. The Rossi couple was on their way up. Mike grabbed his case file and met them at the door. They looked exhausted.

"Mr. and Mrs. Rossi, I'm Detective Mike Romano and I've been assigned to your case. Sorry to you meet like this. First, let me congratulate you on our wedding. Second, allow me to express how sorry I am that your special day was ruined, but I promise, we will try our hardest to bring those responsible to justice."

Frank Pigro had previously left the office to confer with the Six Oh Squad on a joint case, leaving only Charlie with Mike and Tony in the office.

Mike introduced Charlie to the couple and asked, "Charlie, do you want to sit in on this?"

Detective Wilson was enjoying Mike's enthusiasm and opted out, "No Mike, it's your case but I'm available to help if necessary."

Mike gently guided the couple, "Please folks; let's go into the break room. Would either of you like some coffee?"

Before they could answer, he indicated a large table and three chairs, "Please sit here."

Doug declined anything, but Janet accepted a cup of 'regular'.

"Detective, we hardly got two hours of sleep because we were up all night reliving the horror and trying to figure out how much we lost."

Doug added, "Once our parents heard about it, they were calling relatives and friends to stop any checks and asking if they would replace their wedding gifts. That sounds kind of greedy doesn't it?"

Mike, trying to ease their guilt answered, "Not at all. That would have been my first suggestion. It will give us an idea as to the physical value of the theft. Have you arrived at some kind of estimate?"

"Not completely. Our parents are still waiting for return calls. Maybe later today or tomorrow we can answer that question."

"That's fine; I can add the details later on. Now, let's start with anything you can remember about yesterday. Your report doesn't say if any of the men wore masks. Did they?"

Doug took the lead, "No Detective, not that I remember, Janet, how about you? John and I were down on the ground and didn't get a chance to see them very well?"

Janet Rossi began to shake as she responded, "No, I don't remember any mask. We thought we were going to die. They had guns and we saw their faces. That's what robbers do when you see them, they kill you, right?"

Romano tried to reassure them both with, "Not usually in the case of this kind of crime. They obviously chose that corner because it's rather dark there and you have to stop. They were quick and kept the men down. They only wanted to get your money and leave quickly. Please try not to worry."

Doug put his arm around his wife and spoke softly, "Honey, please listen to the detective. He knows about this kind of stuff."

"Thank you Doug. You two will be fine. We have a fridge with soft drinks downstairs, would either of you like something cold instead?"

They both shook their heads and leaned forward as if to say, "What do you want to ask?"

Mike started slowly. "First, I'd like to know if either of you felt or saw any unusual activity around you during the reception."

Doug asked, "What do you mean by unusual?"

"Well, if anyone was taking a personal interest in either one of you; like a waiter, waitress, or a busboy."

"That's a hard one Detective. We were the bride and groom, everyone catered to our every whim. After all they all wanted a big tip."

"Yes, I know, but did anyone stand out? Think about it for a minute, I'll be right back." Mike went to get himself some coffee.

When he returned to the couple, Doug pensively asked, "There was one waiter that was always around us. It seems that he never left, especially after the cake was served when people came to us with their gift envelopes."

Mike heard celestial voices say, *you can do this Mike. You're on track.*

He answered the groom. "That's exactly what I mean. Do you remember his name?"

"Doug answered, "Detri or something. I got upset because he hovered over Janet all night."

At that point, Janet Rossi hugged her husband.

"Silly, he just wanted a big tip. He's not even my type. Wait, I kept calling him 'Waiter, and he kept saying, 'please call me Demetri. That's his name! Yeah that's it! Do you think he's involved, Detective Romano?"

"I don't know. Does he speak with an accent?"

"Yes! Now I remember, it sounds Slavic, maybe from Hungry, Russia or something like that. My Grandparents are Romanian and he sounded a little like some of my family does."

Mike focused his attention, "Now, both of you, think back to the men in the street; was Demetri or someone who sounded like him there?"

Doug answered, "The guy who said, 'keep still or we take the women,' kind of had the same accent. The black guy was American and I'm not sure about the other two, but they were white."

Janet added, "I think at least one other man spoke like our waiter."

Mike heard wings beating in his head. He hid his excitement.

"Okay, now I may have something to work with. That's all for now."

He then handed each of them his business card that he had rushed through the local print shop on his second day in the squad and said, "Please call when you have figured your monetary loss or have something else to add. I'll touch base with you tomorrow."

As they were leaving the room, Mike stopped them. "Just one more thing; your report says the robbers were in a black Chevy. It must have been a four door sedan and who do you think was driving?"

Janet looked at Doug, who responded, "Yeah, all the doors were opened. One of the white guys. I think the man who threatened us. The black guy came out first and fast when they stopped. Why?"

"I'm trying to gather all the information that I can. You never know when a little thing cracks a case."

My God, I sound like a TV detective. Hope they didn't notice. He smiled inwardly.

Charlie Wilson walked over to comment on his interview technique. "You have style Michael Romano. You did great. It seems that you read the book, "Interview 101.""

"Thanks Charlie. It was fun, a little different from narcotics. Now I have to find the dirt bags. I'm going over to the catering hall. Care to come along?"

"Not really. Go do your thing. It's just right across the street; you should be safe. I'll be here when you get back. Good luck."

Mike grabbed his case folder, he told Scala where he was going and didn't sign out to the field.

***

Inside the building lobby, an attractive raven-haired

young woman greeted Mike. "Hello Sir, good morning and thank you for considering Colonnade Catering. My name is Clare. How may we help you?"

Mike smiled at her assumption and answered, "No, I'm not looking for a caterer, but perhaps you can help me. My name is Detective Romano from the station house across the street."

Before he could withdraw his identification, she cheerfully responded, "Opps, sorry. I assumed that you might be a customer. Are you here because of what happened last night?"

"No problem and yes. Is the owner or manager in? I need to speak to him or her, please."

"He is and he's my Dad. Please follow me."

"Thank you," Mike answered as he followed her through a rather ornate doorway.

Once inside what was obviously the "closing office" for potential clients, Clare announced, "Bernie, this is Detective Romano about the robbery last night. Excuse me."

She then promptly left the room.

Romano thought, *Must be used to calling him that when in business mode.*

The pleasant looking man behind the fancy desk rose and extended his hand in Mike's direction, "I'm Bernie Shapiro. Detective, how can I be of help?"

"Mr. Shapiro, I'm here because I've been assigned to investigate the robbery of last night's bride and groom. I've already spoken to them and need your assistance."

"Sure Detective, please call me Bernie."

"Fine, Bernie. First, has anything like this ever happened before?"

"I'm sure it has somewhere in this city, but never

here or during my twenty five years in the business."

"Let me get right down to it then, do you think that one or more of your staff may have been involved?"

"You're kidding. You must be new here to ask that question. We've been here over eighteen years and even had some local police officers get married here or have booked other affairs over the years. My staff is hand-picked."

"Sorry, but you must understand that I have to ask. It's no reflection on you."

Bernie looked hurt as he answered, "Yeah, but what can I do to help. You obviously have something in mind to come here."

"Yes, I do. Would you please give me a complete list of your entire staff and any other info you might have on them, like employee photos; if you take any?"

"Sure can. Clare!" he bellowed.

Clare walked in scant seconds later, "Yes, Daddy. What do you need?"

Mike noticed that she answered calling him Daddy. *Now she calls him Daddy. Guess because I'm no longer a potential paying customer.*

"Please get Detective Romano a complete list of all our employees and any other info we have on each of them."

Before she could answer, Mike added, "Clare, can you make it from the beginning of last year to date?"

Shapiro looked at his daughter, "Please don't take too long. I'm sure the detective is in a hurry. Thank you."

Turning back to Romano he asked, "Detective, Mike, while we wait, can I offer you a sandwich or a drink?"

"No thanks, I'm fine for now, it's not even noon yet."

"Well, I'm having one, don't let me drink alone. It's bad luck."

Mike chuckled, "That's a new one. I never heard the bad luck thing before. It's cocktail hour somewhere in the world. Only to be polite, please make mine Dewars and water, loads of ice and water. I still have to work."

The two men sipped their drinks and chatted about mundane things while they awaited Clare's return.

During their conversation, Mike wondered if Bernie was involved. *Damn, I like this guy and I think he's okay. I hope he's clean. I would hate to lock him up.*

Mike learned that Bernie inherited the business from his father. The family roots were from the 11th century Ashkenazi Jewish population of Central Germany. His family emigrated from Frankfurt, to the United States in 1933. He had no idea how the business began but could recall being inside a hall around non-family celebrations and weddings as a child. After high school, his father sent him to the University of Pennsylvania.

After graduation, Bernie returned home and began working part time in the family business that gathering experience that led to his current success.

Clare had no interest in additional education and started in the business as a waitress right after high school and worked her way up.

"She's my right hand now. She gets her brains from her mother. My son, Mark, just wants to play big shot and chase girls," Bernie quipped.

Fifteen minutes had passed before Clare brought a folder containing the information that the detective had requested. She was handing it to Bernie when he spoke.

"Thank you Clare. Will you please hand the folder to Detective Romano?"

"I made copies of our employee records Detective," she stated offering the folder, 'including a copy of our employees' photos. We always take a polaroid too."

Mike took the folder. "Thank you Clare. Your dad has said some nice things about you."

Clare smiled in response and quickly turned to leave the room as her face began to glow a bright pink.

Mike thought, *Wow, a modern young woman who can still blush. He certainly raised her properly. I like Bernie even more.*

Romano opened the folder. "Bernie, please excuse me a minute or two while I look through. I might have a couple of questions for you before I leave with this."

Holding up his empty glass, the Caterer said, "Sure Mike, I'm at your service; another drink?"

"Not for me but you go ahead."

It took Romano only fifteen seconds to find what he was looking for. Dimitri Titov, 23 years old, hired as a waiter. His visa stated he was from the city of Minsk in the state of Belarus. The file listed that his residence was in the Gravesend section of Brooklyn, along with a street and house number.

"Bernie, is this kid Dimitri Titov well-liked by your other employees? What kind of worker is he? Would you let him date your daughter?"

Bernie leaned back in his chair with an expression of surprise. "Detective, first let me say, no, I would not let him date my daughter. His background makes him a probable Lithuanian, maybe Russian. Minsk was at one time part of the USSR. They spoke several Slavic languages in that city, including Russian. I'm not that fond of Russians, generally, I don't trust them."

"Why did you hire him if you feel that way?"

"This neighborhood is getting a large influx of them. It seems that the Russians are the new immigrant wave here. I will only hire the younger ones because the young Russians are more Americanized than the old folks and I need them, sometimes as an interpreter. Usually they're okay, but not as a son-in-law."

Mike responded with, "Oh, and I always thought Bensonhurst was all Italian."

Bernie chuckled to hide his embarrassment at what he just said, then continued. "He seems to be okay. The guests like him, ethnic lines not withstanding, and it seems that the employees do too. Why, you know something?"

"No, nothing except that he might have some information for me. The bride and groom said that he hovered around them through most of the night. I just wanted your opinion of the man."

"Is he a suspect?"

"When is he scheduled to work again? I'd like to spend some time with the guy."

Bernie, once again called out for Clare to join them. "Clare, when is Dimitri Titov scheduled to work again?"

"He's up for a small mid-week anniversary party this coming Wednesday. Is there a problem?"

"Detective Romano asked is all."

She turned to Mike and asked, "Detective, did he do it? Was he involved?"

"No, he didn't do it and I don't know. It's just part of my investigation to get all the pieces of the puzzle together."

Clare appeared uneasy at his answer and asked, "Do you still need me?"

Wonder if and just how well she knows him. Maybe Daddy doesn't know and it appears that he certainly would not approve.

Romano reshuffled the contents of the folder before closing it. Then he stood up to leave, "Thank you both. I have to get back now. I'll keep you informed as to the progress of the investigation."

***

Romano returned to the squad and went right in to Scala's office. "I'm back Sarge."

Tony smiled and asked, "I know it's a little early in the investigation but, did you get lucky?"

"I don't know if I did or not, but I have some info that I may be able to work. I'll have a DD-5 for you in a couple of hours."

"That's all I ask for Mike; timely paper work, although it would be nice to solve it with a collar too. Good Luck."

After separating the employees by past and present, Mike broke them down by ethnicity. He was going to make photo arrays in the hopes of getting a suspect identified by the bridal party.

At the end of his workday, Mike had assembled several photo arrays. One of them gave the same residence as Titov.

He dropped them into a case folder and was set to swing out and return for a set of 4 x 12's on Wednesday. To be thorough, he planned to interview all the victims and also speak with Dimitri Titov and his roommate.

CHAPTER FOUR

Mike always drove into Manhattan both Monday and Tuesday evening to meet Lillian as she left her job. They had drinks and dinner at *The Atrium,* a better than average local restaurant-bar within a short walking distance of her office. Giovanni, the owner maintained a well-stocked bar and employed a world class chef specializing in Continental Cuisine. It had become "their place."

Adding to the convenience of the establishment, Detective Romano was able to park in the same block using his cardboard, command-parking permit without feeding the parking meters. The first time he displayed it, for an unknown reason, it was honored as if it was an official laminated Department Plate. He continued using it without reservation, never giving it another thought, and it was always honored without fail.

One Wednesday morning, full of nervous energy, Mike, was anxious to get to work and back to his *bridal case.* To keep busy, instead of sitting home, he drove Lilly to her office.

When they parted, it was only 9:30 and with energy and time to spare, he decided to visit his old narcotics office. After quietly visiting with some of his old team members, he excused himself and went around to the office of "The Taz."

Lou Tazzara was surprised to see him. "Hey Romano, you clean up nicely."

"Thanks Loo, it's the suit. I'm still the same guy underneath."

Lieutenant Tazzara liked Mike and showed it once again with a touch of sarcasm and humor.

With a serious face he stated, "I suppose by now you know that I got a call about a week ago from your sergeant, Tony Scala. He seems like a terrific guy, even though I've never met him, but I like his style. He was curious about you. He wanted to know if I thought that you could cut the mustard in his squad. Naturally, I only had bad things to say about you, like your ability to piss me off on a daily basis."

"Yeah, I heard. Did you tell him that I almost kicked your ass a couple of times?"

Louie embraced his former team member and almost crushed his ribs. "You crazy SOB, I'd like to see you try. Let's go get some perogies at that Polish restaurant on Avenue B, just the two of us."

When Michael agreed, Louie finally released him.

"It's only 11:30 in the morning, but you're on. When we get back, if we can still stand, I'll kick your ass for crushing my rib cage and wrinkling my suit."

The two friends dined on perogies of every description while reliving their time together, especially the case when Mike and his partner Alex played drug dealers. After many anecdotes and a few belly laughs, they topped off their meal with several slices of Makowiec, a poppy seed cake/loaf and several glasses of strong tea brewed in an old Samovar that looked like it had survived the Russian Revolution.

Both men were pleasantly surprised when they realized that they had burned three hours sitting in the Old Poland Restaurant and could now hardly move as they rose to leave.

After seeing a few old team members and promising to visit again, Mike left his old office then drove to the Six-Four in Brooklyn, arriving half an hour before the start of his scheduled tour.

Tony Scala walked in behind him just as he was signing in.

"Romano, glad to see you here early, the squad C.O. is back from vacation and should be in his office. Come, I'll introduce you."

Mike had previously met all the other squad members during change of tour overlaps, but he had never met Timothy Fitzpatrick. As he followed his sergeant, he waved acknowledgement to Battle and Levy, the two detectives present in the office

Finding the door to the Sergeants' Office closed, Tony Scala turned toward Mike and said, "He's kind of a hermit and usually does this unless he's in the mood to listen to what the men are doing." Tony knocked.

"Enter," was heard from what sounded like a disembodied voice from within.

Scala entered and said, "Hello Tim, hope you had a nice vacation. I'm sure you'll be pleased with the new man in the office."

Tony then put his hand on Mike's shoulder as he continued, "Tim, meet Michael Romano from OCCB, Narcotics. I believe he'll be an asset to our office and comes highly recommended. Mike, meet our Commanding Officer, Sergeant Timothy Fitzpatrick."

Fitz stood and reached out to shake Romano's hand. Mike took his and quickly added, "It's my pleasure Boss. I already like working here. Sergeant Scala has been invaluable in getting me settled in."

"Another Italian I see. Well, it's appropriate in this

neighborhood. Sergeant Scala likes you. That's good. You should do well here. Please have a seat; I'd like to chat with you."

Tony Scala took the comment as a dismissal and said, "Excuse me gentlemen, I have something that I must do. See you later."

During the short conversation, Mike was evaluating his commander. The man was obviously Irish and stood well over six foot tall. His diction was impeccable as was his mode of dress. There wasn't a hair out of place or a wrinkle in his clothes. *He looks a little like that bastard Bryan but doesn't have his heavy drinker coloring and demeanor. One thing for sure, he only tolerates Italians. Bastard is another bigot.*

The celestial voices in his head were telling him not to judge too quickly.

As Mike eased into the chair alongside Tim's desk he replied, "Ask away Boss. What do you want to know?"

"Well, I read your jacket and learned that you have almost seventeen years on the job and served both in plainclothes and uniform. Your last command was in OCCB, Narcotics. This is different. Here we work on cases that need to be solved or the perpetrator is known and we have to build a case against him. I see that while I was on vacation you already closed a kidnapping case with an arrest. That was good work. It could have been a mess."

"Thank you."

"Romano, Wilson and Pigro are getting their team mate, Detective Daniel Reyes back in the morning."

"Oh?"

"In light of that, I'm going to assign you to another team, a permanent team. They're doing their second eight by four tomorrow. Sorry to have you come in so early but I always try to have three man squads whenever possible. I believe you are already acquainted with them; Samuel Battle and Richard Levy, their third man is on loan to Homicide for a while. Do you have any questions?"

"No problem, but I do have one question. Do I keep the cases that are already assigned to me?"

Fitz responded emotionless with, "Yes, you do and please don't forget to submit timely DD-5's. It's one of my priorities. Now welcome aboard and go to work."

Mike returned to the outer office. Levy and Battle had already left. Charlie and Frank were now occupying the room.

Only tolerating Frank, Mike nodded in his direction and went directly to Charlie asking, "Hey, Charlie is the boss always so business like and straight laced. I got mixed vibes from him. What's up?"

Frankie laughed and quietly answered, "He's Irish, genetics. He can't help it. Imagine how I feel."

Charlie looked at Pigro and said, "Hey Frankie, cover your pinky ring, you're blinding me."

Pigro answered, "You're just jealous because you don't have one."

Charlie then leaned closer to Mike, "I'll tell you about Fitz, Mike, but not in the office. How are you doing with the bride case? Got any outside interviews to do?"

"Yes, as a matter of fact, I do. I want to go see Bernie across the street and maybe go visit one of his staff, a guy named Dimitri Titov. The kid is my prime suspect. Give me a minute to get my file. Please sign us out."

"Done and I'll grab a radio, we can come back for a car if we need one."

When the two men crossed the street, Mike gave in to his inner voice and stopped as they mounted the sidewalk.

"Charlie, hold on. I can't stand it, just what can you tell be about Sergeant Fitz?"

"Many things; he's smart, graduated Columbia, majored in English Literature, so don't misspell any words on your DD-5's. He'll make you re-write them before he signs off on them. His brother is a big super chief downtown in the Puzzle Palace and he gets Squad Commander's pay. That's lieutenant's money. He doesn't micro manage your cases unless he sees something he doesn't like and then he's on your ass like white on rice, forever."

"Sounds like a charmer."

"Also be careful, if you catch a case that may get controversial, dot your I's and cross your T's because he will blame you for aanything that goes wrong. He was scheduled for vacation when the Robinson Case broke. Now, with something like that one, any squad commander would want to be present, but not Fitz, you're a firsthand witness, he went on vacation anyway."

"He wanted to avoid the controversy?"

"Yup, in other words, he has no balls. Rumor has it that his brother covered for him by saying he had already paid for a cruise and couldn't cancel. Otherwise he's not so bad; he's never loud and pushy and never belittles his men in public like some bosses."

Mike chuckled as he said, "Sorry I asked. Thanks."

Bernie was in the building's lobby as they entered the Colonnade.

"Detective Romano, Mike, I see that you brought reinforcements. I recognized Detective Wilson. Any break in the case?"

Mike responded, "Not really but I'm curious, is Dimitri still scheduled to work tonight?"

"Actually he called in yesterday saying that he had a family emergency and would be away. Why? Do you think he's involved?'

"Maybe, here's my card, call me if you hear from him. I'll keep in touch. Thanks."

As they left the building, Charlie asked, "What do you have on this kid, Mike?"

"Well, one of the stick up men was black and Dimitri and one other of Bernie's employees, a black man, share an apartment. The black kid wasn't implicated as a player but you never know. I want to interview both of them. Let's get a car and go visit."

According to Bernie's records, Dimitri and his roommate, Ronald Lewis, shared an apartment at 2107 Cropsey Avenue within the confines of the command. Before they went to the location, Mike stopped at a street phone and called the number that Titov had given as his own. There was no answer. The partners continued to the apartment building, a rather small four story old red brick building that may have once been rather nice.

After checking the mail boxes for either name with negative results, they sought out the building superintendent who confirmed that, "A Russian kid who works at one of the caterers on Bath Avenue, I think the one near the police station. He was living in apartment 3A, but disappeared yesterday owing me rent. If you find him, let me know. I want my money. I don't know if he's coming back. So in two weeks, he loses the apartment."

Charlie asked, "Did he live with a black kid, you know, someone who looks like me?"

"Yes, a nice yong man. But I haven't seen him in a couple of days."

Mike turned to his partner, "Suspicions confirmed.

They're on the run. There's nothing to be gained here. Let's go back to the office Charlie."

"Hey Mike, what about the balls on the super, let him know when we find the kid. Does he think we're a damn collection agency?"

Back in the office, Mike remembered a connection he had made inside the New York Telephone Company's security section when he had worked in plainclothes back on The Apple, Joe Lipor. The two men had become fast friends. He decided to use the relationship to help in his investigation, after all, Joe had told him to call anytime, and he did.

After exchanging pleasantries, Mike gave his friend the telephone number that he had for Dimitri and asked for any available residential records for the subject and all listings for similar names in Brooklyn, both past and present. Joe explained that it would take some time and he would call back in two days.

It's possible they're in the system somewhere, he thought. Anxious to keep going, Romano's next call was to the DMV liaison at One Police Plaza. He requested anything in the system for Titov and Lewis. Next, he contacted BCI requesting if there were any fingerprint records available for either of the men.

Less than an hour later, Mike received a return phone call. The search had produced negative results.

Mike typed his DD-5 follow-up report on the case and dropped it into Fitz's in basket for his signature. When he then checked the catching sheet, he saw that he had picked up two new cases. After pulling them from the in basket, he sat down at his usual desk to review them.

The first one was for violation of a court order. The second, intrigued him, It was for assault 2nd Degree.

The complaint explained that a local man was working on his small garden in front of his home and felt a sting followed by mild pain in his right buttock. He turned to see a car pull away from the curb and a young male laughing at him. The injured man recited the license plate number, committing it to memory as the car pulled away. The narration went on to say that after he reached back to touch the area, he saw some blood on his hand, then rushed inside to call 911 saying that he may have been shot.

An ambulance and a patrol car responded. It was determined by the EMS team that he was shot with a pellet gun when they saw the projectile half buried in his skin. Patrol sent the complaint up to the squad for investigation after running the plate. The car's owner was listed.

Romano, not wanting to get involved with a possible arrest situation, shelved the case aside for his next tour, it was only a pellet gun and could wait. He busied himself with his older cases until end of tour.

As the clock on the wall inched forward, he signed out and went home to his beloved Lillian.

CHAPTER FIVE

At exactly 7:30 a.m., the following morning Mike signed into the squad's command log. Tony Scala was already at his own desk. Fitz would be coming in for a 4 x 12 tour.

Mike greeted him with, "Morning Sarge," before going to his desk. Remembering that he had seen Battle and Levy sitting, at the first two, he had planned to claim the last one as his; it gave him full view of the entire squad room.

He smiled inwardly as he sat down to begin looking over his cases. *Gee, I hope that Frankie Pigro doesn't rub off on me.*

"*Buongiorno*, Detective Romano, *e benvenuti* in the team."

Slightly startled, Mike looked up and was surprised to see Richie Levy.

"Hey Richie, good morning to you too. I didn't know you could speak Italian."

"Until I went into the Marines, I was the only Jewish kid in my neighborhood. It was learn or be left out; so I learned. Sam should be here any minute."

As Richie spoke, Sam Battle walked in.

"I see an old friend from the Three Two made it to our team. Except for Charlie, who may be as old as dirt, we're known as the Dinosaur Team. There are so many youngsters on the job today, you're right up there with us so welcome, Dinosaur. Now there are three."

"Thanks, I think."

Sam released a short deep laugh before continuing, "But we're not extinct by any means and can kick ass any day. Is that fresh coffee I smell?"

From inside his head, mike heard a voice ask, *"What do you think of this team Michael?"*

Silently he thanked his celestial benefactor, vowing to stay put until he retired, knowing that he had found a home away from home.

Sam went into the break room for coffee even before he signed in.

Placing a cup down on his desk, he asked, "Mike, anything you have to go out on today? I have one case I want to check out and Richie is working with Homicide on the Robinson thing, so it's just us catching for a while."

"Well, yes I do. On one of them, I have to wait for some info to come back and my new one is a pellet gun shooting that I want to check out, maybe there's a quick collar involved too."

Sam responded with, "Let me finish my coffee and make some calls on a few old cases, then we can go. Okay with you?"

"Whenever you're ready, just holler."

***

Two hours later, the new partners were out in the squad's Gold Chevy Caprice. Mike drove at Sam's request. They began their time together with small talk, as new teammates usually do.

"Sam Battle, that's some name. Sorry, but it sounds like a rock band," Romano told his partner.

"It does, and I will rock-n-roll. Battle is my name and battle I will do. One time a few years ago, in a different command, the Seven Four, place was a shit hole."

"Yeah, I know it."

"Anyway, I was walking back to my car after a four by twelve and some home boys blocked my path. They had knives and one had a gun in his hand. They asked for everything I had saying that they didn't want to hurt me because I was 'a brother.' I asked if they were sure that they wanted everything. They said yes, so I gave it to them. I emptied my off duty in their direction."

"Wow. Get any problems from the job?"

"None, it was a good shooting. One died and two were taken to the hospital. I gave them all I had. If I had an automatic, I would have given them more. That's the way I roll, I learned it in the Marines."

"You're a piece of work. I remember you from the Three Two. You were in Anti-crime when I worked on patrol. My old partner said you're named after the first black cop ever appointed to the New York Police Department. Is that true?"

"Yep, he was my great grandfather, Samuel J. Battle, appointed as a Patrolman on March, 6, 1911. He was born in New Bern, North Carolina and moved to New York City after a short time in Connecticut. Great-granddad was also the first black sergeant and first black lieutenant. Sometime later on he became the first black Commissioner of Parole."

"Wow, that's some history. You must be proud."

"I am and remember him at family gatherings when I was a kid. He was a big guy. Stood six three and my father said he was 280 pounds when he worked the street. I was only nine or ten when he died. To me he was *the* real Paul Bunyan. Everybody called him 'Big Sam' back in those days. I honor his name whenever I can."

"That's a great story. I wish that I had a famous person in my family."

"You may and don't know about it; or, you can be the first one. Work on it."

Sam had been working a case regarding the theft of stolen coins and jewelry. He planned to check the local pawnshops and estate jewelers. After stopping at several locations and interviewing the owners, with negative results, they went to work on Mike's gun case.

They began at the residence of the owner of the car used by the pellet gun shooters.

Both detectives went to the front door of the modest home. Romano felt as comfortable with Sam Battle as he had with his old narcotics partner, Alex Summers. There was no need to discuss how to approach a closed door. Each man stood on the side of the doorway as Mike rang the bell.

His training officer, who later became his partner, when he was a rookie in Harlem, taught him the tactic as a survival skill. *Sometimes, there's a bad guy on the other side willing to shoot a cop, standing out of the line of fire gives reaction time.*

The door had a window. Behind the lace curtain hanging on the inside of the glass panel, they were able to see a pretty, relatively young woman, looking through the curtain.

The cautious maneuver was not necessary in that particular instance, but a good habit is a good habit.

"Yes, can I help you?" she asked through the door.

Mike and Sam had their shields in their hands. Mike answered, "Detectives, Mrs. Prego, can we have a minute of your time please?"

She opened the door and asked, "Just what is this about? Is my family alright?"

Sam responded with, "Yes ma'am. I'm sure everyone's fine. My partner, Detective Romano and I would like to speak to your husband if we may."

"About what?"

Mike picked up the ball, "Your car may have been involved in an accident; a witness gave us a plate number that belongs to your husband's car. We would like to speak with him and see his car. Oh, by the way, does your son drive?"

"Paulie does have a license. Why that question?"

Mike responded, "Well, our witness said that a young man was driving. Do you only have one son?"

"No, my other son, Joey, is a year younger and does not have a license."

"Are they home Mrs. Prego?"

"No. They're both in school. Why do you want them? They're good kids."

It was Sam's turn. "Oh I see. What school? Can we speak to your husband please?"

"They go to James Madison. Dom is at our pork store on 13th Avenue, Prego's Italian Meats and Deli. I'll call him if you'd like."

"No, thank you ma'am," Mike answered. We'll just stop by the store. Thank you. Sorry to bother you."

Back at their car, Mike stated, "Sam, I'd like to go to the pork store if you don't mind. I'm sure he's expecting us."

"Let's do it partner."

Luckily, there was a fire hydrant in front of Prego's shop. Mike pulled into the space and moved back enough to keep the actual stanchion clear. He put their red bullet light and the vehicle log book on the dashboard before locking the vehicle.

Once inside, Sam acted as if he was fascinated with the layout and variety of foodstuffs inside the shop. Actually, he was looking around for anything that might trigger his built in safety alert system.

There were two men behind the service counter. Mike flashed his shield at the closest counter man and asked for the owner, Dominic Prego.

Seeing the gold shield and assuming that the second man in his shop was also a cop, Prego answered, "I'm Dominic Prego. How can I help you, Detectives?"

Romano introduced himself and told him that a witness had identified his car as being used in a drive by shooting. *If he's been alerted by his wife, he hides it well. He's dealt with police before.*

Prego acted shocked. "What, you're crazy."

Mike continued, "Look Mr. Prego, yesterday afternoon a man was shot in the butt by a very powerful pellet gun. He required treatment because the pellet was stuck in his skin, luckily there was no real damage and he's home now. The shooter fired from inside a car and a witness saw a young man laughing and waving the handgun. The license plate on that vehicle is yours."

"It's impossible. There must be some mistake."

"We know that you have two boys and that one of them drives. Do the math, your plate, two young men. Where are your boys now?"

"In school; you can't be serious. What are you going to do?"

Prego was getting nervous and agitated, "Yes, at Madison High now, but you guys can't go there, you can't."

Mike was becoming annoyed, "We can and we will. Now, do you know if either of your sons owns a pellet gun or is it yours?"

His face showed strain as he answered, "I own one that we use when we go to our country house. It's in my hall closet at home."

Romano pushed, "We're going to the school now. Meet us back at your house in one hour so we can see the weapon. If it disappears, I **will** charge you with several crimes. Thank you."

"Romano, you're crazy."

Without any further conversation, Mike and Sam left.

Once in their department auto, Sam commented, "Michael, you have some kind of style. We are going be great partners ! What now?"

"First, we go to the school and ask that the boys be sent to the guidance counselor's office; without being specific, we tell him or her that we need the kids to help with something back at their house."

"How do you know the school guy will cooperate?"

"If he doesn't, I'll threaten him with arrest too. We know the mother is home and if he calls her, it will check out."

"That Prego guy is right; you are crazy, but like a fox."

"We take the kids home and interview them in front of their parents as required by law. If we can get them to admit what they did, we arrest them with the parents as witnesses. Then, we transport the little guys. The parents can meet us in our office. How does that sound?"

"Like a bulldog playing with a bone, a man after my own heart."

When the Prego boys saw two detectives waiting for them, they began to shake and looked down at the floor. The siblings knew that nothing pleasant would come of the meeting and they might now pay for yesterday's actions.

Mike and Sam were easy with them and only repeated what they had told the school official, that they were needed back home to assist in a police investigation and their parents were expecting them.

When the two detectives arrived at the Prego home with the boys, Dom's car was already in the driveway. It was a perfect match to the description given in the complaint.

The boys acted as if they were going to the gallows. Now it was only necessary to get an admission from the boys and recover the weapon.

***

Dominic Prego was standing next to the kitchen table and holding a wooden case as his wife led the entourage in.

"My pellet gun is in here. It's really a good one and was expensive."

Sam gently ordered, "Please put the box down on the table sir."

Prego did. Sam then slid the case closer to where Mike was.

Mrs. Prego was off to one side, sitting on a high chrome stool and mumbling to herself. Dominic Prego was looking directly at Romano; his face was rapidly changing expressions, first anger then a pleading expression as if he wanted to say something, but didn't.

After opening the box and carefully examining the weapon without removing it, Mike began, "Boys, I think that you both know why we're here. Yesterday, you two drove past a man's house and shot him in the ass with your dad's pellet gun. Do you know how dangerous that could be? What if a police officer saw it happen or stopped you just after the shooting and saw the gun. He would have been within his rights to defend himself. What if he shot you?"

At the sound of the question, Mrs. Prego gasped and Dominic's Italian machismo surfaced instantly.

"Theresa, if you can't control yourself, please leave the room. Even better, leave now. I have to talk privately with these men.'

Theresa sniffed and left in a huff.

The actual interview continued for twenty minutes without incident. The boys admitted to taking the gun and father's car. They drove around looking for what they considered a suitable target. It was the younger boy who actually shot the complainant. Only after Mike informed Mr. Prego, that his two sons were about to be officially arrested and charged with Assault and Possession of a firearm did everything take a surprised turn.

Being a father himself, Mike naturally expected Dominic Prego to defend his kids and plead for him to go easy, but what he had to say surprised him.

"Romano, what the hell are you doing? You're gonna ruin my kids lives with this. The gun is an air pistol not a real gun. Come on, I know who you are, you're family for God's sake."

The voices in Romano's head told him to remain calm and go with the flow, but continue to ask questions.

"Excuse me Mr. Prego; I don't understand what you're talking about."

"Don't play dumb Romano. This is Brooklyn and you know exactly what I mean. After you left, I made some calls. You're related to half the wise guys in this borough. Out of respect, you gotta let this go. Here, take the gun, but leave my kids out of this. "I'll even take care of you, if you know what I mean."

Sam looked at his partner. By the look on the Italian detective's face and though it was their first day actually working together, Battle knew that a button had just been pushed; he just smiled at his partner and waited to enjoy the response.

Mike Romano had never backed down from a challenge is his entire life and Prego's last comment could be taken several ways. The voices in Mike's head shouted a demand for clarification.

"Listen Prego, don't threaten or try to influence me in any way, you'll lose. For one thing, I can charge you with a misdemeanor for the gun. It's illegal in New York City. Second, if you are threatening me, I'll just make up some other charges to add against you, Bribery, for one. Now I know why your kids are such assholes. The apple never falls far from the tree."

Prego, taken aback, stammered as he tried to explain, "Bu... but Detective, what I'm trying to say is that you're Italian too and probably related to people in this neighborhood, friends of mine. Out of common heritage, blood is blood. Can you give the kids summonses or something; or even Desk Appearance Tickets. I promise they'll be in court. If you can see your way to do that, I'll make sure you're compensated for it."

Romano was furious but delivered his next answer ice cold.

"There you go again Mr. Prego. Just because I'm Italian, doesn't mean that I'm connected and take bribes. I always do my job according to the rules and the rules just happen to coincide with my personal moral code. Is that clear?"

"Very clear, I'm just trying to do right by my kids. I guess I've been fed the wrong information about you. I'm sorry."

Mike didn't answer him. His brain was speeding along trying to digest everything Prego had said.

Sam answered instead, "Mr. Prego, the best thing that you can do for your kids is to let us do our job. Both your boys are over sixteen, so they will go through the system. Meet us at the station house and make sure you get a good attorney for your kids. They should make night court sometime before midnight today. My partner is obviously not happy with your comments and frankly, neither am I."

By the time his partner had finished, Romano calmed down enough to be professionally cold again and turned his attention to the two boys.

"Fellas, please turn around, we're going to pat you down and handcuff you. It's procedure, so don't break our shoes, okay?"

After he and Sam cuffed the pair, Mike, without saying a word picked up the case containing the pistol and began to lead them out of the kitchen.

Sam spoke, "Mr. Prego, please meet us at the station. Thank you. We'll explain the next step to you there."

***

The Prego brothers, after a thorough search were put into the holding cage. Mike then explained the circumstance surrounding their arrest to Sergeant Scala and vouchered the pellet gun. He listed Dominic Prego as the rightful owner.

Sam and Mike began to fill out an arrest report, each man taking one of the kids.

When Dominic and Theresa Prego walked in and saw their children in the cage, tears began to run down her face. She began mumbling and turned away, unable to see them penned up.

Sam met them as they came into the room, guiding them away from the source of their pain and asked, "Will you please come with me into the break room? You'll be more comfortable there."

Romano, still upset with Dominick, only spoke to the boys, temporally ignoring the couple. He completed all the paperwork without any conversation between himself and the Prego parents.

When finished, he took the papers and the pistol in to Scala for his review signature.

"Well done Mike, and fast too."

Entering the break room, Romano finally addressed the parents.

"Your boys will be transported downtown to central booking where they will be processed and wait to appear in night court. I suggest that you have their attorney there by six o'clock the latest. They will see a judge in night court at 60 Center Street. I'll try to push their case through quickly."

Mrs. Prego alone, acknowledged his statement with a nod.

Mike then handed a copy of the gun voucher to Dominic, as the owner and said, "You can go now and give the particulars to your attorney. We'll transport them as soon as my boss is finished with his review. Thank you."

Sam escorted them out and returned with sodas for the two kids. It was something for them to do besides sit there and shake; besides they looked thirsty and gratefully accepted them.

With the kids' parents gone, Sam playfully asked, "Michael, are all you Italian guys connected? Prego seems to think so. Maybe he has you mixed up with someone else."

"No, you shit head, we're not all connected; at least I'm pretty sure that I'm not."

Sam was showing his age when he answered, "Good, because I don't want to worry about Tommy Guns."

Mike, happy for the release of tension, got caught up in the game. "We don't do that anymore. Now, its car bombs as you know,"

He was referring to an infamous incident several years earlier when a "made man" was blown to bits within the command. The incident made national news for weeks and later was incorporated into a popular movie about the Brooklyn disco crowd of the Seventies.

"Sergeant Scala called out, "Romano, all your paper is ready. Your collars can go downtown now."

"Sure thing Sarge, will do."

Mike went down to the desk officer and requested a patrol car team to transport his prisoners to the ground floor of One Police Plaza for booking. The lieutenant on duty was more than happy to help and grabbed two men for the job.

Romano planned to go downtown with his own car and sign out from the field. He had something to do.

***

Mike met the transporting team just inside the

entrance to Central Booking and took control of his prisoners. Procedure dictated that the Prego kids were searched again. The boys weren't very happy about it.

Romano then brought them over to the holding pen, a large safety glass enclosed area for prisoners awaiting transportation to cells within the Criminal Court Building.

"After you spend some time in there fellas, let's see if you act like shit heads again. I sure hope that your parents got you a good lawyer to meet you in court later. Young guys like you have trouble on the overnight. Good luck."

As he logged out, he smiled inside and thought, *I sure hope they learn something after some time with society's miscreants and real tough guys. I'll bet they never come back here.*

Romano went to the complaint room in the District Attorney's Office for an interview with an Assistant DA and the formal charging of the Prego boys. It was now about 4:30 p.m. The case would most likely come up later in night court.

Due to budget considerations, there had been some changes in the court system regarding arraignments in New York City. It was no longer required for the arresting officer to be present in front of a judge at the formal reading of charges to a defendant and a plea first entered. The sworn affidavit of the arresting officer was sufficient.

Before he signed out, Mike went to find a pay phone. He had two calls to make, first to Lillian to say that he would be home late as the result of making an arrest and the second, to Rocco Banducci to ask for a meeting at their usual diner in Queens that evening if it was at all possible.

CHAPTER SIX

Rocco Banducci, answered his telephone on the fifth ring. As usual, he was vague and cautious when speaking on any phone.

"Yes, who is this please?"

"Hey, Rocco, it's Mike, your almost brother-in-law."

There was little caution in the response. "Michael, long time since we last spoke. How are you my friend? Is your ex-wife breaking your balls? She's not interfering with your new life is she? Your current wife, Lillian, is indeed a lovely girl."

Romano, over the years learned to always skirt around the real reason for the call. He answered accordingly, "No, not really, but I would like an update on my family if possible. I haven't heard anything about my kids in months. Do you have time to fill me in?"

"When?"

"Today, if possible, I'm kind of in a hurry and free now. Are you available?"

"You are so lucky, I was just going out. Mikey, give me an hour and we can have a drink at our place. You do remember?"

"Yes and thanks. See you there," he said into a dead phone line. That was Rocco's usual telephone style.

It was 4:40 p.m. when Mike signed out of the court processing room.

Once outside, he lightly tapped the breast pocket of

his suit jacket. He felt better feeling the cylindrical shape of a cigar. He withdrew it and quickly peeled off the cellophane wrapper. The detective needed a good smoke to ease the frustration that was building up inside regarding Prego's statements and his impatience at not having answers. Cupping both of his hands to guard the flickering flame flaring from his Zippo, he lit his smoke.

For Mike Romano, cigars and scotch were necessary to relax him when agitated, upset or in a celebratory mood. They were better than ice cream on a hot day in August. Better than all of those things combined, was being with his wife, Lillian, but she wasn't with him at that point in time.

Sitting in his Chevy, he spent a few minutes in deep thought while blowing smoke rings.

What does Dominic Prego know that I don't? Could he know about my relationship with Rocco? No, that's not even remotely possible. Rocco always referred to me as family. Is there more? Well, I'll soon know.

Mike put his car into gear and began his ride to the Privateer Diner on Astoria Boulevard in Jackson Heights, Queens.

As usual, Romano parked in the rear lot and walked around to the front entrance. He headed straight to the rear dining room and was disappointed to see that Rocco had not arrived yet. Off in the right rear corned was a small bar with three stools. He sat on one, ordered a Dewars on the rocks and anxiously waited for his friend.

It was 6:45 p.m.; Romano was sipping his second drink when Rocco walked in. After a silent cursory greeting, Rocco motioned with his head indicating his usual table, the last booth on the left. Banducci slid in first, facing the door as usual. Romano took the seat facing him.

The cop inside him was silently arguing with another adversary, *Damn, I don't like it with my back to the door. Don't worry, you can trust Rocco to see any potential problem coming in. All these years and it's always been fine. Relax.*

Rocco, a fair judge of people, was able to see the tension in his friend.

He began with, "Michael, is that your first drink? I better order three more, another for you and two for me. I want to catch up. Allow me to apologize for my lateness. I had to shake a tail. Some Federal guy was on my ass."

"You what?" the last remark brought Mike to full alert.

Rocco smiled and replied, "He's like an old friend. From time to time, he attempts to follow me. We play a cat and mouse game. Today, the cat lost and the mouse won. We even leave birthday cards on each other's car. It's been going on for years."

"That sounds crazy. Some day you have to tell me all about it. Right now I have to ask a serious question."

"You're a good friend, ask away."

Mike was feeling better and couldn't resist a tease.

"With all that action, you must be hungry. Are you hungry? I sure would like a double cheeseburger, anything for you?"

"Very funny Michael, I'll have a BLT. Thanks."

After they ordered, Romano finally began to explain the reason for the requested meeting. He began by relating the story about the pellet gun shooting and the father's demand for leniency from him towards the two boys.

He emphasized the parent's comment that Mike was, "Italian and related to half the wise-guys in the borough."

Rocco smiled as he responded, "I wondered when you would finally ask that very question. After our long association, I guess it's time for an explanation. Yes, Michael, you're *Family*, in the New York Italian sense. While you and I are not actually related by blood, but some of my associates are."

"Holy shit!" was Mike's response to the bombshell.

"Don't get all excited and paranoid, some of the people in the Costello family group are your cousins. It goes back to your grandfather's old town in Italy. As you know Sam, actually Samuele Costello is *Capo Di Tutti Capi* and the Banducci's along with the Romano's and several others are part of that group. Naturally, not every relative is in the life, there are many relatives who lead normal lives. Occasionally, one comes along that those members in my line of work respect. You my friend, are one of the rare few."

"How long have you known this?"

"I knew of your background since I began dating your former sister-in-law, Kelly. I learned just how righteous you were when you saw me in the cage in Midtown and later you unselfishly gave me advice. You immediately earned my respect and that of all my associates."

"So you're telling me that I'm directly related to *made men*?"

"Yes, but you're fine. You made it to the police force didn't you? Never cross over the line and you'll be okay. Everyone respects you because you're a straight guy. You're just on the o ther side, that's all. You do your job and never make it personal, my people know that and that's what they like about you. Did I answer your question?"

"My head is still trying to wrap itself around this. It's kind of scary. What about Prego and others like him? I don't want to lose my job, I like it."

"Just stay the way you are Michael and you never will; plus you have the knowledge that you'll never be hassled unjustly by most people you might come into contact with. It's power, enjoy it."

"Holy shit Rocco, this sounds like a television show but it's real. I'm at a loss for words."

"Just remember, if you're ever questioned about it, deny, deny, deny. If it gets too crazy, you can always call me for clarification. You're like a brother to me."

"Wow, I need time to get used to this. How do I thank you for being honest with me?"

Rocco chuckled before answering, "By picking up the check this time."

"Done," Mike answered with a snap.

"I'm only kidding my friend; I assure you that I can afford it better than you and it's my pleasure. Now about your ex…"

The two men shared another drink before they left. Mike drove home anxious to share the information with his Lillian.

***

Lillian was at home alone when Mike arrived. He grabbed a Dewars and water and detailed the circumstances that led to the cryptic conversation with Dominic Prego. Next, he explained what Rocco Banducci had told him. He had just found out that not only was he now *connected*, but *family*.

"Lilly, as you know, Rocco has always been a friend. I sometimes walk a very thin line maintaining the friendship. Logically, I should sever it, but my instinct or inner voices tell me it will be okay. Do you have any opinion?"

Lilly smiled at him and gave him a gentle peck on the cheek, then answered, "Michael, my Michael, you're a good person and a moral one. You've always followed your heart, I'm sure you'll choose the right thing to do."

"Yeah, but now I have you and I don't want to jeopardize our comfort by me losing my job."

Lillian grabbed Mike's hand and spoke softly, "You have always trusted your *inner voice*, trust it now. Remember what you told me? That Rocco always tells you to never change your ways, well, that goes double for me, Mister Saint Michael"

Mike embraced his wife, "Thanks for always saying something to make me feel better. I love you, Lilly."

***

When Romano returned to work the following day, Sam Battle was already there and Sergeant Fitzpatrick was in his office.

Sam said, "Good Morning Mike. Are you over that shithead's accusations yet?"

"Yeah, now I realize that he was just trying to do right by his kids by blowing smoke out of his ass. It's all good. Is Richie coming in today?"

"No, Fitz said that he's over in Coney Island with Detective Schroder on the Robinson case. It's just us, once again."

"Sam, after I catch up on my paperwork from yesterday's collar and do some 5's, I'm going to go across the street and ask Bernie if he has a new address for the Lewis kid. If he has one or my hook at the phone company comes up with one, I'd like to go out and interview him. Are you up for that in a couple of hours?"

"Sure Mike. I enjoyed the show yesterday." Sam then emitted what was his signature deep chuckle and continued, "Maybe we can both have fun today, but of course, I'm not an *Eye-talian* like you."

Two hours later, Mike paid a visit to Bernie and returned with the latest address they had on the Lewis kid.

"Sam, Bernie came up with an address for Lemar. He gave me 1799 Stillwell Avenue apartment three, with a phone number that is supposed to belong to his sister, Keisha Lewis. I don't want to call her but I do want to talk to the kid. Are you ready to take a ride, partner?"

"Hey, Mike, do you think she's a looker?"

"It doesn't matter; we're going there to see Lemar."

Twenty minutes later the partners pulled up in front of a small three story, red brick apartment building.

Finding the door front locked, Sam pushed all six of the apartment bell buttons. The door lock buzzed and the men went inside. They found a small bank of mailboxes with apartment numbers and took a chance, ringing the doorbell on what they thought was apartment three and they got lucky.

From behind the closed door a male asked, "Who's there and what do you want?"

Sam answered, "We're detectives and we want to get your help in finding somebody. Got a few minutes?"

"Hold up badges to the peep hole."

"Sure thing; get a good look little brother."

Satisfied, Lemar opened the door with, "Sorry, can't be too careful. Come on in."

Mike spoke first. "Lemar, you're not in any trouble or anything, but we need some information on the bride robbery."

"Yeah, I worked that night and so did my old roommate, Dimitri. Are you here because of him?"

"Sam questioned, "Why do you ask?"

Lemar was quick with his reply. "Well, you two DT's visit me and ask for help on the robbery of a bride on a night that I worked. My former roommate then gets a sucky attitude and throws me out the next day. I gotta be stupid to think anything else. Wh'da wanna know?"

Mike picked up the questioning at that point.

"Lemar, do you know if Titov had anything to do with the robbery?"

"No sir, but I guess he did, because he threw me out and Bernie says he disappeared."

"Okay, just what can you tell me about the guy? Did you ever see him with friends or anyone outside of work? Did the other workers like him?"

Lemar looked past the two detectives for a moment before answering, as if deciding what to say.

Finally he spoke, "He tried to introduce me to some of his friends. It started at the hall, you know. Sometimes, a couple of them would meet him outside after work. They'd be sitting in a car and blowing a joint. Dimitri tried to get me to hang with them but I always said no."

Mike thought, *damn, this kid has something to say but is holding back,* "Listen lemar, we're not here about you or weed smoking. We're here to find Dimitri and need your help. What are you holding back?"

"Dimitri hung out with two black dudes and a couple of Russians. He sold pot and pills that they supplied to him from somewhere in Coney Island. That's all I know."

Mike and Sam exchanged glances before Sam

asked, "Little brother, did he sell anything at work, at the Colonnade?"

"Yeah, sometimes, some weed and mabye pills.'

"Do you know who bought the stuff?"

"Yeah, but I don't want to say. I don't wanna lose my job. You understand?"

Holy shit, Bernie's daughter. "That's fine kid. We do understand and we'll be going now." Mike offered one of his business cards. "Here, call me if you remember anything else.

Outside Mike asked, "Sam, do you think what I think, that Bernie's daughter might be buying weed or whatever from Dimitri?"

"Sure enough, partner. That's what it sounded like. Lemar threw us a big enough hint. Just how are you gonna handle it?"

"It shouldn't come into play. I'll only use the information if we come up dry on the pursuit of Dimitri and his friends."

Mike and Sam had just sat down at their respective desks when Mike's phone rang. Putting the receiver to his ear he heard, "Detective Romano please."

"This is Romano, can I help you?"

"Mike, Joe Lipor here. I have some results regarding those names you gave me, not the best but it's something. Got a pen and paper?"

Mike rustled around for a clean pad before saying, "Ready, shoot."

"First, I have nothing on Dimitri Titov. There are several Titovs in your area of Brooklyn; here they are..."

Joe recited six Titov listings. After hearing Romano repeat the list, he continued, "As to Lewis, the list is quite extensive; there are 127 names in Brooklyn alone. Do you want them?"

"It's not necessary, Joe. I've already met with Lemar Lewis. Currently he lives with his sister. I'm good on that one. Thank you so much for your help with Titov. Now, I have something to work with."

"Mike, it was my pleasure. Talk to you soon." The line went dead.

Sam asked, "Mike, Was that your phone guy?" Did you get some results?"

"Yeah, six listings for Titov and over one hundred for Lewis, and that's just near our command. I don't need Lewis anymore, but now we have something to work with regarding Titov. Tomorrow, I want to visit all the locations."

Sam responded, "Terrific and while we're out, I can hit some pawn shops and jewelers for my burglary case. It's a date. I'll pick you up at your office."

In an answer to Sam's silliness, Mike responded, "Oh, big boy, I can't wait. Is it your treat?"

CHAPTER SEVEN

The following morning, all three of the Dinosaurs were present and started their work in the squad as usual, first, coffee, small talk and such. After several minutes, Richie Levy got called into the sergeants' office to discuss the latest developments in the Robinson case.

While Levy was sequestered inside with the two supervisors, Romano and Battle gathered up their papers, grabbed a set of car keys and a portable radio before signing out to the field.

Their first stop was to be one of the addresses for one of the Titovs listed in the Brighton Beach section of Coney Island, known to the locals as Little Odessa because almost all the inhabitants were immigrants from Russia. Sam had planned to canvas that area's pawn shops while out with Mike.

The ebony detective took the wheel and asked, "Okay partner, where's our first stop?"

"I might as well start at the top of the list. The first one is, 3105 Brighton 5th Street, apartment 6A. Maybe I'll get lucky."

"Good, those apartment houses are near the Brighton Beach Station of the "B" Line. There's plenty of activity nearby; a few pawn shops and some Russian clubs. Maybe it'll work out for both of us."

***

Sam Battle drove to the area and stopped across the street from a storefront that had a sign with three words written in Cyrillic characters. Because of the items in the shop's windows and the universal three golden balls suspended over the doorway, Romano knew that was to be their first stop.

Sam, put the *bubble light* on the dashboard and announced, "First pawn shop, let's go partner."

The team sprinted across the street avoiding two speeding cars.

Mike commented, "Were they trying to kill us?"

Without answering, Sam motioned for Mike to enter the business first.

Behind the counter was a bear of a man. He looked like a Hollywood version of a Russian. He was big, bulky, dark haired and had hairy arms.

The place had three glass enclosed display cases set in a horseshoe pattern along three walls. At first the counter man only looked up and smiled, generally ignoring Romano's presence but went on full alert when he noticed Battle. He cleared his throat as if mustering his courage before speaking and then went into an obviously well perfected act.

"Welcome gentlemens to my humble business. Is something you would like to see, yes?! I am Mishka, the owner." His thick accent revealed that he was obviously a relatively new arrival to the United States.

Pointing to his partner, Mike answered, "My friend is looking for something. He'll tell you."

Mishka put his hands together in a humble gesture coupled with a slight bow. He had perfected his act in an effort to diminish any appearance of being a threat because of his size. He didn't want to piss off the men who were obviously cops.

"Ahh, yes, Mister. You see something you like perhaps."

Sam smiled as he held his shield up, "Yes, there is. I'm looking for a man who may have sold you some stolen goods."

Mishka's face drained of all color. "Mishka does not deal in theft merchandise."

"I didn't say that, you did. Maybe the guy came in to sell something. I would like to show you a picture of some items. You may remember them."

Continuing to act nervous, Mishka responded, "Yes, yes, as in Russia, I always are eady to help police. What you looking for?"

Sam reached into the breast pocket of his suit to get some photos to show to him.

As he did, wide eyed, the Russian bear softly muttered, "No, please, no."

Mike thought, *Damn he's good.*

Sam laughed, "We don't shoot people in this country unless they are a threat first. Are you a threat to us Mishka?"

"No, Mr. Detectives. I only want to help. Show pictures please."

Sam produced two sheets of paper, photocopies of pictures of stolen jewelry and coins. The complainant in the case had supplied two original pictures. He then placed them on the counter and slid them in front of Mishka.

The Russian slid them around on the counter in an effort to convince the detectives that he was examining them closely and also tried to act as if he didn't recognize anything, but the two detectives could tell that he was acting.

Mike in particular noticed the man's breathing had

increased.

"Sam, you hang out and talk with Mishka, I'm gonna have a look in the cases and maybe find something for my wife," he said before moving to another counter.

Mishka looked up and said, "Yes, good, I give you good deal. No problem."

While Sam continued his verbal jousting with Mishka, Mike examined the cases. He stopped when he noticed a commemorative coin that looked like something on Sam's list, a 1988 Olympiad Silver Dollar coin.

He called out, "Mishka, if you and my partner are finished, I see something that I want to look at."

Sam and Mishka came over, Sam was grinning. To hide his enthusiasm, he covered with, "Hey, Mikey, you're finally going to spring and buy your wife something?"

When the big man was in front of him, Mike asked to see a gold bracelet that was on the same shelf as the coin.

Two hands, the size of catcher's mitts, flipped *the* bracelet around to show it off before handing it to Mike who feigned interest for a few seconds, then asked to look at the silver coin.

Mishka answered any question Romano might have had as he reluctantly reached for it and said, "But why of looking at silver when women like gold so much. Wife will like gold bracelet much better."

Mike responded, "Oh, it's not for my wife, it's for me. Can I see it?"

Mishka hesitated as he handed it to Mike.

Romano turned to his partner with the coin in his hand. "Hey Sam, does this look like something from your list?"

Battle took the coin, "It sure does." Turning his attention to the big Russian, he asked, "My friend, who sold this to you?"

The genuinely nervous reply was, "Detective, I do not remember. There are so many people to sell me things. I cannot remember."

Sam, annoyed at playing the game responded, "Look my Russian friend. We are New York City Detectives so don't bullshit us. By law, you must record everything that you buy along with who sold it to you. I want to see the list."

"Detective, sometimes on small things like this, I forget. You know it's only one piece silver coin."

"Listen to me, cooperate with us or we'll place uniform police inside your store, get a warrant to search and close you down. We both know that in your counters or your safe are stolen goods. What do you have to say to that?"

"Of course, Mishka will cooperate. You want the coin? Take it, it is yours."

Mike spoke, "No Mishka, we don't want the coin. We want the man who sold it to you."

"I remember face, because he is Russian and came in with a black man. Black man sold coin to me. Both peoples say, they have many more coins and will bring them to me. If it is your wish, take coin now and I will call when more come. Yes?"

Mike's mind snapped to attention at the off chance that the Russian accompanied by a black male was Dimitri Titov. Could he get that lucky?

"Sam, please give me the car keys. I want to get something to show Mishka."

Sam responded in a tone that implied that the big guy would get his ass busted if he got stupid, "Sure, Mike. I'll keep our friend company."

Romano returned with the "Bride" case folder. He dropped two photo arrays on the counter and directed Mishka, "Look at these pictures and tell us if you see anybody that you know."

Apparently taking his time to decide if he should give up any information, the big man slowly looked over each sheet twice. Having made his decision, he pointed to two photos.

"This man is Russian also who come in with other Russian and this black man. Russian in picture gave coin to black man. Other man say they have many more and could bring soon. I say yes to them but they not come yet."

Mike and Sam exchanged glances that said, *"We got lucky, now we have to work it."*

Romano asked, "Do you know the name of the white man in the picture?"

"Da, he is know to me as Dimitri. The other man I see here."

"What about the black man? Do you know him?"

"Sometime he comes in with Dimitri and other Russian young people to sell things. Only name I know is him," he answered poking Titov's photo for a second time.

Sam gently pulled on Mike's arm while saying, "Come outside a minute will you?"

The two cops stepped just outside the door, closing it to block their conversation. They continued to watch Mishka through the class door to make sure he didn't get on a phone or disappear into the nonpublic recess of the store.

Sam quickly said, "Go with me here. We can both close our cases by getting these shitheads. Okay? I want to set up an arrest situation. Act as if we had a disagreement."

"Sure, you have the floor."

Back inside, Sam approached Mishka and put the silver coin on the counter, sliding it towards him. "Thank you for your help my friend. You can keep the coin but I want something in return."

"What it is? You want bracelet, ring or watch?"

"No, nothing like that. First, I need your full name and don't lie, we'll check."

The counterman was too nervous not to cooperate. "Mishka Kaminsky."

"You have been dealing in stolen goods. Now I personally don't want to arrest you even though my partner does. So in the spirit of *Glasnost* I'll tell you exactly what I want."

"Of course Detective Sam, I will help any way I am able."

"Okay. When those boys come in again, I want you to tell them that you will buy all the coins and whatever other stuff they are willing to sell you in one big bunch. You must somehow tell them that they must first give you time to get the cash ready, maybe two hours. At that time, you are to call my office and ask for me, only me. I will give you exact instructions as to what I want you to do. Understand?"

Mishka had been watching Mike pace the room as he spoke with Sam.

"Yes, but I do not want to have problem with gang. They maybe be part of Russian Mafia, you know, *Bratva*. I do not need that kind problem. You will keep me out of any problems, yes?"

"You'll be fine, don't worry. You must trust me in this and you can keep your shop and continue your successful business here."

"Your partner, Detective Mike, does not look happy

about arrangement. You will speak to him?"

Sam gave Mishka one of his business cards and answered, "He'll follow what I say. In your country, senior officers give orders to younger officers. Is that not true?"

"Yes, of course, that is the proper way."

Sam smiled broadly at his subject and then cast a menacing look at Mike before answering, "Well, I am the senior officer!"

***

Once back in their car, Mike commented, "Well, that went well." He chuckled and continued, "Mr. Senior Officer, do you think that he'll keep his word?"

"I've been in this command for over two years Mike and I've had to deal with the influx of new immigrants besides you Eye-talians, and frankly, I get along better with the Russians."

"Bullshit. Italians and blacks are related; didn't Hannibal invade Italy using elephants back in the day? Conquering soldiers always intermingle with the locals. Don't they? Shit, we may be blood relatives."

An observer would be hard pressed to etermine which partner was enjoying the exchange more. Maybe they were indeed related somewhere or somehow during the creating of the universe.

CHAPTER EIGHT

Two uneventful workdays and a swing (regular days off) passed without any extraordinary new cases for the "Dinosaurs." Only two of them would be present for that set because Richie had been assigned over to work the Robinson case with Schroder 6th Homicide in Coney Island. There were rumors of progress in the case, but nothing on paper. This workweek was to be Romano's first set of four to midnights with his new team.

Sam and Mike had settled down at their respective desks to begin the sometimes-boring paperwork of formulating and writing follow-up reports, sorting through the squad's in basket and the like. they had been at it an hour when the phone on Sam's desk rang.

Mike looked up as he heard Sam's voice.

"Detective Battle, Six-Four Squad... Yeah, that's great. What time?" Okay. We'll be ready. Now here's what will happen..."

Mike listened to Sam's end of the conversation. It was Mishka from Coney Island.

Dimitri Vitov had just left his shop and had carried in several boxes of the silver commemorative coins listed as stolen by the complainant in Sam's case.

The subject was asking $5000 for the coins that he claimed were valued at $42,000.

The Russian shopkeeper managed to put him off for an hour claiming that he didn't have enough cash on hand. He had explained to the thief that he would go to a fellow shopkeeper for some money.

Mishka had left his brother behind to mind the shop as he left. Once inside his friend's business, he went into the back room with the owner to call the detectives on the off chance one of the thieves was watching him.

Mike listened as Sam explained to the big man that he as the owner, would be arrested with the others and that would hide the fact that he was working with the police. His brother was not directly involved and would not be taken allowing him to keep the shop open.

Once in the station house a false call to a district attorney would release him from custody.

The shopkeeper's reluctant response was, "Da, I will inform this to my brother."

The two detectives, with Sergeant Scala's blessings, left the office.

The first thing the team did was to use their portable radio and ask the police dispatcher for a patrol car team to meet them a few blocks away from the pawnshop as a precautionary measure. The detectives anticipated multiple arrests and would need them to help with apprehension and transport. They did not want Mishka with other prisoners during the ride to their office.

The uniformed men were to stay out of sight, but close enough to be instantly available if needed. They were to use the tac 5 channel for point to point communication.

Brooklyn, always notorious for double-parking, allowed two men sitting in a Chevy to blend in and not attract much attention. They took a position across from, but not directly in front of the shop.

Mike, always impatient, asked, "Sam, just how long do you think it will take the bad guys to return?"

"I don't know Mike, but look, there's our Russian

buddy. He just came out of the store; look at him, he's as nervous as a cat watching out for a pack of dogs. I guess he's as anxious as we are."

"Yeah, for such a big man he looks scared and like he's about to pee himself."

"He'll be fine. Please, just sit back and enjoy the view. You must have had lots of wait time working narcotics."

"Yeah, but that was different. It was always, the State of New York against the bad guys. Now I have real complainants. I feel so sorry for the bride and groom in my case. I'd like to get their money back, or at least whatever the shitheads didn't spend."

"Look my friend, we're not social workers, we're cops. Our job is to lock up the criminals we encounter, if at all possible; it's not our job to find and return property."

"I know, but why can't we do it all?"

"Listen Mike, we can't always recover and return property. We can do it only about half the times, because the thieves still have all or some of what they stole, or we have to track it down, as we're doing now. You know that after the DA is finished with it, the victims get a release and then can go get their stuff."

The voice inside Romano's head told him, *you're gonna do well in this case. Relax.*

An additional twenty more minutes passed before they saw Dimitri Vitov and a black man walking towards their target location; each carrying a satchel that appeared to be heavy. Two other young men, both white, walked closely behind them.

Romano blurted out with, "We got 'em Sam, they're carrying something awfully heavy."

Battle picked up his portable and announced, "Squad

here. Be alert. Our two subjects are approaching our target, followed by two male whites that are probably with them. Roll up to the shop slowly until you can see our car but do not approach."

The answer was almost instantaneous, "Patrol, ten-four. Rolling," seconds later, "we see you now. Advise."

"When we leave our car, move up on anyone that might be out front."

"We're on it guys. We'll move up as if we're pulling a foot post and are bored shitless."

Romano pulled on his door handle.

"Easy Mike. Wait until the door closes behind them, then walk, but walk quickly, as if you're avoiding traffic as we cross the street. We don't want them to get nervous and run. When we hit the sidewalk, rush into the store."

"Let's do it."

"Keep an eye on the other two as we move, in case they have weapons to protect the two target dirt bags. Hopefully the uniform guys will grab them as we hit the doorway."

The satchel carrying bad guys entered the store.

Mike and Sam quickly, yet stealthfully, slid out of their car as they had planned and sprinted across the street, looking right and left as if they were dodging vehicular traffic.

They could see the two uniformed backup men walking along the sidewalk towards their location as if on normal foot patrol and in normal conversation. Just as the detectives hit the sidewalk, the uniforms grabbed the other two men, without incident.

Nano seconds later, the two detectives entered the location. Everything worked like a good Swiss watch.

Inside the location, Mishka gasped and threw his

hands up as the two detectives pulled their weapons and shouted, "Police, don't move!!"

Sam ordered, "All hands flat on the counter and you two, drop the bags."

Before Titov could react, Mike reached around his neck grabbing his larynx and applying some mild pressure with his left hand, he ordered, "Don't move until I tell you."

Mike heard Sam deal with the man in possession of the second satchel. "I said, drop the bag you sonna bitch," along with the sounds of a scuffle.

The two detectives jumped when they heard the street door open. It was the uniformed backup team.

"Go easy Detectives, it's Jones and Carter behind you and we're bringing in two under arrest, with weapons recovered."

No more than 10 seconds passed before all four bad guys were cuffed and under control.

Sam asked, "Who has extra cuffs? I'm taking the counter man too."

Jones handed him another set of the sliver bracelets.

Sam continued as scripted and informed Mishka that he was under arrest too, for knowingly receiving stolen property. In keeping with the program, he protested like a wounded bull.

At that point, Uri entered the sales area from the rear of the store. He did his part and acted quite indignant.

"What is happening? For why is my brother being arrested? You American pigs just want to lock up Russians. Release him and Get fuck out!"

Romano held back a laugh and thought, *acting must be a family tradition. Someday I have to ask what they did in Russia.*

Mike responded with, "You, pain in the ass, get

over next to your brother, lock your fingers together, and keep your hands on top of your head. One move and I'll blow you out of your shoes." *I can act too.*

Detective Battle then reached down and brought the two satchels up from the floor, putting them on the counter top. "Damn, these are heavy."

He opened the top of both and looked inside.

"Jackpot! The silver coins, lots of them are in this one; more coin, jewelry and a semi-auto in the other."

He turned to the man who had hesitated before dropping the bag and shouted, "No wonder you didn't want to drop it. Boy, I wish that you tried to run or open the bag. Your ass would have been in pieces. No more crap. Got it?"

Sam, grabbing only the grips, removed the gun; a brush finished, stainless steel, Colt Mustang .380 semi-automatic.

"It's heavy; the thing is loaded and looks ready to go. Maybe we'll print it later," he said, replacing it and closing the bag.

Mike added, "Maybe my complainants can identify the gun. That would be a score."

Battle then asked the uniformed men, "What did you guys take off your two shitheads?"

Each cop handed a weapon to Sam, one .38 Colt Detective Special and a Browning 9 MM semi-auto, both black finished. They also identified who had which gun. The rounds were visible in the revolver and the 9MM was heavy enough to be loaded too. Sam put them into the second satchel. Multiple handling negated use of latent prints, but getting a gun off the street is always good.

"You guys were terrific. Thank you. Now, if one of you will get your car and give us a hand, we can transport these shitheads to the Six-Four."

Officer Carter jokingly asked, "Can you three handle this crowd while I get the RMP?"

He then left the store returning with his patrol car about a minute later.

Officer Carter walked into the pawn shop smiling, "Ready for transport fellas."

Mike pulled his portable out from under his jacket. "Six-Four Squad to Central, K."

"Central here, go ahead Six-Four Squad, K."

"Central, we have five under and will transport all back to the Six-Four from 606 Brighton Beach Avenue to the Six-Four. Be advised we have two uniform members with RMP 1133 from the Six Five assisting us with transport. They will be 10-62 out of service as needed, K"

"Received and acknowledged, Squad."

Mike turned to Uri, "You can stay here to run the shop. Behave and someone will call to inform you when we send your brother downtown and where to meet him with a lawyer."

The only reply was, "Da."

The two uniformed cops again frisked all involved. Then the two gunmen and the yet unidentified black man were brought outside and stuffed into the patrol car.

Uri asked, "You take Mishka now?"

Romano answered, "Yes."

Continuing to hide Mishka's involvement, Sam said, "Look you, your brother is involved with stolen goods. Keep quiet, don't ask questions and we won't take you too. Understand?"

"Da."

The detectives gave another pat down to both

Dimitri and Mishka in the interest of safety. Then they each grabbed a satchel loaded with the contraband and walked across the street with their charges.

After putting the satchels into the trunk, the two prisoners were unceremoniously stuffed into the rear seat of their car.

Sam drove as Mike positioned himself sideways to watch the arrestees. The uniform car followed.

CHAPTER NINE

The five men arrested by Romano and Battle, with the assistance of officers Jones and Carter were herded into the Six-Four Squad's office.

After the prisoners were separated and re-secured with handcuffs belonging to the squad, the assisting uniformed team from Coney Island got their hardware returned to them. After some hand shaking, they were heartily thanked for their assistance and released to return to their own duties.

With five prisoners in the office, Sergeant Scala asked the desk officer to send up a man to assist controlling the multiple detainees. Mishka, still handcuffed, was placed in a chair in the corner of the break room.

The young black man now claimed that his name was Willie Mayes.

"Ya, know like the ball player," and "I didn't rob nobody."

He remained cuffed and dropped into another chair in the opposite corner of the room and was hooked to the wire mesh window guard. Dimitri and the others were brought to the cage where they were released from their bonds and locked inside.

As required, Sam gave Miranda warnings to Mayes and the big Russian, while Mike attended the other three.

Feeling comfortable that their criminals were properly attended to, the partners donned latex gloves, to protect any fingerprints, before making the recovered firearms safe. After doing so, they then took Polaroid photos of all the property, including the guns. The work was tedious and they were growing tired. They spent more time than anticipated while marking and cross referencing everything.

The busy detectives spent the next hour vouchering and bagging everything, including the recovered coins and jewelry.

The firearms were brought into the Sergeants' office and locked in a file cabinet on the possibility a complainant could identify a weapon as belonging to one of their assailants.

The other items were brought down to the desk lieutenant who logged everything in and put it all in the property room.

After returning to the office, the two detectives photographed the five arrested men. They would be used in photo arrays if it became necessary on the chance that one or more of the *Bride and Groom* victims were unable to respond for a "show up" identification of the arrestees.

Romano reached out to his complainants by phone. Both couples promised that they would all arrive together within two hours.

Sam also reached his complainant who promised that he would, "Be right over."

The first process to prepare them for transportation to Brooklyn Central Booking was fingerprinting of the men beginning with Mishka. He was now genuinely protesting because he had expected to have been released much sooner.

Mike printed the big Russian shopkeeper first and then returned him to a seat in the corner of the outer office that was actually, at Romano's own desk, in plain sight of the caged group.

After cuffing the man to the metal grate covering the window, Mike made the previously planned, *call to the*

District Attorney. Mike spent several minutes explaining the parameters of Mishka's involvement in the case to a disembodied voice that was repeating the current weather report.

"Yes Sir, I understand. Correct, I can't prove that the coin I saw in his display case was one of the stolen ones. Yes, Sir, there was six million of them minted and it was not in a box with the others. Yes Sir. I will release him and give him his fingerprint cards. Yes, thank you."

Turning back to Mishka he said, "You are one lucky guy. You heard some of the conversation. The District Attorney ordered me to let you go. Relax while I take the handcuffs off."

"Da, I told you I was not involved with these men. I not a gangster."

As he handed all but one of the fingerprint cards to the big man, Mike shouted to his sergeant, "Sarge, I'll be right back. I'm gonna escort this guy outside. The DA says we gotta let him go."

Scala answered with, "Four out of five and two cases closed ain't bad. Good work fellas. Get on it."

Once outside, Mike asked, "Mishka, do you have a way to get back to your store?"

"Yes; Detective Mike, I will call friend for a ride. You are an honorable man, just like Mishka. You sure you not Russian?" he added with a laugh and a handshake followed by a loosley executed man hug.

As Mike re-entered his office, young Mayes was trying to cut a deal with Sam Battle. With only four prisoners left, Tony Scala had sent the uniformed man back down to the regular command.

From inside the cage, his two Russians cohorts were arguing with Dimitri in the native language. Occasionally a highly accented threat in English was hurled in Mayes' direction.

Battle and Scala, both seasoned investigators, were smiling; each man knowing that they were making progress towards entirely completing every aspect of both cases.

The detectives and their sergeant allowed the action to continue for several minutes while sharing coffee with the eager to cooperate, Mr. Mayes.

***

The phone on Sam's desk rang and he rushed to answer it.

"Detective Battle, Six-Four Squad, can I help you?"

"Detective Battle, it's Officer Cummings on the TS (telephone switchboard), I have two complainants here that say you're expecting them. Can I send them up?"

Sam chuckled as he answered, "Just at the right time. Please send them up at once." After replacing the receiver, he turned and strode to the office door to meet them.

Several seconds later, a distinguished looking man with skin the color of Café au lait approached the office accompanied by an attractive woman of similar color; both were neatly dressed in clothing that indicated upper middle class status.

Sam stopped them outside the door just before they entered. "Thank you for coming so quickly Doctor. One moment please."

The man said, "Detective, please meet my wife, Parsaud."

"Mrs. Singh, it's my pleasure." Without hesitation he continued, "As I told you when I telephoned, we have arrested some men that were in possession of coins and jewelry. They appear to be the same as items you listed in your Burglary complaint.

"I see," said the doctor.

"I'm going to walk you past them on the possibility that you may recognize one or more of them. They have no idea why you're here, so don't be afraid."

The couple nodded in acknowledgement.

"Next, I'm going to take you to a closed room for our conversation. Once inside, I'll show you pictures of property that we recovered and hope that you can identify some or all of the items. They will not be able to hear us. Ready?"

Singh answered for both of them, "Yes, please lead the way."

The men in the cage were still having noisy discussion and appeared to be arguing. Sam quickly led the couple past the cage, but as planned, hesitated for a second to announce, "Sarge, I have to speak with a complainant inside on another matter. I'll only be a few minutes."

Sam led the couple into the records room adjacent to the Sargent's Office. After closing the door behind them, he gave the Singhs ample time to look at the photos of the coins and jewelry. He told them that he had listed the doctor as the owner of the property on all the vouchers. He also explained that at some point in the prosecution of the defendants, after the District Attorney's Office was satisfied the property was no longer needed, they would be instructed as to how they could retrieve their property; of course, only if it was proven to be the Singh's property.

Excitedly, the doctor produced a list of the serial numbers that he had recorded from the storage/shipping boxes when his coins arrived from the issuing mint.

The detectives matched both the photos and the box numbers listed on the prepared vouchers against Singh's list. There was no doubt that the recovered coins belonged to them. Mrs. Singh recognized two bracelets as hers, leaving four other pieces of jewelry unidentified.

The bags containing the Singh bracelets were to be opened. New vouchers reflecting the identifications would be prepared along with a new set of property bags.

Sam asked if they possibly recognized any of the men that they had passed. They both answered, "No."

Ten minutes later, Detective Battle escorted them downstairs.

***

While his partner was downstairs with the Singhs, Mike, impatient as usual asked, "Sarge, would you be okay if I took Mr. Mayes to another office to have a private conversation with him? The three Russians are still in the cage."

Tony Scala, never the type of supervisor to stifle the enthusiasm of one of his men responded with, "I'm old enough to keep an eye on them alone. Sam just vacated the records room. You can use it, close the door and turn on the TV to mask your conversation if you're concerned about unauthorized eavesdropping."

"Sure thing Sarge, will do."

Mike walked over to Mayes and said, "Let's go kid, time for a talk."

Mayes, after trying to make a deal with Battle, was reluctant to be alone with Romano. Mike had to physically grab his arm and convince the young man to move.

"Listen kid, I want Dimitri and the Russians for

armed robbery. I'll talk to my partner for you. Work with me, will you?"

"Yeah, sure, Detective, I only know Dimitri from the neighborhood. He asked me to go with him because he needed help to carry stuff that he wanted to sell. I didn't know it was stolen.

"Oh sure!"

The kid was begging, "I also had no idea that there was a gun in my bag; and those two guys with guns... I never saw them before in my life. I swear."

"Fine Willie, if that's your real name. Remember, we have your fingerprints and you're going to be booked for possession of stolen property and gun possession. We can add lying to the police as another charge. Now help me and I'll speak to the District Attorney."

"You'll see Detective, it's my real name, I swear. My momma was a big baseball fan."

Romano's instinct was working like a well-oiled wristwatch. The voice inside his head kept saying, *Michael, the boy is lying. Don't let his friendly ways cloud your vision.*

Eager to begin the Q and A, Mike snapped, "Sure she was!"

Before Mike could begin his questioning, someone knocked on the office door. It was Sam.

Urgently he announced, "Hey partner, there's four people downstairs, a couple and their two cousins. They said it's important. Come on out. I'll sit with the famous Willie Mayes."

Mike understood and almost threw the office door off its hinges. He couldn't move quick enough; "He's all yours Sam. Thanks," he replied and almost ran to the stairway.

Reaching the bottom of the steps, Romano quickly

slid around the cold drink machine that was next to the final landing and into the station lobby. He saw all four of the complainants in his *Bride Case.*

The victims were nervously milling about, paired off in couples; the bride and groom, Doug and Janet Rossi, and their cousins, the best man and maid of honor, John and Kim Segar.

When they saw Romano, they surged forward, everyone began speaking at once, "Did you get the guys? Did you get our money back? Are they all here? Was Demetri involved?"

Mike chuckled and reached out to shake the men's hands. "Thank you all for coming. I understand that you're excited at the prospect of seeing the robbers arrested and jailed; that's fine, but there is a way to do it correctly."

Doug Rossi answered for the group. "Tell us what we have to do. We want the bastards to go to jail forever."

Will you all please follow me upstairs? We'll find an empty room and I'll explain just what we're going to do." He turned and led the way.

After securing the clerical staff lunchroom for his group, Mike explained just what he had planned for them. He would begin with each one viewing the subjects as an individual. The identification couldn't be tainted in any way. He would sit down with them all later in the squad office.

"Before we begin, I first have to go into my office to speak to my partner. I'll be right back, please excuse me," he said as he walked away.

Quickly, he went back to Sam, "Hey partner, I need the room. Can you please take Mr. Mayes into our coffee room and sit with him. Put him against the far window so I can see him from the doorway as I pass the cage. Thanks."

No explanation was necessary. Sam knew exactly what Mike was about to do. "Sure thing, you go do what you gotta do."

Normally, the proper way for a victim to identify a suspect would be with a proper line-up. In this case, with all the arrestees already locked into a burglary, possession of stolen property and possession of firearms. They would see jail time for sure and he had a plan B.

Romano decided that a *show-up* would be sufficient for his needs. After all, his complainants would see them *by accident.* If he was lucky and any of his complainants made a positive identification, he would use it to gather even further information about Dimitri's role if any.

As far as Mike was concerned, Titov was the mastermind behind the robbery and the link to finding the missing man.

***

"Now, Mrs. Rossi, Janet, please come with me to my office. There's something that I would like to discuss with you. As I explained before, we can't chance you being influenced by the other victims."

Janet gave her husband a quick peck on the cheek and left with Mike.

As they entered the office, Romano stopped to open the barrier gate and hold the door for her. It was just enough time for Janet to see the men in the cage.

"You! You set us up you bastard," she shouted, pointing at Dimitri.

Mike said, "Easy, we'll talk about that inside."

Janet was on a roll. "Those other two gorillas,

they're two more of them. The bigger guy is the one who threatened to take us away from our husbands. Can you charge him with threatening kidnapping?"

"Easy Janet, it's okay. No, there is no such charge."

His plan was working well. Mike moved her forward about two feet and pointed into the coffee room, "Would you like some coffee?"

Her eyes followed his hand and she shouted, "You got him too. Him, that one, was waving a black revolver. Good! There's one white guy missing. Are you going to get him too?"

Sergeant Tony Scala was standing in the doorway that led from the coffee room to his office. He was smiling because he had witnessed the identification. He had no doubt that his detective was going to walk every complainant past the cage. He decided to remain quiet and watch knowing that he would have to sign all the DD-5 reports for both detectives.

At that point, Scala decided that the two detectives made a great team, perhaps the best in the office.

Janet Rossi, getting no answer to her last question turned to Mike and apologized, "Sorry Detective Romano. I know you're doing your best. Thank you. Will the others see them too?"

"Yes, they will Janet, one at a time. Please come inside with me."

Turning to Sam, he asked, "Sam, do you think that we can stuff Willie into the cage with the other guys now? Pretty soon, it's gonna get crowded in here."

Sam answered with his signature laugh and removed Maye's handcuffs as he stuffed him into the crowed cage. "Have fun boys and play nice."

Scala said, "Romano, I'll bring Mrs. Rossi into the

record room, you go get your next witness," obviously enjoying the game he added, "and don't forget to offer them coffee."

"Thank you Sarge. I'll get right on it."

Mike repeated his identification process three more time with the same success; the only differences were the words uttered by the complainants. All of the complainants were then brought to the larger break room. There they milled about as the detective closed the double doors to the squad room.

The detective explained that the next step in the prosecution of the men already arrested, would be for the complainants to tell their story to a writing ADA.

It was important that all of them were required to be downtown at the DA's office on Schemerhorn Street at 10:00 the next morning where they were to be interviewed by the writing ADA. The interview was necessary to properly articulate the crime and formally charge the defendants. He also assured them that he would try to find and arrest the missing man.

He told them that he planned to use Dimitri to try to recover some or all of their money, but he didn't mention that he knew it was almost impossible.

Ten minutes later, all the *Bride Case* complainants were gone. Mike and Sam sat in the record room to discuss what charges they could substantiate for each defendant.

Sam spoke first. "Well, let's see, we have each of the monkeys in the cage except Dimitri on gun charges. Dimitri and Willie are guilty of possession of stolen property. All charges apply to all my guys as co-conspirators. If any prints come back to match those recovered in my complainant's home, then I'll have the owners of those hands on the burglary also."

It was Mike's turn. "Happily, I have three out of four of my robbers. I'll add the weapons charges to elevate the charge to armed robbery, one count for each victim. Mayes is a lock for armed robbery. Now if I can work Dimitri to give up the last man, I'll have them all."

"Don't play around too long. You know that the geniuses in the Puzzle Palace want all arrestees in Central Booking within two hours whenever possible."

"Screw them. This is an ongoing investigation. I'll see if the Sarge will approve the time disparity. If he doesn't, I'll call an ADA and explain the situation, if they agree, the bosses won't dare complain then."

Mike went to speak to Scala. "Sarge, I'd like to play around with Titov. I really believe that he set up my robbery. Maybe I can get him to name the last stickup man before we take them downtown."

"Go ahead. Since when do you need permission to play a subject?"

"We're awful close to the two hour limit. It's gonna put us over and some high ranking boss who thinks he's a lawyer might bitch about it. I don't want either one of us to get caught up in any crap. I'll get ADA clearance if you want me to."

"Mike, I'm the supervisor and have witnessed your interviews or signed off on your paperwork so far and will continue to do so. You and Sam are doing a great job on this. Go for it and good luck!"

***

Romano went to the cage and removed Dimitri. He was going to set the hook in his fish now and took him into the record room, closing the door behind them.

Mike slid a chair into a corner between a file cabinet and a wall. Forcefully he ordered, "Sit."

The young Russian hesitated. Sitting down, he regressed into a heavy accent and asked, "What you vant? You already arrest me?"

Go ahead Mike, use acting lie number seven.

Mike began with, "First let me explain something. I didn't put handcuffs back on you because I want to help you. This is a Detective Office and we are detaining you. New York State Law says that I can shoot you if you try to escape from a detention facility. Because we are holding you here, that is what this is regarding you. Try to run and I will shoot you. Keep that in mind. Do you understand?"

"Da."

"Okay, now listen to me and don't interrupt."

"Da, you speak, I listen."

"As of this minute, right now, you're being formally arrested and charged with burglary, criminal possession of stolen property, illegal possession of firearms and armed robbery. They are all felonies and each is punishable by at least five years in jail. We have three guns, four victims on the robbery and two victims on the burglary and possession of stolen property. Do the math; it's about fifty five years total jail time."

Indignantly Titov answered, "What? I am only guilty of setting up theft of bride on night of wedding. I have no gun. What is burglary?"

Got you, you stupid ass. You just admitted to acting in consort on the robbery.

"Burglary is breaking into a person's home or business and taking property."

"I steal from nobody. I sell marijuana sometimes to guest at job. Dimitri is no thief." *Got ya again, keep going.*

"Listen to me. You got caught with the people who broke into the couple's house and had their property. You carried that property to sell it. These same people had guns with them. They were identified as being the stickup men and one gun was identified; you get charged with it all. That's the law."

Dimitri shrunk down into his chair. He looked like he just received a prison sentence. Romano knew that he had him.

After several moments of silence, the slick detective could see a glimmer of hope in the face of his subject.

"You bring me in this room to talk. You want something from Dimitri? I ask again. What is vant?"

Mike paused for effect. *Got him now. The game is on and it's called, human chess.*

"Okay Dimitri, here's what I want. I want the name of the missing stickup man. I also want whatever money that you guys took from the bride and groom."

"Detective, you are crazy. I tell people about big wedding and they do what they did. I do not even know those men. How do you expect that I can find taken money? I am not a Suka."

"What the hell is a Suka, Dimitri?"

Mike could see sweat forming on his brow. The kid was crapping his pants.

"I think you call such a person a bitch, no, a snitch, that is it, that is the word, a person who gives information to government person, a mussor, a cop. The word is not nice, it means garbage. That is what police are called in Russia. Nobody likes police."

Mike knew that he took the bait and continued acting.

"Listen, don't bullshit me. You know exactly who

those men are and also the name of the fourth man. I'll make you a deal; reach out and get the couples' money back, or what's left of it and tell me the name of the other man I want, then I'll ask the District Attorney to go easy on you. I'll ask him to charge you with the crime that carries the least jail time, maybe even probation, no jail time at all."

As he spoke, Mike was studying Titov's eyes and decided that he needed another push.

"If you don't give me the name of the last man in this robbery, not only will I do everything in my power to put you away. I'll let it slip in the prison that you're child molester and a homosexual. You can guess the rest."

"Detective you are a devious man and worthy of to be in KGB. That is not proper at all. How will you do this?"

Cold as ice, Mike continued his routine, "Dimitri, just know that I have my ways. I have many connections here in this Italian community and I am Italian. Your mafia started after World War II, we Italians invented it. Use your head, mabe I wear two hats; maybe I go back and forth across the line. Do you want to try me out? Is your manhood worth the risk?"

Titov was silent for several minutes. Romano pulled his own chair up to a file cabinet, opened a drawer and rummaged through the contents as if he was looking for something, yet watching his subject's expression and body language as the perp was deciding what to do.

From the door leading to the sergeants' office, Scala knocked and asked, "Detective Romano, how are you doing in there? It's awful quite. Is everything alright?"

When Scala knocked, Titov was startled and answered before Mike did.

"Da, Sergeant, I am tinking over a deal offer that

Detective Romano said to me. I believe that I take it and help him."

Inside his office, Tony Scala had overheard most of the conversation and smiled.

Without being asked, he announced, "Okay guys, I'm coming in to officially work it out."

Scala then entered the room and half-sat on the Tabletop next to the office computer. "Okay Romano, what does your prisoner have for us?"

Mike knew that his sergeant had probably heard the conversation that had just transpired. He knew that Tony Scala was covering all bases by acting as a witness to any further information that Titov was about to give. That's how the game was played.

"Well Sergeant, Dimitri here was about to give us the name of the fourth man in the *bride robbery case* in exchange for a good word to the District Attorney. He admits to giving information about the expensive wedding to the stickup team. He also admits to selling marijuana to guests at the catering place, but only sometimes."

Scala laughed, "Nice admission, another charge against him, selling drugs."

Both Mike and Tony knew that his admission would go nowhere without any evidence, but did this Russian immigrant know that? They assumed not.

"Dimitri, with my supervisor here in this room, I'll do you another favor. It's only been a couple days since the robbery. You make some calls, say whatever you have to say and have the stolen money delivered to Bernie at your old job, with the word, 'Bride' written on the package and I'll leave out the drug charges. Deal?"

"Why would someone give back money for to bride? It is maybe gone by now."

"As I told you, there are many people of power in this neighborhood. The bride and groom and their cousins, the other couple that you and your boys robbed, belong to a family that's connected. Do you know what connected means?"

Mike was on a roll, and without waiting for an answer, he took another shot with, "In your country and over in Brighton Beach, I think you call it a Brigade; is that the correct word for a crew of gangsters?"

Titov's eyes revealed the fact that Mike had just struck a nerve. The young novice criminal wanted no part of an Italian type payback. He knew that any problems between the two factions would cause him untold grief.

Mike glanced at is supervisor. Tony Scala had a serious look on his face but his eyes were smiling back at his detective. He gave a barely noticeable nod giving authorization for his detective to continue.

Romano ominously said, "Listen, I don't care how you do it, but some or all of that money has to get back to those kids. Your life and well-being depends on it."

Mike cautioned himself as he heard his own words. *Shit, I'm getting a little carried away. Gotta calm down and lighten up.*

"Dimitri, before we continue, would you like some coffee or a cold drink?"

"No Detective. I wish to finish this and get the process of your court system to begin. I would like how you call it, bail?"

"We do not give bail, a judge does. Just as soon as you give me the name of the last man, we'll get you downtown to see one."

Romano knew the writing ADA would not want to include the sale of drugs in the court affidavit without corroborative evidence, yet he thought that an admission from the defendant would at least get the charge to arraignment.

He continued to push Titov, "Remember, when you get bail, find the kid's money and I'll drop the drug charges before your next court date."

"Da. I give you name, Boris Kozlov from Kiev."

With his interview concluded, Mike returned his prisoner to the cage and filed a wanted card for the fourth man in his case.

Mike arranged with the desk officer to have the vouchered firearms transported to the police lab for forensic analysis, hopefully fingerprints belonging to the perps.

Sergeant Scala signed off on the arrest reports and officially ordered the prisoners to be brought downtown. He was extremely pleased with both of his detectives; four arrests, two cases closed and another collar in the works.

Sam and Mike herded Mayes and Titov into one of the two cars assigned to the squad. Uniformed cops would transport the other two. They were all to meet inside Central Booking where the four men would be processed in preparation for their court arraignment.

Before they left the office, Mike called home to tell Lilly that he would be several hours late because he made arrests in the *Bridge and Groom Case.*

Lillian responded with, "Good for you Michael. I can't wait to hear about it. I know that you worked hard on it; you deserve a reward", giggling, she continued, "if I'm asleep, wake me gently and we'll have a conversation about it." He knew what that meant; it was their euphemism for a sexual romp.

***

Mike arrived home at 2:00 a.m. and stealthfully ascended to their second floor bedroom. As he quietly removed his shoes, he glanced over to his apparently sleeping wife, resting peacefully. He almost felt guilty to awaken her, even though it was her request.

Mike moved to her side of the bed and gently kissed her. Lillian stirred and threw down the bedcovers revealing her alabaster nakedness in the glow of the television screen. He remained transfixed at her beauty.

Suddenly she reached up and clutched his neck pulling him down to her. "Tell me about the *Bride Case* after you take care of this bride first," she squealed.

"Quiet, you'll wake one kids, and they might get jealous," he admonished.

Their *conversation* was lengthy. Finally, Lilly asked, "Are you going to tell me about your day or do you want to converse some more?"

"Honey, thanks, but it was a long day, I'd rather tell you all about it."

Lilly nestled against his chest as he detailed his work day events.

"That's terrific but how can you ever expect the planner, Dimitri to send money back to those kids?"

"Well, Lil, you had to be there and see his face. He appeared terrified at the prospect of having the Italian mob after him. I think he'll come through with something."

Lillian smiled at her husband and responded with, "My, my, Saint Michael, always righting wrongs. You certainly are one dedicated cop. Now let's get some sleep."

***

Mike was awakened by the two oldest children, Paul and Bob, as they left the house laughing and carrying on like two little boys leaving for school. No one complained because Mike was usually an early riser. Sometimes, when they were excessively boisterous in the morning, their sister would complain or the dog would growl. He pulled on a pair of pajama bottoms and padded downstairs to the kitchen. Also as usual, neither of them put on the coffee pot. It was kind of an unwritten rule, Mike made coffee for himself and the women. The two brothers got theirs on the way to work.

Mike let the dog out into the rear yard while he waited for the electric perk to prepare the magical dark brown elixir. Once the coffee was ready, Romano poured himself a cup, black, and prepared a regular for Lillian, trying not to spill any on his way up to their bedroom.

Lillian rose from bed by 7:00 a.m., thanked her husband for the coffee and began getting ready to travel into Manhattan to her employment. Romano just propped himself against the headboard as he did every morning that he was home and watched Lilly get herself ready to face the day. He never got tired of drinking in her beauty. At 8:15, they said their goodbyes at the front door and he returned to the kitchen for a second cup of Java.

***

Anxious to begin the last tour before he swung out, Mike kept busy puttering around the yard until 2:00 p.m.

After a quick shave and a shower, he picked a suit from the closet along with a fresh shirt and tie. By 2:45, he was on his way to the squad office.

Charlie Wilson handed him a message as he walked in and said, "Hey Mike, got a call from Bernie across the street. He said that somebody left a Post Office express mail envelope with his name on it this morning. He didn't say anything else except to tell you right away."

"Yeah, I hoped he would call. I'll go see him soon as I sign in. Thanks."

Romano was pleased and thought, *I guess my story took hold inside Dimitri's brain after all.*

As Romano entered Bernie's office, the caterer stood and executed a mock salute towards Mike. "Detective Romano, my hat is off to you. Never in the entire time that I spent in this neighborhood and this business have I ever experienced anything like this. How in hell did you do it? Please sit."

Romano acted surprised. "What Bernie? I have no idea what you're talking about."

"You are obviously one of the most resourceful detectives on the force", he said as he slid the red, white and blue Express Mail envelope towards Mike.

He picked it up and examined it without looking at its contents. "What's inside Bernie? It looks like it wasn't even mailed, but the word *Bride* is on it."

"Inside is $11,200.00 in cash and a note to you. Read it," Bernie said while extending the envelope to Mike.

Removing only the note, Mike read, "Det., here is all that I could get. It is unfortunate that we chose such a couple. We, in the Russian community hope that they and their connections will accept this as an apology. We are truly sorry and many thanks for no drug charges. Please explain to family." It was unsigned.

"Romano, what do you think about that? How did you do it? Please take the money and give it to the kids."

Mike pocketed the note, "No Bernie, it was brought to you. You be the hero. Call them and have them pick it up. As to the rest of the note, I don't know what that thief is even talking about. I'm happy for the kids. I gotta go."

Back in the office, Sam had arrived and asked, "Hey Mike, I saw that you signed in but were nowhere in sight. Charlie said that you went across to see Bernie. What's up?"

"Seems like somebody delivered eleven grand this morning to give to my complainants in the *Bride Case.*"

Sam was surprised, "Holy crap, I thought that you were all wet when you told him to return the money. Did he say anything else?'

"Yeah, he thanked me for not charging him with drug sales, but I knew that it was a safe bet and would never get written by the ADA."

Sam laughed as he responded, "He must be afraid of the Mafia and knows for a fact that all you Italian guys are connected. I always wondered about you."

It was Mike's turn to chuckle.

The balance of the squad's tour was uneventful and routine. Richard Levy was still out on loan working the Robinson case. They signed out and began a two day swing.

CHAPTER TEN

When Mike returned to work after his two days off, he was called into the boss' office.

Sargent Fitzpatrick bellowed, "Romano, come in here please, now."

"Coming Sarge", Mike went right in.

I read all the DD-5's on the last two cases you and your partner had. It was good work but I heard something odd and unusual about the final results regarding your case. Maybe you can explain it for me."

"Sure Boss."

"In Sam's burglary case, property was recovered and identified to be ultimately returned to the complainants. In your bride and groom , some of the people from Sam's case were also involved in your robbery. They had the property from Battle's case. Am I correct so far?"

"Yes, a bit unusual and lucky but no explanation is needed."

"Well here is what I found odd. I got a phone call from the complainants in your case who wished to thank me for having such a good detective assigned to them. They made it a point to say to thank you for the return of almost half of the stolen money, in cash. There is no paper on that little item. Why?"

Romano knew he would need some time and asked, "Can I sit down and explain it Sarge?"

Fitz, indicating Scala's empty chair, with a tone of sarcasm responded, "Please do."

Romano explained about his interview with Dimitri Titov and his admission to selling drugs in the catering hall. Mike explained that he knew the ADA would never write a charge for drug sales without any evidence and using that knowledge, he subsequently cajoled Titov to return what was left of the spoils of the crime in return for not being charged with drug sales.

He was reluctant to mention his play regarding the rumored Italian connection of the two couples but did so anyway.

Fitz listened quietly, and then sat back in his chair for a moment before speaking.

"That was a slick and ballsy move on your part, playing on what you hoped was his fears. Let me ask, how sure were you? Are you related to some of the people in our command? You know tthe Wise Guys?"

"What?"

Fitz never skipped a beat. "After all you are Italian, and if you turn around you'll see a locked file cabinet and a drawer labeled Romano."

Mike had noticed the cabinet before but never thought about it.

"Yeah, I know Sarge. The guy was blown up a couple of years ago. Am I right?"

"Yes and you have the same last name and I was wondering if there is a bloodline, if you're related."

Mike had trouble controlling his temper.

"Not that I know of; Romano is a common name and the job would have never hired me. Correct?"

Fitz just listened and smile. He was totally enjoying Romano's agitation.

Mike continued, "Listen, I just played on the current Street dynamics. The Russian mobs, aided by the crazy

Armenians, are slowly taking some of the Italian guys' earnings, particularly in gambling and prostitution. Because they don't have a tight organization like the Italians and they confine their enterprises to the new immigrants, like those in Brighton and Coney Island. In a turf war, the Italians would win. I just played on that."

Fitz smiled crookedly and answered, "You seem to know a lot. Just curious, is all. I've been the CO of this office for years and every Italian I ever met claims to be connected."

Annoyed at the ethnic remark, Mike responded, "Well, not this one!"

"Now, don't get testy. Go back to work."

Sam, hearing his partner's voice could hardly wait for his return to the outer office. "Mike, what did Fitz say to raise your fighting instinct?"

"He's an ass. He made an ethnic statement saying all Italians that he ever met are mobbed up. It was a stupid thing to say, so I got a little loud."

Sam's patented chuckle erupted followed by, "Well, aren't you?"

"No, but some of my relatives are, I just don't know which ones. Years ago, when I did the fingerprints back on Staten Island, some butthole impersonated me at a homicide scene. Maybe he was the shooter for all I know. I never found out for sure."

***

Several weeks passed with the team receiving the usual mundane cases; minor assault, harassment, violations of order of protection and the like.

Richie was still working with 6th Homicide and the

salt and pepper partners were getting bored.

One early morning Fitz was at a Borough Command meeting, leaving the two partners alone marking the fact that it was a sunny day even better.

After wasting an hour philosophically solving the ills of the world, the two partners got down to the task of logging in cases on the assignment sheet and dispersing the squad copies in the proper catching order.

Coincidently, the next new case would be assigned to Romano, when a uniformed officer escorted a young woman into the squad office. He was carrying the squad's pink copy of a complaint report, a UF-61.

The escorting cop, Paul Warren spoke first. "Detectives, this is Anya Dorian and she is the victim of an assault, several in fact, one of which occurred yesterday. I was the officer of record on that one. She wants to report another one."

The young woman looked embarrassed and angry as hell at the same time. She turned to Warren and in a pleading manner said, "You were there the first time, please tell them about it."

Mike and Sam were all ears.

Romano was closer to the cop so he offered the copy of the first complaint to the detective as he spoke.

"Yesterday, my partner and I responded to a call of a past assault. When we arrived at the location, the witnesses on the scene said that the victim, Anya, and the perpetrators had already left the scene with the victim. Another young woman, a friend of Anya's handed me a lady's pocketbook saying it was the victims'. I looked inside and found her name and address."

Sam jumped in, "Tell us about the assault."

Officer Warren looked at Anya, who nodded, giving him the floor.

"Well, when we got there, the assailant and the victim, Anya, were already gone. Besides the lady who gave us the purse, Eva, other witnesses told us that Anya was dragged out of a ground floor apartment by two men and forced into a waiting car. After watching Anya try to fight off two men assailants, she was kicked and stuffed into the rear seat, followed by one of the males; the older one. The driver, a female then sped off."

Mike asked, "Anything else. Did anyone try to follow them?"

"That's the weird part, the second assailant jumped into a second car, driven by a lone male, and followed the first one. According to the witnesses, it looked like they were together and the second car was a chase car, you know, to block any pursuers; kind of strange, isn't it? Anyway, Eva told us that the apartment Anya was ripped from was hers. Anya was there because she ran away from her parents and husband."

"What did you guys do next?"

Naturally, we went to the address that we found in the wallet inside."

"How come there was no arrest? Did you do a complaint report?" Romano asked.

"Yes, we did. That one marked; closed to patrol. You have the copy."

"Why close it?"

"Well, when we got there, we sort of bullied our way into the house. The occupants wanted no part of us. We threatened them with arrest and they let us in."

Anya was sobbing as Warren told the story. Sam kept handing her tissues.

Warren continued, "Sitting inside the family's

living room were Anya's parents, her brother and her husband. There was also a little six-year-old girl and a boy about two years old. An older woman, Anya's mother, was holding him. The little girl was sitting next to Anya with one arm around her mother's waist. Anya's face was all red and flushed. She obviously had been crying."

The older guy identified himself as Louis Dorian, said he was the father and that they were having a family discussion and there was no need for police.

"I explained that we were told by witnesses that the people in this room were described as having kidnapped Anya, and viciously beat her in the process. The father denied everything."

"Did you guys speak to Anya at that time?"

"Yes, and she said that her father was telling the truth. She added that they were sitting around and talking about her having gone to a girl friend's house without asking permission. She said that her mother slapped her because they argued about it. We explained that we would make a report about our visit and come back the next day to check on everyone. We left and resumed patrol, turning in the 61 when we went off duty."

"Okay, tell us about what brought you here now."

"Today when we went back to the house to check on Anya, she said that everyone except her and the kids were out at work. When the little girl saw us, she ran up to me, wrapped herself around my leg and begged, 'Don't let my Mommy get hurt again. Please take us with you, please.' I knew at that point that we should bring them all here."

Anya was sitting and staring at the ceiling while wiping a tear from her cheek.

"My partner is down in the lunchroom with the kids. If you don't need me now, I'll be downstairs with him and the little ones."

***

The two detectives were anxious to hear the poor woman's story, but waited until she was ready to begin.

The voice in Mike's head told him, *Mike, go slowly and pay attention. This girl needs you.*

Silently he answered, *yeah but I can't wait and when I find them, I think I'm gonna kick some ass.*

Deciding that he waited long enough, Romano asked, "Anya, what happened after the two cops left?"

Do you have something cold for me to drink? Please, my mouth is dry."

Sam jumped up, "Sure Miss Anya, I'll be right back."

Mike impatiently tapped his pen on his notepad and waited. After almost a full minute, Anya began her story.

"Please, I must go slowly because it is difficult for me to speak about what happened. First I must show you something."

Turning her head to avoid Romano's eyes, she lifted her skirt to expose the middle of her right thigh. Mike could not believe what he saw. There, in shades of purple and black surrounded by a red welt, was the perfect outline of the heel of a shoe.

Mike could feel the pain that must have followed that mark, and thought, *holy shit, I can almost see the Cat's Paw logo.*

He couldn't help saying, "Oomph! Are you okay now? Do you want a doctor? Which of those idiots did that?"

She quickly dropped her skirt before answering.

"Yes, I am okay, I think, but there are more marks

that I am embarrassed to show. Please get a woman police and I will show her in private."

Sam had walked into the room as she spoke. He froze when he heard the request. He pulled open the tab and handed her the frosty can.
"Here you go Anya, ice cold Coca Cola"

Mike quietly asked, Sam, would you please go down and ask the desk for a young female officer. Tell the desk that we need her for about an hour. Thanks."

"Sure Mikey. What's going on?"

To ease Anya's growing embarrassment, he simply stated, "We need a female to document the results of the first and maybe a second assault. Thanks."

Mike, responding to a voice in his head that told him to proceed gently, opened a manila folder and put a yellow legal pad inside along with the original complaint report.

"Anya, if you can, please tell me about that mark got on your thigh and who put it there while we wait for a lady cop."

"You see Detective Mike, my family is very old world. We all are new to this country. Back in Armenia, my parents promised me to my husband's family when I was very young. It is a tradition still practiced by many. I was promised at the age of fourteen to my husband, Ari Abujian. Ari, it means brave in Armenian."

"Brave, he assaulted a woman. That's not bravery."

Easy Michael, you'll get your chance.

Mike was full of questions, but he patiently waited.

Anya continued, "We were married when I was fifteen. Ari was eighteen years old. At first, we lived in his parents' home. My mother and father wanted to go against tradition and have us live with them but his people had much power in our village. They won."

She paused to sip from the soda can.

"When was your daughter born? Here or in Armenia?"

"One year after our marriage, my little girl, Sonia was born. Ari's people were disappointed because they wanted a boy. My father said something must be wrong with me because every woman in the family has boys first."

"That's stupid," the Italian cop replied.

"Anyway, we left one year later and came to America. Now my family keeps me like a pet."

At that point, Sam and a young female police officer entered the room.

Mike looked at her nameplate and before she could speak gently explained, "Officer Rayos, soon as I get film in our Polaroid, will you please go with this young woman and photograph, as discreetly as possible, any bruises and or injuries that she shows you."

Romano saw Anya stiffen as he instructed the cop. He felt her embarrassment and decided to ease her pain with a half-truth.

"Anya, this officer has done this before and will do everything she can to maintain your modesty. The photos are necessary to prosecute the people who caused them. Try not to worry. Only a few people will ever see them."

"Do you not want to hear the rest of my story first?

"We can finish that after you go with this officer. I know that it might be uncomfortable, so let's get it over with. Yes?"

She nodded.

Talking to the lady cop as he reloaded the camera, Mike explained, "Please be careful to only photograph the marks and bruises and if possible, try not to show her face.

It will help her accept this uncomfortable situation with a degree of anonymity. Thanks."

The two women went into the records room where both doors locked from the inside and they could have privacy.

Sam took the opportunity to ask his partner, "What kind of assault do you have here?"

"Based on a horrible bruise she showed me on her upper thigh, a serious one, probably a felony and of course the kidnapping itself. I suspect there's other damage that is worse. We'll have to wait."

***

While Officer Rayos was inside with his complainant, Mike tried to organize his notes and began filling in a new complaint form. He would add time, date and story as necessary.

Ten minutes later, Rayos and Anya returned to the main squad room. Anya, trying to distance herself from the men, went directly over to the Coke can and finished whatever was inside as she wandered into the break room.

Rayos handed the photos to Mike with, "Detective, what these people, her own family did to her is disgusting. Beat the shit out of them when you get them and call me in too. She's a brave girl. Is there anything else I can do?"

"Yes, please mark these on the back with date and time and initial each one. You may be called into court."

"Yes sir."

"Sir, is not necessary but thanks. Then please hang out while I look at these and finish my interview. Your presence will help her."

"Absolutely, glad to be able to help!" I'd like to get my hands on the people that did this and return the favor."

Before speaking to his complainant, Mike looked over the photos. He was shocked to see what were clearly bite marks on both her breasts. Rayos had done a good job and made sure that the areola was hidden by her bra.

On both of her arms and shoulders were bruises consistent with being forcibly restrained by one or more persons.

On the inside of her thighs were several marks that might have been caused by a hand or hands of those same people.

Her panties were pulled aside to expose large purple marks on her buttocks as if she was struck with a belt or similar object. In short, the girl was beaten or worse.

As Rayos initialed the back of each photo along with the date and time, he added the victim's name and the next case number.

Sam's eyes widened and his face grimaced as he viewed the photos. "Michael, we have to find these people and kick their collective asses."

"We will Sam, you can count on it."

Romano went into the break room alone, carrying the photos.

"Anya, please let's sit down and talk. I can't imagine how painful this is for you, but it has to be done. You have to tell me who did what."

"I know Detective Mike. The worst is over and you are a kind man. Can the lady cop be here too?"

"Certainly. Rayos, come in here please."

Mike sat on one side of the table indicating that Anya and Rayos should sit together opposite him.

Before he got to the photos and the assault, he asked a puzzling question, "Anya, why do you still call yourself Anya Dorian and not Anya Abajian?"

"In Armenia, it is tradition for girls to keep their ffamily name. The custom is fading out but my family still follows it. It keeps old ties."

"Okay; thank you for explaining it."

The girl seemed to relax a little. The first photo he chose to show her was of the bruise that she had actually showed to him earlier; he would ease into the rest. Slowly he slid the photo of the heel mark forward.

Reluctantly, she looked down at it.

"Who did this Anya?"

With a quiver in her voice, she answered. "That was done by my father. I tried to fight when he forced me into his car by putting my leg against the door and he struck me by smashing down with his foot. I fell and he forced me in."

Mike tagged the photo as number 1, Father as per victim statement.

"And these two pictures of your arms, who did this?"

She angrily answered, "My brother and my pig of a husband each held me down on my bed as my father bit my breasts."

"Which side was your husband on?" "Sorry, I do not remember."

Next, he pushed forward the photo of her thighs.

"And this?"

"My father did that after he tore my panties off, then he exposed my breasts, bit them and then he pried my legs open. Next, he held a scissor to my vagina and said that he would fix it so I could not ever enjoy sex again. I continued to struggle.'

"That's disgusting."

"My mother was holding my son in her arms and telling him to cut me. I kept screaming and the baby kept screaming. The baby and my little girl were screaming and crying. There was a lot of shouting. I remember my mother pulling my hair out of my head while the men held be down. The lady police took a picture of what is missing."

Mike found the photo and marked it.

"I'm so sorry. Please tell me what these marks are," as the final photo was placed before her.

Anya looked embarrassed at first, then her expression again quickly turned to anger.

"My mother finally yelled for him to stop. My daughter was pulling at her leg screaming and asking her to make my father stop. I guess that she finally felt guilty because she told him not to cut me. He dropped the scissor and then he turned me over and beat me with his belt, calling me a whore with every hit."

Unable to catch her breath Anya, then visibly shrunk into the shoulder of Officer Rayos, and sobbed.

After what seemed like a full minute, she continued, "Those two pigs held me down and laughed. I hate them all. Please find them and kill them."

Anya began hyperventilating and needed time to calm down. Officer Rayos put her arm around her.

Mike gathered up the photos and said "Thank you, I'll be back shortly."

***

When Romano finished making notes to finish the list of assailants against his victim, he again sat opposite Anya. He remained silent for several minutes digesting what he had just heard.

Go ahead and ask her Mike, there's more.

"Anya, I know that this may sound like an accusation but, there must be a reason for your family to assault you in that manner, besides the fact that you ran away. Will you share it with me? Did you stray away from your husband?"

He could see her expression change from angry determination to see her family punished, to a weak smile of a guilty person hiding a secret. Once again, the voices inside his head were apparently correct.

"Anya? Did you hear me?"

"Yes Detective, I heard you. There was someone, a cousin back in Armenia. I knew him since childhood, before Ari. He is the man I wanted to marry. Two months ago, my brother Panos and I went back to visit family. Ari stayed home because of work. We were there for three weeks. It was then that I renewed my love for my sweetheart. We spent some time alone and well, you know."

"You had an affair? What is your cousin's name?"

"Erik, but it was just one time."

"Okay, what happened next?"

"When it was time to return home, I hid away with friends and Panos came back alone."

"But you all live together in the same house now. I don't understand."

"They begged me to return home. Ari begged too. I refused. Last month, I got a telephone call from my mother. She said that Father had a heart attack and was going to die. She told me that he wished to see me. Stupidly, I came back."

She paused again to catch her breath.

"I was shocked to see my father at the airport with my husband when I came home. The first thing he did was slap me and call me names."

"Who slapped you?"

"My father did. That is the day that they started treating me like a prisoner. The entire family became like jailers. No telephone if I was home alone and things like that. They took the phone from the wall. When they sent me to the stores, if possible someone was always with me or they gave me a time limit. Ari also hits me."

"And you never tried to get away before yesterday?" "No, I stayed for the sake of my children. I knew it was wrong to remain in Armenia without them. When I got back and the family treated me badly, I believed that God was punishing me for what I did to take a lover."

Romano took a few silent moments to digest what he heard. An office phone rang and Sam answered it.

"Michael, excuse me for interrupting, but the Sergeant at the desk wants his girl back."

After cautioning her not to discuss what she heard and possibly hinder catching the Dorian family members, he sent the young cop back downstairs.

Mike returned to his interview of Anya.

"When did your family find out?"

"Three days ago when a relative telephoned and said that they had seen me with Pitor, my friend, in Armenia. It got violent. I snuck away to the apartment where that nice cop was coming to help me. The rest you know now."

Mike fought to remain professional. "Anya, please give me a few minutes to make some calls and we'll find a safe place for you and your children to stay."

"That will not be necessary Detective. If I can use the telephone, I can call a friend that my family does not know and ask her to take me into her home until you get them."

"Anya, are you sure?"

"Yes. I will give you the location and telephone number to keep in contact. If anything happens, I will call 911 and tell them your name and that you are the detective assigned to me."

Sam went downstairs to get Officer Warren and his partner to bring the children upstairs.

After meeting the kids, Mike, with Sam's help, tried to convince Anya to go to a shelter instead of a friend's home but she was insistent.

After obtaining the name, address and phone number of her "safe house," the two uniformed men drove her to her destination.

The two detectives filed their notes after filing the complaint report for the second incident that named her family members as the guilty party.

Now all that remained was to go out and arrest them.

CHAPTER ELEVEN

The two detectives knew that they would have to wait until after 5 o'clock in the evening before they could expect the Dorian men to be at the family residence. It would extend their tour and that would require consent from the squad supervisor.

Not knowing when Fitz would return, they decided to bring in the mother, Katya, first. Any overtime resulting from her arrest or any person involved, would fall under a continuing investigation that just happened to go beyond tour. It was an accepted practice. Planning to wait beyond your scheduled tour to collar up was not.

They were signing out a portable radio when the telephone rang at 2:30 p.m. Mike lunged to pick up the call on the off chance that it was Anya and that something was wrong.

"Detective Romano, is this Anya?"

The reply both embarrassed him and calmed his fear.

"Detective Romano, this is not Anya, whoever she is. This is appearance Control with a notification for you and Detective Battle to appear before a Grand Jury tomorrow at 9:00 a.m., for the case of Titov and co- defendants. Notification number GJ31485-64. Please be prompt. Thank you."

"Damn it Sam, we've just got notified for Grand Jury tomorrow. We have to wait before we get the Momma Monster or anyone else."

Sam's deep chuckle rolled before he spoke. "That's fine Mike. Maybe the old lady will call here looking for her daughter and then we can ask her in for an interview and not have to chase her. Tomorrow is another day. We got lots of DD-5's to write and we can use the rest of the tour to go over the two cases we have with our Russian friends and the famous ball player."

"That'll work; let's get to it.

***

Sergeant Scala was present the following morning at 8:00 a.m. when the two partners walked in. "Battle, Romano, front and center please." They entered his office together.

"I see by the case log that this is your baby Romano. It's quite something. Do you want to refer it to Sex Crimes?"

Mike quickly answered, "No Sir. We have it all under control. In fact yesterday we were ready to go out and make collars on it but a court notification got in the way."

"Yes, I saw the notification. Go and get that out of the way quickl, come back and lock up these animals."

***

The two detectives signed in at the Grand Jury by 8:45 and were briefed by George Sirocco, the ADA in charge.

He spoke to both cops at once. "Gentlemen, I will begin chronologically in regard to the time of occurrence of these cases. Detective Battle, you will go first with Mayes and Titov; Burglary, stolen property and a weapon on Mayes.

"So I'm on first?" Battle asked.

"Next we switch to Romano's case. I intend to indict; Mayes, Kozlov, Bulgar and Keiv for armed robbery, including Titov for planning the whole thing."

Mike replied, Sorry to rush you but we have something hot going on and need to get back quickly. Can our case be the first to go on?"

"Sure. It's going to be complicated with the bad guys being in both cases and you each having to testify both as arresting officers and assisting officers. We'll sort it out and I'll try to get you out quickly."

It was 11:00 o'clock when the officers were notified that a true bill was voted for both cases. They would be notified if and when they were needed. The ADA hinted that all defendants would probably plead guilty to lesser charges before trial.

Complementing them on their work, he further assured the detectives that his office would only accept a plea to felony charges. The cops were excused and they rushed back to their command.

After a quick lunch of two slices of pizza each and coffee in their office, the partners set out to arrest Katya Dorian at her home with the blessings of Sergeant Scala.

***

The team pulled their car in front of the neat red brick colonial style home and parked. Before exiting their vehicle, they took a few seconds to look at the property.

Mike spoke, "Sure doesn't look like the home of a bunch of crazies; does it?"

"Nope, it just blends right in to the neighborhood and I don't see any cars around. Do you think that anyone is home?"

"I have no idea. Maybe they're all out looking for Anya and the kids, odd that nobody called the station or the squad on a missing person. Got any ideas?"

"No, let's play it by ear."

The team walked up to the front door and rang the bell.

It took almost a minute and a second ring before the front door opened. Standing before them was a blonde woman about 5'-7" modestly dressed and wearing an apron. Her face appeared to be that of a woman in her late 40's and she was nervous as hell.

After mumbling something unintelligible, she stated, with a heavy accent, "Are you the police, yes? I was just going to call you."

The voice in Mike's head said, *you got her. She's the key go slowly. She's lying and knows why you're here.*

Sam answered first, "Yes ma'am. Are you Mrs. Katya Dorian?"

"Yes, please help me. My daughter is missing."

It was Mike's turn, "How old is your daughter?"

"This is not the first time. She is twenty six years and has our two grandchildren with her, wherever she is. Will you help us find her?"

"May we come in? This will take some time."

Opening the door wide, she stepped aside and waved her arm, "Please come in and sit down."

Once seated, Sam looked at his partner and signaled with his hand to proceed slowly. With a slight nod, Mike indicated that he understood.

He began, "Mrs. Dorian, who else lives here with you?"

"My missing daughter, her two children and of course my husband Petos lives here too. He is a building custodian for that building on the corner of Bath Avenue."

"Do you have any other children?" Sam asked

"Yes, a son, Panos. He is older than my daughter."

"Does he live here too?"

"Sometimes he stays here. He lives where my Petos and Panos work. My husband gets an apartment in the building and Panos lives there most of the time. Why do you ask about my family? I only want to find my daughter."

Ignoring the question Mike continued, "One last question; where is Anya's husband? Does he live here and where does he work?"

"You are scaring me. Are you going to help me or not?"

"Well, to find your daughter, we may need to speak to all family members. It will be easier to know where to reach them to get their help. You do understand?"

"Yes, I suppose it is correct."

"Well, what is her husband's name and where can we find him?"

"His name is Ari and he works on pier number twenty seven for a shipping company. I have his phone number and can call him."

"Before you do, can we have the number please?"

After Katya recited the phone number, Mike rose and stood next to her. Sam rose too.

Mike spoke, "Katya, we know where your daughter is. She and the children are safe and you are under arrest for assaulting her. Please stand and turn around."

She looked like she was going to faint. Sam had to steady her. He also put chrome braclets on her.

Katya kept a blank expression on her face.

"Where are your house keys?"

Silently, she indicated a purse on a small table by pointing with her chin.

Reaching inside, the detectives obtained her house keys and raised them up, making a show of removing nothing else.

After securing her home, they brought her to their car. She remained silent during the transport to the squad office.

Once upstairs in the office, Mike asked Scala to witness the reciting of the Miranda Warnings to Katya Dorian. At that point, she broke down, dropping to her knees and sobbing.

"Please officers, we did nothing wrong. We only disciplined my daughter. She has shamed our family. She gave herself to another man who was not her husband. We did nothing wrong. It is our way. Cannot a parent give discipline to their child?

Scala ordered, "One of you put this unhinged woman in the cage and call down for a female officer to search her."

Romano and Battle lifted her as gently as possible, and put her into the cage. Mike picked up the phone and called for a lady cop.

Scala said, "Good work guys. Soon as this woman is frisked, go get the rest of them."

Later they privately admitted that they wanted to drop her on her face after lifting her from the floor.

***

Connected

The detectives left their charge with Scala and went to 8640 Bay Parkway to look for the Dorian men.

After locating the superintendent's apartment, they knocked on the door of 1D with no results.

They turned, about to leave, when a young, dark haired man walked towards them. As he got close, Mike could see beads of sweat forming on his brow and silently indicated for his partner to cut off any chance for the man to run.

Romano was thinking of what he felt like doing. *Administering some Christian Healing, a laying of the hands upon the man for his sins, something Saint Michael might do. Will he give me a chance? Yeah, I know. Don't get too brutal.*

Mike said, "Panos Dorian, police, please give us a minute of your time."

Panos' eyes gave him away. They flipped around as he sought an escape route.

Sam was quicker and gripped his lightweight jacket. Panos spun around and slipped out of it. Sam slapped him on the back of his neck at the same time causing him to stumble forward.

Mike was waiting. He gave an upper cut to his jaw. There was a loud click as his teeth came together. At the same time, Sam kicked his feet out from under him and the man went down with a thud.

Each lawman took an arm and twisted them behind his back while kneeling on his legs. He was handcuffed and pulled to his feet. Panos was bleeding from the mouth.

Mike smiled at his partner, "Hey that was fun, should we take the cuffs off and do it again?"

Panos screamed, "No, no I did nothing. She is my sister and I love her. I never hurt her."

Mike jerked the handcuffs and said, "Two down and two to go."

Sam asked, "Hey do you think the other two will resist too."

They were enjoying the verbal intimidation. It continued as they stuffed Panos into their car.

Mike was first. "Do you think that this guy loves his old man as much as he does his sister? When we find his father, maybe we can beat the shit out of him and not worry."

"Yeah, sounds like fun to me," Sam replied.

Mike added, "Yeah, we can get two cops to hold him down, then we can take turns just like Panos here did to his sister. Don't forget to bring a big pair of scissors."

Panos' lips were swelling, yet he felt compelled to answer. "I did not take turns to hurt my sister. I only held her arm. Her husband, Ari, held the other one and my father is the person who did things, but it is his right to punish her. We held her to prevent her from hitting my father."

"Thank you for that statement."

Mike turned to Sam, "Would you consider that a spontaneous utterance upon arrest?"

"I most certainly would. Should I give him Miranda as you drive?"

"Yes please do."

Putting the car into gear, Mike thought, *Saint Michael would be proud. We're some team.*

⸪ ⸪ ⸪

Back in the squad room, when Katya saw her son, she screamed and collapsed into the corner of the cage. They called for EMS to respond for their prisoners. The woman appeared to be unconscious.

The Swollen Lip man was put into the cage with his

mother yelling in his native language. Momma stirred. She was alive.

After the medical techs treated him and cleared his mom, they sat with their locked arms together.

Katya, after examining her son's cut lip, shouted, "You men have wronged my son, you will be punished for this by God."

"Where is your husband, Petos?"

"I tell nothing except to say, we did nothing wrong and you are oppressors like KGB."

Mike replied, "If you know where he is, call him for us and ask him to come here. It might save him some problems."

"He has no problems except harlot for a daughter."

Sam tried, "Listen Katya, we are trying to save your husband from upsetting us when we do find him. Maybe he'll fight too or try to run like your son did. That would not be smart. One cut lip in the family is enough. Do you understand what I'm trying to tell you?"

"You men are animals. You do not understand our traditions. It is our right as parents to discipline our daughter. She has become a whore. God will punish you."

Mike couldn't resist, "No, you will be punished and we will help God me do it. Now shut up, we have work to do."

Scala had come out of his office when the EMS people had arrived. He was still standing quietly in the far corner of the squad room and had just witnessed the entire exchange. He motioned that his two men should follow him into the break room.

"Guys, you got two out of four. I should have asked before, how come the second man is banged up?"

Sam answered, "He tried to run when Mike called his name and he ran into me. I slapped him and when he turned, he ran into Mike. Sorry, but you gotta ask Mike about the rest."

"Romano?

"Sarge, I thought that he hit Sam so I clocked him. That's about it."

"Sounds like justified use of force and don't forget to put it into your DD-5. What about the other two?"

"The girl's husband, Ari, is at work on the docks in Red Hook. If you don't mind us leaving the prisoners here, we'll go and try to bring him in too."

"You two are something else. Go ahead. I'll get a uniform man to come up and stay with me until the next team comes in. You two should be back by then. Good luck."

CHAPTER TWELVE

With two of the Dorian family members safely tucked out of the way in the squad's cage and blessings from Sergeant Scala, the team of Romano and Battle quickly drove to Pier 27 at the foot of Verona Street, in Red Hook, Brooklyn, to arrest Ari Abajian.

They were stopped at a security gate.

Sam, in the driver's seat, pulled down the sun visor to reveal the blue Police Department Identification plaque. The guard waved them through.

He returned the visor to its original position.

The actual waterfront consisted of a long weather beaten warehouse with numerous business markings on it.

The once red bricks had lost most of their red pigment and were now a dark stained non-descript brown, giving visual testimony as to its time in service.

Parallel to the warehouse was the actual water's edge with ample length to accommodate at least three or four freighter ships. At ninety degrees to one end of the building was the shorter edge of the pier, only long enough to accommodate the single moored to it. There were no other ships present.

As the detectives halted in front of the section marked "27, Café D'Oro Import Company," a helmeted man in blue overalls drove his fork lift toward their car and stopped next to them.

"Afternoon, I'm Tim Cassidy, shop steward for the men employed here. We're not due for inspection until next week."

Sam dropped the visor again. "Police, we need a few minutes of your time. Perhaps you can help us."

"Sure officers. Is there any trouble?"

Both detectives exited the car and Romano picked up the conversation.

"We're here to see one of your members, Ari Abajian, were told that he works here."

Like all shop stewards, everywhere he asked, "Why?"

"One of his family members needs him, but we need to speak to him first. Is he here?"

At first it appeared that the steward was about to stonewall the detectives, but then thought better of it.

"Yes he is. Over on that freighter supervising an unloading," and pointed to the end of the pier.

Romano asked, "Can you please send word that someone is here to see him and have him respond to this location? We'll wait."

"Get on it right away. He'll be here in less than five minutes."

Cassidy deftly backed up the machine, spun around and speed off towards the ship.

Sam turned to his partner and asked, "What if he decides not to cooperate?"

Mike smiled and said, "Then he goes back to the Our office looking like his brother- his-in-law"

"Ten four; we can do that."

Romano again turned to his partner and said, "I'm gonna relax and light up a cigar. I want to give the impression that this is not an adversarial situation."

Mike had just had about three pulls on his smoke before Sam announced, "Here he comes. He's riding on the fork lift with the shop steward."

"Yeah, I see him too. Hope we don't have to run; I don't want to waste a cigar."

As the words left Mike's lips, Ari jumped off the back of the lift and sprinted towards the far entrance of the warehouse.

"Shit, he's trying to give us the slip," Mike yelled as he threw down his smoke and took off running. Sam already was several steps ahead of him.

Battle ran to the doorway that Ari ran into. Romano, seeing his partner's move, entered the first entrance he came upon, hoping to cut off Ari's flight.

The warehouse was cavernous with row upon row of steel racks containing pallets piled high with sacks of coffee beans, the floor littered with loose beans.

The crisp odor of the dark ebony beans permeated the atmosphere within the building. Although it was not unpleasant odor, Romano's nostrils tingled.

Realizing that it was almost impossible not to crunch beans while moving about and seeing no other persons in sight, Romano froze and listened.

He heard the sound of their target running in his direction, the beans crunching beneath his feet, with the sounds of Sam pounding in hot pursuit.

Mike tried to determine what exact direction the sound was coming from and secreted himself between piles of the burlap sacks, in what he hoped was the fleeing suspects' path.

As the footfalls got louder, he knew that he had made the right choice and braced himself.

He told himself, *any second, now, wait for it* and then jumped out into the fleeing felons' path, his right arm level with the man's neck.

"Police, got you now you son of a bitch."

Twisting his own body around before Ari could react and using his own momentum, Mike locked his right arm around his quarry's neck and gripped the man's left wrist using his own left.

As Ari struggled in an attempt to get away, Sam strode up, grabbed the arm that Mike held, snapped a braclet on it, and using the loose cuff, pulled the arm behind the back of the struggling criminal. Mike released his grip on Ari's neck and forced his right arm to join the other one.

Ari yelled in pain, as Sam snapped the remaining cuff onto his other wrist.

"Who are you people, Cossacks, immigration? I am legal."

Romano answered, "We are the detectives who are arresting you for your part in the physical abuse and mental abuse of your wife. That's who."

"The bitch is a lying whore. She brought me shame. I trusted her and she had sex on a visit to Armenia while I remained at home working. She is a disrespectful woman and lucky that I do not divorce her. I did nothing. Her father punished her, not me. You can ask her."

Battle answered, "We did; also your mother-in-law and brother-in-law. They gave you right up. Now we're gonna bring you to our office. Your family is waiting for you."

"Anya is there? She will tell you the truth."

Mike spoke, "Listen asshole, she already did and we have photos to prove it. Now shut up and relax and we won't beat the crap out of you just for the exercise."

"Hey partner, let's stop somewhere and tune this piece of shit up," Sam bellowed.

Romano took on the classic 'good cop' persona; "See, my partner is just looking for an excuse; he's more pissed off than I am."

The team frisked him and Romano, for the third time that day, recited Miranda warnings to his latest prisoner.

He sat in the rear with his man as Sam drove them back to their office, grumbling that he was disappointed he didn't get a chance to re-adjust Ari's personality.

During the ride back, Mike attempted to get information from Ari.

"Listen, I know how aggravating women can be, but to help someone beat down on your wife while you hold her is beyond my understanding."

"Kiss my ass. I tell you nothing."

"Fine, but you can make your trip to court easier by appearing as a family. You can even save money by using one lawyer. With us, we have three out of four. Now we need to find your father-in-law."

Ari defiantly laughed as he answered, "So, go look for him. Good luck."

Mike smiled and said, "It's your ass; especially in lockup."

Sam thought it was funny, "Oh yeah, good one."

***

It was just about 3:45 p.m. when Romano and Battle herded Ari Abajian into the Six-Four Squad Office. Charlie Wilson and Frank Pigro were already present to begin their shift. Sergeant Scala had returned his uniform assistant back down to his command.

Pigro looked up as the team brought Ari in and was ready to comment as he heard an unearthly noise.

Katya howled when she saw Ari. "Ohoooo, yeow, not Ari too! Are you trying to destroy my family?"

"Well, you boys have been busy, two in the cage and another collar to squeeze in. It's gonna be tight. Hope they're all related, with the woman and all."

Romano answered, "They are Smartass; mother, son and son-in-law."

Battle was next. "This is how good detectives work; they go out and get their man and woman. You two are jealous."

Scala came into the room and remarked, "You two certainly know how to get the job done. Mike, I see that your old Lieutenant was on the mark, you are a bulldog."
Pigro was jealous and actually gave a, "Woof, woof.

Sam removed the prisoner's cuffs and announced, "He's clean. He's been tossed Sarge, and Mike rode in the back with him on the way here."

He then undid the cage door's slide bolts and almost tossed his prisoner in.

Katya wailed again while she clung to both men.

Tony asked, "How fast can you get his paperwork done? I want this group brought down to Central Booking as soon as possible."

Mike answered quickly, "I think we can do it in about forty minutes. Our new man got a little bruised from falling when he ran and refused medical attention. We'll cover it in the arrest report. Tomorrow we can catch up on our DD-5's."

"Good, get cracking."

The caged trio was quiet and forty minutes passed quickly.

Tony was an intuitive supervisor and knew his men were not satisfied with a perpetrator still loose. He quickly reviewed the arrest reports, walked into the outer room and issued an order.

"Reyes, since you and Pigro have no stake in this case, you will transport two of these fine people. Romano, you and yourr partner pick which one you're going to take and get the hell out of here."

"We'll take the woman Sarge. You know, her being a mom and all."

"I understand. Get moving."

***

Once settled in their car, Romano began to interrogate Katya as Sam drove them to Brooklyn Central booking. They would meet the other team inside when they arrived.

"So Katya, tell me why your daughter uses your family name and not that of her husband."

"We have done nothing wrong, but I will answer you to make you understand our culture."

"Thank you."

From behind the wheel, Sam mumbled, "Your culture? You're Barbarians."

Only Mike had heard the remark. He turned to Katya and asked, "Please continue, will you?"

Back in my country, the girl always keeps her family name. It is proper. Her husband naturally uses his own name. In our village as the rest of the country, when keeping her family name, she is maintaining the ties with her family even though she has left the household. Usually the girl and husband live with his family. We love our daughter, so in America, they live with us."

"I see. Now explain why you all feel the right to abuse her like you did."

She instantly reverted to being uncooperative. "I do not wish to discuss that with you at all." Romano tried to change the subject and appear to be on her side.

"I see. Can you tell me where I can find your husband, Petos? It's necessary to clean up this whole confusing mess. We can bring you all into court as a family and find you an Armenian attorney who understands your ways."

"My son lives in the building where Petos is in charge. Panos does the work. Petos was a barber back in our country. He goes to various customers and cuts hair."

"Do you know any of his customers or where I can find him?

"No. That is your job. You found my son, Panos, now go find my husband, but you will not. You will be unable for to find him because he has friends in Brighton Beach Bratva, what you call mob."

Mike was still trying to understand why this woman, a mother, would stand for and encourage abuse against her own daughter. He was anxious to book her.

"Don't even give it a thought. We'll find your animal husband and arrest him too.

***

Once inside the booking facility, Romano and Battle took charge of Ari and Panos. Detectives Reyes and Pigro returned to the Squad.

Each male prisoner was photographed and searched again before being put into a large holding pen for transport to court.

The woman was chained to a bench to wait for the arresting officer while waiting for processing.

The holding area was one of the rooms in the booking complex that was windowless with three block-tiled walls lined with slab type benches on three sides.

In the center of each bench was a six-foot long horizontal steel bar anchored to the wall where unruly poisoners were attached with handcuffs.

The entrance door was the only door in the room in the center of a reinforced wall that faced to working cops.

The room was dingy and appeared as if it wasn't cleaned in a week.

Directly opposite the booking camera, in the center of a large open area was a steel cage, constructed in the same manner as the one in the Six-Four Squad's office, only much larger. Inside were two benches. The room could hold at least twenty people. The prisoners inside could be viewed from all four sides.

It was used for only female prisoners and usually loaded with streetwalkers, due to its location, the occupants could sometimes overhear bits of conversations during the booking process.

When Katya was finally booked, the women in the cage had obviously overheard some of the conversation.

"Hey DT, what you got that nice white woman in here for anyway? You can tell us. When you put her inside wit us, we is gonna find out 'bout it anyway."

Romano saw an opportunity to administer some justice to his prisoner. *Can't hit her because she's a woman but forgive me, I have to do this,* he silently said to the celestial beings that he often spoke to.

When Katya heard the woman speak to Mike, her eyes widened in fear. The woman that was asking for the explanation for her presence was the largest, meanest looking of the cage occupants. Mike could feel her body tense up and begin shaking. He handed her off to Sam and motioned for him to move her away, but not out of earshot.

"Please Mister Detective, don't put me in there. I'm afraid. Please don't make me go in there."

"Sorry, that's where we put females waiting to be transported to court. You should have thought about that before you hurt your daughter."

The big woman in the cage responded,"Oh my DT, we be whores and crooks but what kind of bitch would hurt her own child? Put her in here and we gonna do God's work upon her ass."

Katya emitted a sound reminiscent of a crying puppy and then tried to hide behind Sam; they looked like they were dancing.

Mike addressed the women.

"What she do?" the woman asked.

He motioned for the big woman to come forward and she did.

Quietly Romano said, "Listen, she deserves an ass beating, but I'm telling all of you, if any harm comes to her while she is in here, I'll charge each of you with Felony Assault and make it stick. Play with her on a mental level; she deserves that, but nothing physical. Got it?"

"Sure Mister DT. We be whores but we ain't stupid. I can tell by your eyes that you ain't bullshitting. I don't wanna play with you or that scary black man that's your partner. You got my personal guarantee."

Mike smiled and answered, "Just scare the crap out of her, no touching. Have fun."

He then called out to his partner.

"Okay Sam, bring her here. Inside she goes! These girls will keep her company until she gets to court."

Katya struggled as Sam brought her next to the cage door. Mike opened it and ordered, "Get in Katya, a cage is where you belong."

Sam had to pull the fingers of her right hand open to release the grip that she had on his suit jacket.

"Woman, let go of me or I'll add assault on a police officer to your charges along with resisting arrest. Maybe I'll knock you out too."

The woman in the cage shouted, "Woo woo, my kind of man. Hey, Mr. Good Look'n, Black DT. When I get out, can we go on a date? You can knock me down on my back with my legs in the air." She was having fun.

Another woman jumped in with, "Hey Bitch, I saw him first, you got the white guy."

There were several other similar comments from the other women. For a few moments they all seemed to forget the depressing surroundings.

It took both partners to push their prisoner into the cage. She headed straight for the unoccupied section of bench that was against one of the corners of the enclosure and wedged herself into the corner, into what could be described as an upright fetal position; her vain attempt to disappear.

The big woman walked over and sat down. Leaning close she said, "You just wait until the DT's leave Honey, we gonna have a talk. You gonna learn something special."

Romano quickly moved behind the woman and whispered, "Don't forget what I said."

"We all good DT, don't you worry."

Romano called Tony Scala to inform him that the prisoners were lodged and requested permission to keep Sam with him for the balance of the booking/court perpetration process. It was already past their tour.

Scala agreed to the request. "Romano, you know this is a little out of the ordinary, but you have three perps. Make sure that Battle is listed as the arresting officer for the mother. You take an assist on her and put him down for an assist on the two men with you as the AO. You know what to do."

"Sure, thank you Sarge. We're both tired as hell and will push to get out of here ASAP. To justify staying there were spontaneous utterances made by each of the subjects in front of the AO and his partner. CYA; I got it."

The two partners shot over to the Broolkyn DA's office at 120 Schermerhorn Street, making the drive in five minutes. They were dog tired and wanted to get back to sign off duty and go home to bed. Their next tour would arrive all too quickly.

It took the better part of three hours before the detectives were interviewed by one of the writing Assistant District Attorneys. Finally, just before 8:00 p.m. affidavits of complaint were prepared for each of the defendants.

With the new pre-arraignment system just initiated by the New York City administrators to cut down on police overtime, the two detectives swore to the accuracy of those papers and then were able to return to their command.

With the new system, an officer assigned to the court system would present the defendants before a judge for the formal reading of charges and bail application when appropriate. The actual arresting officers were not necessary. They would be called back to court when needed.

**

It was just after 10:00 p.m. when Mike pulled into his driveway.

He found Lillian sitting on the sofa in the living room watching a talk show on TV when he walked in.

She looked up, "Boy Michael, you look like you've been chasing bad guys."

"I have."

She smiled, patting the sofa. "Sit down and relax I'll bring you a large dose of Doctor Dewar's and a sandwich. When I come back, you can tell me all about it."

She was up and moving before he settled in. As Lilly entered the kitchen, Mike heard their dog, Gidget, bounding down from the second floor. The animal cantered across the kitchen like a Lipizzaner Stallion and into the living room before breaking stride and launching herself into his lap, personally welcoming him home.

Inadvertently, the dog landed with one of her paws on his manhood. He groaned as he attempted to move her. She tried to remain in his lap and her constant shifting within the first few seconds caused multiple hits. Mike was tough, but not that tough and reacted by throwing her off and onto the floor. Rejected, the dog cowered at his feet.

Recovering quickly from the assault, Mike leaned down and gently stroked her ears, her personal favorite. He then readjusted himself and carefully coaxed the dog back into his lap.

It was work; she weighed in excess of fifty pounds but he was rewarded with wet doggy kisses.

Lillian walked in with his drink. With feigned anger she said, "Nice going Romano, I don't even get a hello kiss before the dog does!"

She handed him the glass and he playfully pulled his wife close, right on top of the dog, spilling scotch and ice over the entire sofa. Lilly kissed him passionately as he attempted to move the dog, the remaining ice in his glass tinkled in protest.

Almost unintelligibly Lilly said, "This is nice, but don't spill it all, I'm not moving."

Gidget whined as she wiggled loose and scampered away.

The couple laughed loudly.

From upstairs, their daughter Lucy, who was now nineteen years old, yelled, "Oh my, there they go again. Yuck! Let me know when it's safe to come downstairs. You two are like young lovers, worse than teenagers and we all know how raunchy they can be."

Her mother shouted back, "Watch it young lady, you're still under our roof."

When they finally untangled, Mike drained the last

mouthful of the amber liquid that remained in the glass and rose up from the sofa.

"Lil, I'll be right back. Don't bother with the sandwich; a little more Dewars' is what I need. Then I want to tell you about the crazy day I had. You're gonna be appalled at what people will do to each other. You may even want to go out and kick some woman's ass."

Lillian listened to her husband's account without comment. When Mike was finished, he asked, "Well, what do you think? You know, jaded as I can be, the cruelty of that poor girl's parents really appalled me. I wanted to beat the crap out of them all."

"Michael, I can't even relate to that woman. I can't believe that a mother would treat her own daughter like that. That girl is a woman by God, and her own mother allowed her husband to demean her daughter like that; spreading her out like a chicken, as if she wasn't even human. You're right; I'd like to beat the living crap out of her too. Did any of those people you arrested resist? I know you must have administered some instant justice."

Mike only smiled.

"No, don't tell me if you did; I really don't want to know."

"Okay, how about some *Lilly Lovin'* in place of that sandwich? I'm starving."

"Race you upstairs; and don't spill your drink!!."

CHAPTER THIRTEEN

The following morning, Mike was at his desk catching up on paperwork for yesterday's two collars. He was smiling, remembering last night's "long conversation" with Lilly when Tony Scala called both he and Sam into his office.

"I've just been notified that your collars from yesterday have been released on bail, twenty five thousand each, cash."

"Do we know who put up the money?"

"It was put up by some Russian attorney by the name of Nikolai Kruzhkov. That's seventy five thousand dollars. He might be a Russian wise guy lawyer. Check him out."

"We'll get right on it Sarge. It would explain the wife's bragging that he's somehow connected to the Russian underworld and we'll never find him."

Back outside in their office, Mike took Sam out into the hallway for privacy.

"Sam, do you think that the Russian pawn shop guy Mishka, could shed some light on the matter? He owes us and if we play it right, the guy could be a source of information down the line."

Sure, it can't hurt. Let's visit him, shake him up a little, and see what falls out."

"Great, but first I want to talk with Anya and maybe her mother Katya again before we see him. We need a little more info if possible. I doubt that the crazy mother will give us anything, so give me a minute to call Anya first at the safe house; we'll visit her and maybe won't have to go speak to the crazy woman again.

Twenty minutes later the partners were sitting with Anya in her safe house.

"Detectives, it is nice to see you. Is my family still in jail? What have you come to tell me?"

Mike took the lead, "Well Anya, a lawyer named Nikolai Kruzhkov bailed them out. They're free for now until the next court date. Has the District Attorney spoken to you as to when you must appear in court?"

"No, I have not heard. When will it be?"

Sam answered, "We are not sure, probably within the next couple of days. They will ask you to appear before a Grand Jury to give your story. After that, formal charges are submitted to the courts and the pre-trail process can begin. They'll explain it all to you when you get there."

"Will my family of cruel animals be there too?"

"No."

"Good. For now, even though they are of my blood, I have no family; perhaps someday I will speak to them again."

This girl doesn't' know if she wants to sink her family or not. I had better press on.

"Anya, we still have not located your father. Katya hints that the Bratva in Brighton Beach protects him. Is there any truth to that? What can you tell us about your father's friends?"

"My father is, how do you call it, the building super. He is the person who is paid to maintain the building where my brother lives. There is not much money, but he gets apartment too. My brother Panos lives in apartment there, not my father. Because the pay is not much, he cuts hair for many people like in old country. He has made

168

many friends in Brighton Beach and Bensonhurst. I have not met them but I have heard him to brag to my brother."

"Just what does he say?"

With a hint of disgust in her eye, Anya answered, "He puff up like a rooster in barnyard when he speaks of it to Panos. He says our family will always have food on table because he cuts hair for some men who are Russian gangster. He is proud of it."

"Did he ever say names?"

"I have not heard any."

"Is there anything else you can remember that might help us find him?"

Anya was pensive for a few moments and then she locked eyes with Mike before answering.

"He also goes to cut hair in Manhattan, down in Italian area. I do not know why. It is make no sense if has good business in Brighton."

The two detectives exchanged glances at that bit of information, without comment.

After thanking Anya for her time and reminding her to call whenever she felt the need, the two detectives left.

Sam climbed into the driver's seat of their car. He waited until Mike closed the door before starting the engine.

Sam asked, "What's next?"

Mike answered, "Well partner, do you think that it's time to re-visit the pawn shop and squeeze your friend Mishka. He likes you better than me and that hurts me to the bone."

Sam gave his patented deep throaty chuckle, before commenting, "Can't say that I blame him. Let's go."

"Too bad that old charge we found for possession of stolen property was dismissed giving him a clean record;

we could have used it to shake him up a little."

"Listen Mike, I've been in this command for some time; all pawn shops sell swag, especially the Russian ones. He knows someone or something; we just have to work it right. That's what partners are for."

"Okay, but you start off as the good cop first and we'll play it by ear. Let's go. It should be fun."

Mishka Kaminsky and his brother Uri were all smiles as the two detectives entered his shop.

Mishka quickly stated, "Da, my favorite American Detectives are here. How can I help you?"

Uri quickly added, "Thank you for treating my brother well. We are honest business persons."

Sam spoke first. "Mishka, perhaps you can help us. We need…"

Sam was cut off by his partner in mid-sentence, "Bullshit! We gave him a play. I personally spoke to the District Attorney for him. He will help us."

"Go easy Mike. These two guys know what life is about. They don't want to piss you off. Remember they already cooperated with us by working with us a few days ago. They are our friends. Am I correct?"

Uri backed away as if he was scared or about to become a problem. Maybe because he wasn't arrested with his brother, he only wanted distance in an act of self-preservation.

Romano reacted to the movement by reaching for his weapon. Without extracting it from its holster, he shouted, "Freeze Uri. Don't make me hurt you."

Both of the brothers threw up their hands.

Sam put his arm around his partner and grabbed his gun arm. "Slow down Michael, these two are good people. We need their help. I'm sure they are more than willing to give it."

Mike put his two hands, palms down, on the counter in front of him and shook his head as if embarrassed by his own actions.

The ruse worked.

"Detective Mike, my brother and I are, as Detective Sam said, your friends. We are willing to help in any way that we can because you are honorable men. Please believe that. Yes?"

Romano answered, "Yes, I do."

He then continued with a justifiable lie, "Sorry for my outburst but I'm under some personal stress. Sometimes it just gets too much."

Sam leaned close to his partner's ear and whispered, "Good one. Never heard that one before."

Mike nodded his head two times and shrugged. *I thought those two were gonna crap their pants.* He stifled a chuckle.

Sam continued, "Now Uri, we came here to ask your assistance in locating someone. There's a man we need to find. His name is Petos Dorian and he's a barber. You know what that is? He cuts hair for a living. My partner here wants to arrest him for attempting to cut his daughter's vagina."

Apparently Uri and his brother knew that word because theirs eyes widened instantly. Mike caught their reaction.

"Do either of you guys have children; a daughter?"

Both men shook their heads as an answer.

Uri asked, "Mr. Detective Mike, why do you come here? How could we know this bad man? We are not, how do you say, sick sex animals?"

"We are here because his wife says that he cuts hair for prominent Brighton Beach men, Bratva."

The two shop keepers twitched.

"Detective, we are not part of such group. We not know such people."

Mike returned to the time honored good cop-bad cop scenario.

"Listen dip shit. We gave you a break or did you forget that I personally spoke with the District Attorney to keep you from getting charged with any crime a few days ago?"

"Da, Mishka remembers. But we do not know such men."

Sam took the lead at that point.

"Don't bullshit us. Every pawnshop and second hand dealer since the beginning of time knows or deals with criminals. Just how close they are with them is another story. My partner is Italian and this area of Brooklyn used to belong to his family. They allow you Ruskies to operate here because they now have other interests. Don't pull our chain or we'll shut you down and then find a way to throw both of you in jail. Now answer his question."

"Mister Mike, how can we help; is that true? Her father wanted to alter his daughter's womanhood?"

"Yes, with the help of his son, his son-in-law, and his wife. We have arrested those three, but we can't find him. He is running."

"His actions offend me too. We will try, but you must give us some time."

"You have until this time tomorrow. If you can't locate him, find me someone in the Russian underworld that I can speak to. I need a name and don't bullshit me. You have no idea of how I act when I'm lied to. Got it?"

"Da, I will have information tomorrow. Uri and I

are your friends and will prove such a thing to you."

Sam leaned over the counter and stared at the two Russians as he spoke.

"We'll be back about the same time tomorrow. Have the information because I don't know if I can hold back my partner. You don't want him to get personal with you. Sometimes he scares me. Got it?"

Romano was almost at the door when he turned and spoke, "Let's get the hell out of here before I lose control."

***

Detective Levy was in the office when the partners returned from their visit to the Russian's shop.

Sargent Fitzpatrick, along with Sergeant Scala and Levy, were discussing the Robinson case and the results of the stabbing of Reverend Wallace and his next planned march for justice.

Sam, pleased to see his long time team member in the office asked, "Richie, are you back to stay? Make a collar yet? Mike has proved to be an asset to our team. I think you're gonna enjoy working with him."

Mike spoke, "Richie, we never had any interaction, but I'm happy to have the chance to work with you."

Sergeant Fitz put a quick stop to the small talk with, "Alright, we're all happy to be here. Richie, fill all of us in please."

"Well, after many hours and exhaustive interviews we managed to arrest and charge several perps.'

Mike asked, "How many?"

"There was at least a dozen involved, but we only had substantial evidence to arrest six, one of them a girl, Rosie Rodriguez. She pled out right after arraignment. She was charged with Inciting to Riot because she continued to shout encouragement before and during the assault."

"We heard about a girl being involved. Rumor had it that she dated one of the suspects."

"Yes, she did. Before the incident, the locals were accusing her of bringing blacks and Latinos into the neighborhood because of her heritage. In an effort to get back in good graces with the local crowd, she encouraged the mob as they attacked Lemar Robinson and his friends."

"Crazy broad," fell from Sam's lips.

"In an effort to separate her from the actual assailants, her attorney pled her out to Disorderly Conduct with a year's probation. Frankly, I'm surprised they gave her that much. Hell, Discon is only a violation."

Before any of the other squad members asked for more, Richie continued his narration.

"One kid, Salvatore Minelli, 19, was the shooter. Several witnesses stated that he shot the victim as the others, Brian Conley, an Irish kid, and two Italians, Giuseppe Pasquale and Robert Tetra, beat the kid with baseball bats. We even recovered one of the bats. We found it on the hood of one of our cars. Someone had a conscience. The lab confirmed that it was used on Robinson."

Sam asked, "By chance, did you guys get any info from those elite bastards from the Puzzle Palace as to the outcome of the idiot who stabbed Wallace? You must have heard something."

"Yeah, perp pled guilty to weapon possession and Assault 1st Degree with intent to do serious physical injury at his pre-trail hearing. He didn't want to risk a trial and more serious time. His lawyer advised him to take the offered five years in the slammer. Personally, I would give him a medal for trying to shut the mouth of that phony shit stirrer. Reverend, my ass."

Fitz broke up the meeting with, "Richie, I want details. Please come into my office and close the door. You too Sarge. These guys have work to do."

"Anyway guys, I'm glad to be back. See ya later," Richie said as he entered Fitz's office and closed the door.

Sam and Mike caught up with their paperwork during the rest of their tour, however, Romano found himself stopping frequently to stare at the various papers that littered his desk. Silently, he asked the celestial voices in his head for guidance as to what he would do if Uri came up with a blank.

***

At home that evening, Lilly, ever sensitive to the minute changes in her husband's mood commented, "Michael, you look pre-occupied. What's bothering you, another tough case at work today?"

He didn't answer.

"You usually leave those problems at the office unless they upset your Saint Michael genes...What is it?"

"I'm just frustrated that we still haven't located the father of that abuse case I told you about. You know the one where the girl got pinned to her bed and her father was going to cut her vagina with a pair of scissors. He's still among the missing. There's a rumor that he cuts hair for Russian or Armenian mobsters and they're hiding him. Sam and I went to a Russian shopkeeper to try to get a line on the guy...Nothing yet. It pisses me off. Sorry to bring it home."

Sarcastically, Lilly spit out, "The poor girl is so lucky to have such a loving family."

After a few seconds, with an evil grin, the feisty redhead angrily added, "I still want to kick the old lady's ass. Are they still in jail?"

"No, some fancy Russian attorney got them out on bail...My gut says mob money."

"You be careful Michael, you're not invincible you know. Those people play rough."

"Don't you worry your pretty little head about it. I'm not going after them; I only want to get their barber. I'll be fine and Sam and I are always together."

"Just make sure you come home to me every day and we can continue our conversations."

"Don't worry; I wouldn't miss a single one. Race you upstairs!"

***

The following day, after checking his in basket and finding two new cases that he quickly worked, he typed his first DD-5 for each one and made his mind up that he would lean heavily on Uri if necessary.

Mike was learning about the Russian mob.

They were gaining a foothold in the States since the 70's and taking over Russian Ethnic communities like Brighton Beach. They had a hierarchy, but were not as organized as the traditional Italian Mafia.

Their gunmen and strong-arm guys, *voy,* while tough tattooed survivors of the cruelty of the Russian Gulags, were not the dedicated and loyal soldiers of the Italians. As ruthless as they could be, the local bosses just were not strong enough to tangle with La Cosa Nostra.

Reluctantly, he decided to seek an audience with Rocco Banducci.

CHAPTER FOURTEEN

Just two blocks away from Uri's pawnshop was a dingy looking secondhand junk shop. Rumor on the street claimed it was the location of a "club house" used by the Brighton Beach Russian mob, few people knew for sure.

Rocco Banducci was one of the few.

The rear of the shop was set up as a meeting room and gathering place for the local *Brigade* leaders to meet and discuss business.

The main room was cavernous. The décor was reminiscent of what might have been inside an old Czarist Palace; lots of red, burgundy, ornate green area rugs with heavy drapes covering non-existent windows. The room was detailed with an abundance of gold painted woodwork and such. Along one of the far walls, rather devoid of fancy decoration, were two doorways. The story was that beyond those doors were soundproof rooms where discipline was given and sometimes business dealings were concluded with eliminations.

Rocco Banducci and an associate of his, James Paloma, aka: Jimmy Pigeon, were there to discuss a problem with the distribution of untaxed cigarettes brought up from the southern states, particularly North Carolina. There seemed to be some discrepancy in the latest shipment and exchange of funds. It was one of Rocco's duties in Don Costello's organization to adjudicate and settle such problems.

The two Italians were there to meet with Boris Vorobyov, the Brighton Beach *Pakhan* or *God Father*.

In the center of the room, under a crystal chandelier was a very ornate and expensive looking forest green antique rug. Boris lounged on a maroon leather sofa under the watchful eyes of two very large men. They stood slightly behind the sofa at parade rest, like the soldiers they were.

Rocco sat in an overstuffed matching chair facing the *Pakhan*. Jimmy Pigeon remained standing.

After cursory greetings, Boris, without prompting, began their business conversation by insisting that a trailer load of contraband cigarettes was delivered with a light load and yet he paid in full as required.

"But, Mr. Rocco Banducci, we have counted the cartons twice and I tell you that my people, two separate people have the same number of cases short, fifteen. That is too much of a number to make mistake…Maybe one or two, a minor business error, but fifteen? You, out of all respect must make it right."

Rocco was used to the accusation. It was possible but unlikely and he was ready to counter.

He countered, "Boris, my boss, Don Castello, is disappointed in you. You know that he personally guarantees accurate delivery; his word is gold. You surely must have heard that, even back in Russia."

"Yes, that is true but facts are facts."

"Listen, we seal the trailer when we ship it. Was the lock sealed?"

"I did not myself see the truck. I was told that there was no seal."

"Then you have the problem solved. We did not ship short. Someone in your organization is stealing from you. Perhaps they have gone into a side business?"

"Then, Mr. Rocco, what you are saying to me that

one or more of my people stole my cigarettes? That is impossible."

Rocco thought he wasted enough time, "Listen to me. Don Costello doesn't make mistakes. We have been in business for many years before you and your people came to this country. In the interest of keeping peace in America, we allowed you people to do business as you have in your homeland."

"Da!"

"We gave you control of gambling in your New Odessa, this neighborhood. We have not even asked for tribute. Is this not true?"

"Yes, Mr. Rocco. You have been a friend."

"As long as you and your comrades continue to recognize our superiority, it will continue this way. There is enough for everyone. You buy what we have to sell, in this case cigarettes at a very large discount. You have your gambling operation. We even turn a blind eye towards other enterprises as long as you remain in your own area. Most importantly, we do not take kindly to insults against our honor; do you want to, as we say, rock the boat?"

Vorobyov's face twisted slightly at the question. He was used to dominating every conversation he engaged in regarding business in Brighton Beach. In his mind, the Italians, were but children in a man's world.

Unknown to him was the fact that Rocco Banducci was a true professional in his field, doing his homework before the meeting.

Rocco smiled at the Russian, turned to his companion and said, "Jimmy, please go outside and assist Joey in bringing in the person we brought with us."

"Sure thing," Jimmy snapped, as he threw a pair of menacing looks at each of the two rather large human bookends on either side of Vorobyov on his cushioned perch.

They had slowly advanced forward and were now standing at each end of the sofa that held their boss.

"While we wait for your man, please, may I offer you some Vodka? It is our way of friendly business."

"No thank you, but I will have some tea from that old Samovar I see in that far corner if it is filled and hot.

"It would be my pleasure."

Turning to the man on his left, Boris ordered, "Maxim, some black tea for me and our friend. Bring the vodka and two glasses in case."

Maxim had finished pouring as Jim returned with another of Rocco's men. They flanked a very scared man mumbling in Russian as he walked with his eyes cast down.

Rocco spoke as the two escorts backed away from the obviously nervous man.

"Vlad, tell your Boss why you are here. In English please so that we can all understand."

Vlad kept his eyes down and dropped to his knees, mumbling again in his native language before he began speaking in earnest.

"Pakhan, God Father, Mr. Vorobyov, sir, this was a total mistake on my part. I have three children and a wife to care for. I was going to replace cost of cigarettes after, …when I sold them. Please allow me to remain in your employ. I will do whatever you ask and will remain loyal."

Boris spoke calmly, "My dear Vlad, is it not true that people in my organization may come to me at any time with a problem and I will help them?"

Even though the Pakhan's voice was calm, his red face revealed his true feelings. It was slowly turning the color of borscht.

Vlad responded by babbling in Russian, he was now sweating profusely.

The Pakhan waved his right hand, summoning his two men as he spoke, "Remove him. We will speak again, later perhaps."

The larger of the two said, "Da", as they yanked the man to his feet and shoved him across the room to one of the doors on the far side of the room. After pushing the distraught man inside, a loud click was heard as the door was locked. The big man returned to his post.

***

The Russian mob boss was impressed and said so. "Mr. Rocco, you are obviously a very, how do you say, complete? Ah yes, a thorough man. You came to this meeting at my request for your associates to answer an unfortunate accusation. You came prepared. I truly have a red face. I am, as you say, embarrassed, yes?"

"Yes, you should be Boris. I assume that you will deal with that thief and explain to your organization not to betray your trust or the trust between our organizations?"

"Mr. Rocco, that goes without question. How may I make amends? Is there anything you need of me?"

"No. Our meeting is over and if I need anything from you that I believe is within your power, I will ask. I have other appointments now and must go."

***

It was Mike's third tour of the set and he, along with Sam, visited Uri at the pawnshop.

Sam silently began walking behind the counter.

To get his attention, Mike loudly stated, "Uri, I don't believe for a minute that you are a choir boy."

Uri almost spun around when Sam shouted to his partner.

"Hey Mike, let's go check out the back of this place. I'm sure we can find something that will allow us to close this rat hole."

Uri began to panic. "Mr. Mike, what is choir boy?"

"That is a really good boy who sings hymns with his church group. You my friend are not a boy and not a saint either. Now tell me where I can find that piece of shit barber, Petros Dorian."

"Mister Mike, I do not know a Dorian so how can I help you?"

Sam was in the rear of the shop by that time and slowly knocking things over and generally making a mess.

Uri yelled, "Please Detective Sam, please stop. I will try to find this man for you but it will take some time. I give you my word."

Abruptly, the noise stopped and Sam walked back into the front of the shop.

Romano leaned close to the big Russian and said, "Uri, tomorrow at 3 o'clock we will be back. We expect an answer or you will be out of business. Understand?"

"Yes, yes. Have pity, I am but a shopkeeper only and not Vor."

The detectives left the babbling Uri alone in his shop.

***

Outside, Sam asked, "Mikey, just how in hell are we going to close him down? While I made a mess in there,

182

I saw nothing illegal."

"You gotta trust me Sam. I am Italian you know."

"Yeah partner, but this is Brighton. They're all Russians."

Not wanting to give anything away, Mike laughed and answered, "Well, you know I hear voices in my head, maybe they'll tell me something."

"You're one crazy Eyetai."

The rest of their tour was routine: a few phone calls, some DD-5's and such.

Mike did however go out to a payphone, and called Rocco Banducci to ask for a meeting. He was lucky and Rocco would meet him later that evening at their usual diner spot. His next call was to Lilly at her job explaining to her that he would be meeting Rocco for dinner and she could expect him home before midnight.

***

"Rocco, I know my world is not your world and I'm sorry to bother you, but I want to close a case. I need your help once again."

"First my friend, let's order a drink and you can tell me all about it.

Rocco signaled for the waitress and the men ordered drinks.

After she left, Mike began, "Rocco, I'm still trying to get my head tuned onto the fact that my blood relatives are actually made men. As a young kid, I remember it was always innuendos and hints. Some of my uncles, even though they were blue-collar workers, always had lots of money. My cousins and I always thought it was just stories to entertain us. Can you please fill me in?"

Banducci smiled and asked, "Remember that bad cop, Capelli?"

"Sure, don't tell me I'm related to him."

The waitress returned, placed their drinks down and asked, "Are you gentlemen going to have dinner too? I'll bring some menus."

"Not right now thank you. We need some alone time," was Rocco's answer.

"Now Michael, out of respect for you, here's the rundown, but please never repeat this and once again if questioned, deny, deny, deny. It is for your own good. "

Nervous, yet exhilarated Mike chuckled and to hide his emotions, then answered, "Absolutely, whatever your name is."

"Here is the quick rundown. Capelli, aka, Baggs was a collector for Johnnie Sanducci as you know. Baggs brought grief to him. Victor Sanducci is the New Jersey boss, no secret there. Victor answers to Sam Costello as you know; all that is public information. When you arrested Capelli, you did everyone a favor. Now here's the good stuff."

"I'm all ears," Mike answered and signaled for another round.

they waited for the drinks in silence.

After getting them, Rocco continued his muted conversation.

"Back in the early 1900's, in the mountains of Italy were several small towns. Those towns were each inhabited by three main families; Costello, Sanducci and Banducci. They began to intermarry, one of the old Romano's even married a Banducci, making one very large clan. Soon, your Great Grandfather, Francesco Romano married a Costello. Let's just say that he proved his loyalty."

"Wow, that's some story," Mike commented as he leaned across the table, not wanting to miss a single word.

Rocco answered, "Not a story, just family history."

"Damn, please go on."

"When all the old *Mustache Petes,* as we were labeled at the time, came to this country, each faction of the family was assigned a given area or job. Sometimes a disgruntled member would react violently and made the newspapers, but we always tried to get along and sometimes still do."

"Yeah, sometimes, your disagreements did make the newspapers."

"You my friend, even though you are not in the family business, you don't lie or bullshit us and always extend human dignity to every one of us. For that reason, you are respected, especially by me. So there you have it."

"Holy shit Rocco, it sounds like a movie script. I'm floored, and thank you."

"No problem Mikey, you're family. Now, let's see if I can help you? What about the case you want to close?"

"This is gonna take a little while. Can we order food?"

Mike waited until their dinners of Linguine Pasta Pescadores and two more drinks were on the table before he began his story.

Mike paused between bites to tell his friend about the case that he was currently obsessed with; including the fact he may be serving as a barber to both the Russians and Italians.

Rocco, as usual remained silent as the story unfolded. When Mike was finished, Rocco finally spoke.

"That's disgusting. How could a father do that to his daughter? Shit, I'll take him out myself if you want."

"No, no. I just want to find him. I've been dealing with a Russian pawnshop owner that has been useless up to now. I don't know if you can get me some information on the guy but I thought I would ask anyway."

Rocco smiled and said, "Well, my friends and I have dealings with the Russians in Brighton from time to time. I'll see what I can do. Is there anything you want to discuss? How is your lovely wife, and family?"

"We're all good, thanks. Rocco, what you just explained to me about my family background, just how accurate is it?"

"As accurate as an expensive Swiss wristwatch. Why, are you nervous?"

"Not really. It just explains some things. My Dad's father used to tell stories to me about people trying to muscle in on his ice and coal business that he started when he came to this country. My grandfather said that at one time, he made lots of money and business was good. He used to say that one time he had to "get rough" with the people who tried to move in on him."

Mike paused to get another forkful of linguine. After swallowing it, he took a small sip of his ever present Dewars before continuing.

"That was during World War Two. They wanted a partnership, an uneven one. The story goes that he sold his business after the war and returned to his home town in Italy to show off his wealth and help family with rebuilding their lives."

"Recently, I've heard rumors that he may have lost his business and "got rough' with the thief causing him to go to Italy for some time. Can you shed any light on the story?"

"Not really, but I heard stories about some of the old

timers. Your Grandad was a tough old bird. There's even a story that back in the day, he once saved the life of my father. After that, for whatever reason, he never continued "in the life." I don't know if it's true, but if it is, everything turned out okay because, you my friend are the result."

Rocco signaled for service. He ordered a pot of expresso and two slices of Italian Cheesecake. As the young woman turned to leave, he added, "And please bring us a bottle of Sambuca and two glasses."

***

Back at home that night, after one of their "conversations"; Mike related the entire nature of what he had learned from Banducci to his wife, Lilly.

"Michael, I'm in total agreement with Rocco about your grandfather; if he had remained in with those gangsters maybe you wouldn't even exist and I never would be the happy woman that I am."

Michael just smiled at her before speaking, "I love you Lillian. Anything else to discuss, or do you want to go over our last conversation?"

Lilly just shook her head to indicate no, then grabbed him, furiously nodding yes.

CHAPTER FIFTEEN

The midnight blue Caddy sedan, driven by Jimmy Pigeon, stopped in front of Boris Vorobyov's second hand junk shop.

Alongside the entrance stood a very large bearlike man who appeared that he would not be able to fit through the doorway.

"Da, you have business here?" he asked as the two men exited the glistening auto and coolly walked toward the entrance.

The luxury sedan was not the usual way Rocco traveled, but he wanted to guarantee his entrance. He had no desire to come back, and spoke confidently, making sure to gain the big man's attention.

"Yes, my big friend. We would like to speak with Mr. Vorobyov. Tell him Mr. Rocco is here and would like to request a favor."

The human bear held up his hand indicating that they should wait. He turned slightly, opened the door and spoke loudly in Russian to an unseen person. Within a few seconds, there was an unintelligible response.

The imposing hulk smiled, pushed the door open and said, "Da, you are a friend, welcome. Go in please."

The interior appeared to be filled with a worthless collection of household discards.

Just inside the entrance, another man-bear led them to the rear of the location.

As they entered Boris's den, he rose from his big

red sofa and greeted them.

"Ah, Mr. Banducci and Mr. Jimmy, welcome." Waving his arm toward two matching chairs he continued, "Please sit, thank you.

"Demetri, bring us some tea and vodka with glasses at once."

As the two Italians settled into the chairs, a tray containing the requested drinks was placed on the sofa table in front of the *Pakhan*.

He poured tea and vodka for each of them as he announced, "First we make a toast to friendship, *Za vashe zdorovie*", to your health," he said holding up a glass of the clear liquid.

Rocco leaned forward to pick up his glass.

Without waiting for his guest, Boris gulped his and said, "Drink up", repeated the toast and poured another.

"It is an honor that you come to ask a favor. So tell me, Mr. Banducci, what is it? If it is within my power, it is granted as we speak."

"I'm sure that you're still grateful when, a few days ago, we sat in this room and I presented you with a thief from within your own organization."

"Da, I am. It will not happen again."

"Well, I want to locate someone. I'm told that he's a barber to some people; *vor*, is that the proper term you use, here in Brighton? He does not own a shop but goes to them when he cuts hair. Do you know the name, Petos Dorian?"

"Unfortunately, I do not know the name, but I do know of a local man goes to various establishments within my circle to cut hair. Why do you want him?"

"I want to locate him for a friend, a Detective, Michael Romano. He wishes to arrest him for a disgusting crime.

It would be a personal favor to me."

"I have heard this policeman's name, for what kind of crime is this?"

""'Boris, I'm told that you have daughters, correct?'

"Da, is this a threat?"

"On the contrary, now I know that after you hear my answer, you will understand why my friend wants him so badly. Allow me to explain.

Banducci gave him a quick version of the assault against Anya Dorian, emphasizing the planned cutting of the girl's lady parts.

"Da, my friend, I understand. If someone did that to one of my daughters, I would kill him myself, slowly, I might add. He would beg for death! This man is the girls' father?"

"Yes, he is, my detective friend wants to make him someone's woman in jail."

"It is done. I will have your detective contacted when we locate him. You are welcome to stay and enjoy my hospitality if you wish."

"No, thank you, we must go."

***

When Romano returned to his office two days later, Sergeant Scala informed him that a Russian named Uri Kaminsky wanted a call back.

Tony asked, "Is he the guy who owns the pawn shop in Brighton? I thought that case was over. Do you have any idea why he called? Have you pulled some of your magic on him?"

"Sort of Sarge. I asked him to shake the trees to see if he could get any info on the last remaining subject in the

Dorian case, the main perp, the father. He's been hard to locate and I want the sick bastard to become somebody's bitch in jail. He's earned it."

"Well, good luck and be careful. I don't want you to get jammed up. Make sure you wait for Sam if you're going to Brighton."

Mike returned Uri's call and arranged to be at the shop by noon.

***

Romano and Battle walked into the shop at 11:30 a.m., Uri Kaminsky was alone and waiting.

"Ah, my favorite American police people. Welcome once again to my humble business. I have good news for you Detective Mike."

Sam quickly answered for the team, "Don't waste our time comrade; why did you contact my partner? Don't bullshit or I go back inside and begin taking inventory again."

Boris turned to glance at the rear of his store before answering with a pleading look in his eye. He obviously didn't want Sam to "rearrange" his stock again.

"Detectives, I know of where is Petos Dorian at this time, right now. You may go, how you say, pick him up."

Mike asked, "Where?"

"Before I say, Mr. Mike, Uri must say that I am impressed at how do you say, your connections."

"What the hell are you talking about?" was Romano's response.

"I do not know how you accomplished such a thing but yesterday I get visit from right hand of local brigade boss. You know what is brigade?"

Sam answered, "Yeah, we know. Get on with it."

"Well, I am told that you may pick up Petos at doctor office today at one o'clock. He will be there and will offer no resistance. I give you address" he said as he slid a paper across the counter to Mike.

"This doctor is a friend and will not interfere with police."

Romano's curiosity was peaked, "Why at a doctor's office. Is he ill?"

Uri answered with a sardonic grin.

"No. He is going to be there to tend to his hand. I do not know how, but it was damaged. You will see,"

Sam broke off the meeting with, "Okay Mike, we have some time. Let's go and get some coffee."

Once outside, Romano turned to his partner, "Damn it Sam, I think there was an application of justice applied here. Guess we'll find out soon enough. Let's grab two coffees to go and stake out the doc's office."

The partners parked their car and across the street at a fire hydrant, two doors before the house that served as housed the doctor's office. They put nondescript paperwork across their dashboard as if they were two businessmen taking a break and waited.

At 12:45 p.m., a taxi pulled to the curb in front of the location and a middle-aged man exited.

Mike almost shouted, "Sam. Look at the guy's right hand. It's all taped up or something. He's struggling to pay the fare with his left hand!"

"Yeah, I see it. We'll know in a few seconds just what in hell happened. Do you want to take him now or inside?"

"Well, if he gets treatment from the doctor, we don't have to worry about the injury at Central Booking.

We can take him as he leaves. What do you think?"

"That's one of the things I love about you my man, aalways thinking. Let's wait."

Almost an hour later, after seeing several people exit the office, Petos finally came out and stopped on the top landing just as a taxi pulled to the curb.

Mike got excited, "Let's go Sam, before he gets into the cab. I don't want to chase him across Brooklyn."

The partners separated as they crossed the street and approached Dorian. Just as their subject hit the sidewalk, he noticed Sam approaching and hesitated reaching for the taxi's door.

With all his attention focused on Sam, Mike approached from the rear, announcing, "Petos Dorian; Detectives, you're under arrest."

Mike's "Avenging Angel" gene kicked in and he grabbed the injured hand causing him to pull away in pain.

"Just try it you bastard. Nothing will give me more pleasure that beating the hell out of you for resisting."

Sam grabbed the man's collar, pulling him close, "And when he's finished I'm gonna give you some too."

Dorian's eyes almost popped out of his head. "Nyet, neyt. I am an injured man. Police in this country do not beat prisoners. What for you arrest me?"

Mike silently prayed, *Lord, give me the strength needed to hold back the special brand of justice I want to administer to this man.* "You're arrested for the sexual assault that you and your crappy family perpetrated against your daughter Anya."

The taxi driver began to open his door to get a better view.

Sam growled, as he cuffed Dorian, "Get lost buddy. This guy is going to jail."

Without saying a single word, he slammed the car into gear and accelerated away at a rate that would have made an Indy driver envious.

The two business suited cops almost dragged Dorian across the street and then, roughly threw him into the rear seat of their car.

To continue terrifying his prisoner, Mike asked, "Hey Sam, please sit back there with him. If he acts up, I don't trust myself not to shoot him. Thanks."

Enjoying the game, Battle responded, "Sure thing, I'll only slap him around a little and maybe punch him in the balls for good measure."

The injured barber cowered in the corner of the rear seat all the way to the office.

Once the subject was properly frisked and in the cage, Sergeant Fitzpatrick came out of his office and asked, "Romano, is this man the last perp in the sexual assault case?"

"Yes Sarge. This wonderful individual is the main one, the father, Petos Dorian."

Looking at the man inside the cage, Fitz asked, "What's that obvious injury on his hand about?" not waiting for an answer he continued, "I know how you Italians are, you all act like gangsters, did you do that to him?"

His supervisor might have thought that he was being funny, but Roman was not amused and said so.

"Listen you oversized, red faced leprechaun, I did not, and all Italians are not gangsters, just like all Irishmen are not drunks."

Knowing that he may have stepped over a fine line, he added, "Sir"

To his dismay, Fitz had learned that Detective

Michael Romano was not one of his usual subordinates.

When he felt offended, Mike would come back at him with unbridled vigor. Fitz had mixed emotions regarding that part of the Italian cop's personality. He enjoyed his feistiness, but disliked it at the same time.

Tim's face slowly turned crimson, "Watch it Romano."

Timothy Fitzpatrick knew that over the years, his men thought less of him than he would have liked, but they all gave him respect at all times, unlike the man standing before him.

Fitz could have put his disrespect down on paper and transferred Mike, but Romano helped in keeping the office clearance numbers high. There was always a thought back in the far reaches of his mind that somehow, the Italian detective would make his life hell.

Sam emitted his deep, throaty signature chuckle and finished with, "Easy boys."

To regain some face, Fitz ordered, "Alright you two, process this man quickly, get proof of treatment of that injury and get him downtown. See me before you transport and I'll sign off on everything."

Mike sat at his desk to fill out an arrest report while Sam called the doctor for a copy of the man's chart. The doctor was Russian and seemed very happy to comply with the request. He then added that a uniformed cop would come and pick it up within a half hour. After ending the conversation, Sam went down to the Desk Sergeant to arrange it.

***

Petos Dorian was removed from the cage and sitting across from Mike with Sam beside him.

"Mr. Dorian, you have been informed of your Miranda Rights and I will not ask you to speak about the crime."

"Da, and I will not speak of it until I call lawyer, Mr. Nikolai Kruzhkov. I make call now, yes?"

Mike knew everything he wanted to know about the Russian shyster. After all, he had posted bail for the entire Dorian household.

He played the part with his prisoner, "Sure. Give me the number and I'll dial it for you."

"Why you make call?"

"Procedure, I must include it in my report. What about that hand, did you injure it?"

"Nyet, it is how you say, work hazard."

"Really?"

"Da."

"But you're a barber. Your family says that you cut hair for *voy* in Brighton. Isn't that correct?"

"How do you know that?"

Mike knew that he had him hooked. "They brag about it. That's how I found you, your wife and son gave you up."

"That not true. They tell me you arrested them and you vow to find me. How was it done?"

"How did your hand get broken? it is broken isn't it?"

"I wish to call lawyer now."

By midnight, Petos Dorian was arraigned on various counts of assault against his daughter, all felonies and remanded with a half million dollar bail.

As he drove home, Mike thought, *I have to thank Rocco. I'll call in the morning.*

Romano's next tour of duty was a four to midnight.

Lilly had left for her job at 8:00 a.m.

The two boys were also at their employment, and his stepdaughter, Lucy was at school, leaving him alone. At 11:00 a.m. he phoned Rocco Banducci.

"Hey, Rocco, it's Mike. I have to be in for a four by twelve today, can you meet me for a bite at about one? I just wanted to spend some time with an old friend."

"Sure Michael, at the usual spot?"

"See you then."

Mike arrived first and as usual went directly to the rear dining room.

He was already enjoying a cup of coffee when his friend arrived. They nodded at each other. The waitress chimed, "Good afternoon, coffee sir."

Turning to Mike she asked, "Refill for you?"

"Yes, thank you."

Putting two menus down she asked, "Will you men be ordering something to eat?"

Rocco answered, "Yes as soon as I have some coffee please."

The girl scooted off.

"Banducci smiled and said, "Michael, you look pleased and puzzled. What's up?"

"Well, Rocco, first, thank you for your probable assistance in locating that perverted Armenian barber. We got him yesterday and his right hand was wrapped in a plaster cast. Have any ideas?"

Before he could answer, the server returned with coffee. "Will you order now gentlemen?"

With a wave of his hand, Mike indicated Rocco should go first.

"My first meal of the day, so I'll have two over easy

with crisp bacon and whole wheat toast, thank you."

Mike was next, "Eggs over easy sounds good, but please ask the cook to put mine on top of a medium hamburger steak. Also some rye toast. Thanks."

As the girl turned away, Mike asked, "Well?"

"When I spoke to the local Russian boss and explained the situation, he expressed his disapproval of the man, Dorian, isn't it?"

"Yes."

"Well, my guess is that he was spoken to and you were notified where to pick him up."

"I was told that I could find him at his doctor's office. Paper work we got from the doctor stated his hand was fractured multiple times. All the small bones are broken and he won't say how it happened."

"Michael, what the man did to his own daughter is repulsive; the local *Pakhan* agreed with me. He even said that if something like that happened to a member of his family, he would kill the man himself."

"I bet he would"

"The girl wasn't a relative, so maybe concessions were made. Maybe he sent a messenger to express his opinion, though I'm just guessing."

"Well, however the court action turns out, I'll guess that he won't be cutting hair anymore," Mike answered with a nervous chuckle."

He felt slightly guilty; *Saint Michael, thanks for helping me avenge that poor girl and thank The Boss too. Tell him not to be angry about how I found him.*

"Speaking of broken bones, your ex-wife is now married to the man you caught her with.

Mike spit out, "That low life bastard!"

"Easy, don't get all upset. I attended the wedding

and got a good look at him. He has a nose that hooks to the right. I heard about the night you met him. You sure left your mark."

Mike chuckled, then spoke, "Well, I hope Betty is reminded of that night every time she looks at him. They deserve each other."

"That's some job that you did; your Grandfather would be proud."

Romano smiled. "By the way, is Betty aware of my family ties to you? Does she know that we still have a friendship? I don't trust her and can see her trying to take my job away."

"Don't worry. I have never mentioned it or your name. As far as they know, you're past tense. Besides, our relationship is none of their business."

"Thank you and thanks again for your help with the barber."

Their food arrived and the two friends ate. They chatted about sports and the weather the entire time.

Finishing his meal, Rocco announced, "Michael, I have to go now and you have to go to work. It was nice to see you again. You're like a brother to me."

"And you to me. I just wish we could hang out like normal people do."

Rocco, as usual, indicated to the waitress that he wanted the check. When she placed it on the table, Mike quickly snatched it.

Rocco reached for it. Mike waved his hand away, "This one's on me, I insist."

Banducci stood, smiled and said, "Have it your way. Call again when you need advice or whatever."

Banducci turned and walked out before Mike even got his wallet out.

CHAPTER SIXTEEN

Several months later, Romano entered his office and was as usual, grateful to see that Sergeant Fitz wasn't on duty and Tony Scala was.

"Hey guys, I see Tony's in today. It's gonna be a good tour."

Scala acknowledged him by saying, "Please come into my office Detective Romano, I have a case that needs your relentless talents."

Mike knew it must have been important because Tony used his full name. He signed the logbook and said hello to Battle and Levy. He saw Frank Pigro and ignored him, thinking *he must have had court.* Then he turned towards Scala's office.

As he entered the doorway he heard Pigro comment, "Let's see him handle this one. It's a big bag of shit."

Once inside the office, Tony made an introduction. "Detective Romano, this is Captain Peter Lugo, the acting Chief of the Seawall Police Department." Lugo was in civies.

Mike held out his hand, "Captain."

Lugo shook his hand, "Detective. Your Sergeant says that you're the best man for this job."

"Thank you."

Turning to his boss, Mike continued, "What is the job Sarge?"

Scala handed Mike a Complaint Report listing the

crimes of Arson and Harassment. Peter Lugo was the complainant.

Both men waited until Romano skimmed over the report before Tony began to speak.

"The Captain will explain what he believes happened here and the reason for it. I'm sure that you as our office bulldog, will work the case hard and attempt to bring the perpetrators to justice."

"Captain, isn't Seawall that gated community on the tip of Brooklyn? I knew they had their own security but not that it was an actual police department. How is that?"

Lugo explained, "Seawall is a 'closed, private community' within the Borough of Brooklyn. Back when Brooklyn was not part of New York City, Seawall filed for incorporation as a village. As a village, the community had the right to police itself. The incorporated town formed its own police force. Now, as part of New York City, the residents invoked a 'grandfather clause' allowing them the right to maintain their own police within their community. The town council is very politically connected."

"Wow, something I never knew about New York City. But those big apartment houses on the end; aren't these buildings part of the Starrett City complex in Canarsie?"

"Yes, they are, but the town council allowed them to be built in the township because it was and still is, financially advantageous. Each family pays a tax, similar to a homeowner's association fee to live there.

Our cops only have peace officer powers within Seawall, they are designated as a Special Patrolman and must have gun permits to travel beyond the boundaries of Seawall. The permits are issued by the New York City

Police Department and list them as Peace Officers on their permits. "

Mike held the report up and stated. "This paper names a possible suspect. How did you get his name?"

Lugo was becoming more excited with each breath and continued. "Anyway, I was out visiting relatives last night and got back to my office about an hour ago when I received a telephone call. The guy on the phone asked if I saw the 'little gift' that was left at my apartment."

"Do you know who it was?"

"No, but my instinct tells me it was one of my own men. The voice sounded familiar and didn't sound like either of the two guys on duty. It sounded like the man whose name is on the complaint. Edward Laquin."

Romano wasn't sure he heard right. "Why would one of your own guys want to blow out your windows?"

Lugo answered quickly, "Political infighting."

Scala stated, "Please explain to us."

Lugo was quick, "I've been employed by Seawall for 12 years. In that time I've worked my way up to Captain. Several months ago, the Seawall Association, in an effort to economize, dismissed their Chief of Police, Louis Triano. That brought me up to Acting Chief. Triano was upset. He was livid and voiced his sentiments to close friends, both cops and residents of Seawall. The cops vowed to do what theyy could to get me out and their man back."

"Seems like usual work place vocalizing to me, Captain."

"Yeah, usually I would think so too, but the call and the windows tell me it's them. The blown out window was my bedroom windows. I could have been sleeping there."

"So your apartment is on the ground floor?"

"Yes, in the garden apartments, just outside the village. I drove here and filed a complaint, asking for the squad. It would have made some noise. I put plastic over the damage and I left all the evidence there. They used what looks like an M-80 and duct taped it to the glass.
I can't believe that nobody called it in when it happened.

Mike looked at his sergeant, back at Lugo and stated, "Time is wasting and I don't want anything to disappear. Let me get my partner and have the bomb squad meet us there."

The team left the office at once with Lugo following them. Sam drove and Mike used a Department portable to request the Bomb Squad to meet them.

The men weren't waiting long before the Bomb Squad arrived.

Exiting a marked station wagon, one of the men spoke first. "Sergeant Mitch Sojack here gentlemen. Is anyone hurt? This is Detective Specialist Davis," he said pointing to his partner.

Both men were dressed in black, military type fatigues and NYPD windbreakers with *Bomb Squad* displayed on the back.

Mike informed the sergeant there were no injuries since the intended victim; Seawall Captain Peter Lugo, wasn't home at the time of the incident. Except for the addition of the plastic covering, nothing had been touched since discovery. The time of the incident was unknown.

The bomb team examined the windows, one of which was blown apart and one that still had a device taped to it.

Sergeant Sojack confirmed Lugo's guess.

"This is definitely an M-80 here. The other was probably the same by the looks of the debris. The damn things are the equal to one quarter stick of dynamite. The unexploded piece is too rough for prints but the lab will have to tell us for sure."

"What about the glass?"

"I think the pieces from the broken window are too small, but maybe we can raise some on the window that is still intact."

Mike offered, "I still have my old print kit in the office, it's all I did for several years. Want me to go get it?"

"Thank you, but we have a kit in the car too. Let's see what we can do."

Mike was disappointed, "Have at it then, we'll wait."

The team worked the glass of the undamaged window with negative results. Carefully removing the duct tape, the "specialist" put the pieces into an evidence envelope, nothing more than glorified plastic bags. He was less than careful as he put items into them.

Mike called out, "Hey, easy guy, put that into a box so that it doesn't' stick to the bag and destroy any latents."

The tech ignored him and it subsequently stuck to the bag.

What an asshole. So much for prints.

Lugo waited for a glass man to have his window repaired. Mike and Sam returned to the office knowing there would be a myraid of paperwork to do.

As the team walked into their office, an anxious Tony Scala spoke," Alright guys, put on a pot of coffee and tell me all about it before you put pen to paper."

After fulfilling Scala's informal request, the detectives began their reports. With the exception of stopping for their meal hour, the work consumed the rest of their tour.

***

The following morning, just as Lilly was leaving to go to her job, the telephone rang. She picked it up and listened for a few seconds before responding, "Sure Sergeant, I'll tell him at once."

Lilly secretly wished she could go to work with her husband as she yelled up to him, "Mikey, that was your Sergeant, he said that as of this notification, you're on duty and ordered in."

"Did he say why, Lil?"

"Not really but he said, 'They did it again,' and that you would understand. It must be some case. I wish that I could go with you. Have fun honey. I gotta go. I love you."

Holy crap, I wonder if anyone got hurt this time. His mind raced as he quickly showered and dressed.

Forty minutes later, he walked into the squad office.

Tony Scala was waiting. "There was another bombing at Lugo's apartment about 4:00 a.m. This time he was home, bringing the crime to new levels. You and your Sam are off the chart. Tomorrow you two begin steady day tours until it's solved. I want you to work it hard."

"Ten- four boss."

"Fitz says that you still have to catch cases that come in during what would have been your chart tours and he won't budge. He said Richie Levy will catch everything for your chart. Oh, and notify us if there's any reason to extend your tour."

Battle hadn't arrived yet, so Romano responded for them both, "We got this boss, no problem. Is Sam on his way?"

"Yes, he is. My advice is to treat it like a homicide because it could have been. If the Palace gets involved, Fitz will go crazy."

"Ten Four."

Mike heard the day team; Sam Wilson and Frankie Pigro were acknowledging the arrival of his partner.

After looking over his shoulder, he added, "Here's Sam now."

Mike filled his partner in about what Tony said. He just finished as a very pissed off Pete Lugo stormed into the room. Lugo rambled without taking a breath between words.

"Those bastards did it again. I want them real bad. I'll do whatever I can to help. Let's get on with it. The bastards had the nerve to call too. I was asleep in my bedroom. They blew out the window in my living room. Without thinking I ran into the room and flicked on the light. I flicked it off and ran back for my gun. They must have seen the light go on and off."

Sam, wanting to calm him down spoke first, "Hey Chief, let's all go into the break room for some java and figure out a game plan."

Mike asked, "Was the voice the same one as last call?"

"I think so."

"What did he say?"

"I see that you're okay, maybe next time, if you don't leave."

"I answered, leave where?" then he hung up.

"Did you call 911?"

"No, I called the Bomb Squad direct. They told me to call 911. I didn't."

"Why?"

"I knew that you guys had the first complaint and you would get this one too."

"Okay, what did you do next?"

"When they, the bomb guys, finished I put up plywood over my windows and then came to the station house to wait for you. I'm also in the process of finding another place to stay. How do you guys want to work this?"

Mike and Sam exchanged glances. The look in his partner's eyes said that as it was Mike's case, he should run with it.

"Well Pete, since you don't live in the village, my suggestion is that you go to work and don't mention that we have the case. Can you do that? I know it's gonna be difficult."

"I can but eventually, someone will ask."

"If that happens tell them the Bomb Squad said there's nothing that can be done without evidence and they are having bad luck. These people were stupid enough to call again. They might not know much about real police work. Do you have an answering machine?"

"Yes."

"Well, since you're leaving your apartment empty, let the machine pick up all calls. I intend to put a Pen Register on your line to trap the calls. Maybe we can get some useful information unless they use an outside phone. If they do, at least we'll have an area to work, especially if they used the same phone both times."

"I'll stop by my apartment and set it up right away. I'll get the glass fixed again too. Maybe they'll think that I'm still there or they'll take it as a challenge and do something stupid. I'll get a timer for the TV and lights."

Mike spent the balance of his workday getting background information on the old chief, Louis Triano. He was unable to find anything that led him to believe that Triano would request such action against the new chief.

After his findings with his partner, they both agreed to wait until they could gather more evidence against the perpetrators or there was another incident before they contacted the old Chief.

**

The following morning, Mike picked up a ringing the telephone, "Six-Four Squad, can I help you?"

The caller was Peter Lugo, "Sounds like Detective Romano, is that you Mike?

Mike recognized the voice at once, "Pete Lugo, yes it is. Is there something new?"

Lugo inhaled deeply then spoke rapidly, without pausing to take a breath.

"Detective, last night the alarm on my car woke me up. I was staying at a friend's house and had a clear view of my car. I peered through the window and saw a big guy wearing what looked like a grey jacket and dark baseball cap, jump into a white Chevy pickup. I grabbed my friend's car keys along with my gun and ran outside. My car windows were smashed in, three of them, the rear and both doors. I got a plate number."

Surprised, Mike asked, "How could you? He must have been gone by the time you got outside."

"Yeah, he was, but I got a good look at the truck. It had a dent in the rear quarter panel. I drove around looking for it and found it parked in Seawall near the clubhouse. I have the plate number for you."

"Great. I'll run it and get the owner's information. Give me a contact number and I'll get back to you. Nice assist by the way, thanks."

Romano to went down the precinct computer and got the registered owner name and address. Next, he pulled the man's driver's license information. What was of special interest was that Mr. Danny Clark, at six foot-four inches tall and resided two blocks away from one of the suspect Seawall cops.

Thank you Saint Michael.

Michael returned to his office and spoke to his partner.

"On the Seawall case, the complainant gave me a plate number of a guy that trashed his car last night. I just ran the plate and the guy's height matches with his quick look at the perp. I'm calling my complainant to see if he knows the guy. We might have one of the perps soon. Stay close. We may be going out."

On the third ring, Lugo answered, "Hello?"

"Chief, Romano here, I have a name and according to DMV, he's a match. Do you know a Danny Clark?"

"Yeah, he applied for a position as a cop here. Thank God I didn't hire him. At the time, we had only one position open. If I did, then almost every one of my men would be involved in this crap. You gonna go to his house and arrest him? Maybe he'll give up the other guys."

"Not yet. Can you get me a copy of his application? I want to know if he's employed and where."

"I remember his employment because of the name of the company, Lugo Sales Inc., No relation. Are you going to take him there?"

"I need you to ID him first. Anybody can use another guy's truck. I'd like to take him at his house at about supper time. Are you free about 6:00 p.m. today?"

"To nail those guys I'll make myself free. I have to spend time in Seawall today, but I'll make an excuse to leave. Not to worry."

Romano added, Listen, be here at 5:00 p.m. If his truck isn't at his residence, we'll wait for him to come home."

Excitedly, Lugo answered, "I'll probably be in your office a little before. Thanks."

"Hey, Pete, wear civies."

"Okay Mike, see you soon."

The trio parked two houses away from Clark's home. At exactly 5:22 p.m., they watched Danny Clark approach his home in his white truck.

From the rear seat, Lugo blustered, "In the drivway, that's the truck I saw. Look at the damage. It's got to be the same one. He's here."

The house was a semi-detached modest brick home, typical of the area. The entrance to the house was at the top of a flight of stairs, one level above the street. The ground level had a garage door and perpendicular to it was a street level "basement" door under the entrance stairway.

Romano pulled their car directly against his truck, blocking any movement of the vehicle.

The two detectives and their complaining witness exited their car, taking care not to completely close the car doors.

Quietly Mike ordered, "Listen Chief, stay here and block the downstairs door. We don't want him to run."

The detectives climbed the front steps and took a position on either side of the entrance door. Sam rang the bell. Not getting an answer, he rang a second time.

From a window above the entrance came the voice of a young woman, "Who's there?"

Mike responded, "Detectives, miss. We need to have a few minutes with Mr. Danny Clark. Is he at home?

We only need a few minutes of his time. Please ask him to come down. He may be able to help us with something."

As the inner door opened, Romano was slightly surprised at the young, innocent looking giant that stood before them.

He thought, *that's a big guy. I'm sure happy to have Sam with me. Gotta watch the stairs if this gets messy.*

"Can I see your identification please? I wasn't expecting a visit from police detectives."

After seeing their shields, Clark opened the inner door.

Using his best smile Mike countered, "Can you step outside for a moment please? We need to ask you a few questions about something delicate and your wife may overhear us. We don't want to offend her."

"Sure guys. How can I help?" Clark said as he stepped outside.

An excited Lugo immediately shouted, "That's him. That's the guy who trashed my car."

Danny spun and tried to get back inside by trying to open the outer storm door.

Sam jumped against it as Mike pulled Danny's left arm around to his back and applied upward pressure while snapping on a handcuff; Danny had attempted to break free.

Sam brought the perp's other arm around for Mike and shouted, "I hope I don't have to shoot another one."

Danny stopped struggling. Both cops were relieved.

Romano quickly recited the Miranda Warnings to Clark as they gently encouraged the reluctant man down the steps.

As the cops brought him around to the driveway, he shouted to his wife, who was now standing on the front porch, "Quick, Alice, call my cousin Eddie and my uncle."

Connected

Sam and Mike stuffed their prisoner into the rear of the car. Sam sat in the rear with him, and wearing his meanest expression warned the man to behave. Lugo climbed in front beside Romano.

Five minutes later, ever one was in the squad office. After acknowledging his Miranda warnings, all Clark admitted to was breaking the windows on Logo's car and that, "Some guys" put him up to it. He was waiting for his uncle to tell him what to do. He refused however to identify his uncle stating, "He'll call here and you guys are screwed."

Clark would only give his own his name and date of birth.

Romano began the arrest paperwork and told Peter Lugo that he could leave and he would call if they needed him.

Twenty minutes later a Donald Clark called, said that he was the kid's uncle and that he was a New York City Transit Detective assigned to their Major Case unit.

Danny who was only 22 years old, spent about five minutes on talking the phone with his uncle. At times, the conversation was heated. Finally, he gave the phone to Mike.

Mike, after speaking with the uncle agreed that Lugo and he would tell the DA's Office that Danny was cooperating and he agreed to pay for all repairs and damages.

Clark finallyy gave up the names of the men who "recruited" him to damage Lugo's car.

They were Eddie Laquin, his "cousin", Barry Plitzsor, Harry Goldblum and Richard Goldblum. The Goldblum boys were not related. All four men were Seawall cops.

Romano asked, "Just what were you told by these men to make you commit a crime?"

Danny explained, "They told me that the old Chief, Louis Triano, was very 'heavily connected in New York politics.' They said that he was working to get the police in Seawall similar status as State Police. They would become police officers as well as peace officers. I always wanted to be a cop."

"That's over now. Isn't it?"

Danny remained silent as he hung his head to avoid looking at Mike. Nervously, he started picking his fingernails

Mike pushed "Well, go on Danny, or our deal is off."

"My cousin, Eddie Laquin, he's not really my cousin, we only call each other that, anyway, he told me that if Chief Triano came back, they would get me a job with them and I would eventually be a real cop like them when they got State Police status."

Danny claimed to be a law student. Maybe he was studying on Mars, because he believed those people. It was obvious that the big man was naive to say the least, maybe even not too intelligent, kind of like the giant in Jack and the Beanstalk.

Later that night, Mike processed Danny Clark for Criminal Mischief/Felony, damage in excess of $1000. He had to spend the night in the pens at Central Booking with some of the dredges of human kind.

Early the following day, Mike and Peter Lugo told the story to an Assistant District Attorney, Mark Farlow, in the Complaint Room at court.

After their account regarding the arrest of Clark, Farlow agreed to drop the charges down to a Misdemeanor level, which would allow Clark to offer reparation in lieu of a conviction at arraignment eliminating the need for further court appearances.

After returning to his office, Romano began his quest to locate the men whose names Clark had given him. He obtained all information that Lugo had on the men and then ran each of them through The Department's computers acquiring their auto registrations, handgun and long gun licenses. The results showed that he four "cops" and Clark possessed had long guns.

The following morning, Romano and Battle paid a visit to Clark's home to remove the weapons listed on his New York City Rifle and Shotgun Permit along with the permit itself.

Danny complied without argument stating, "My uncle told me to expect this. Detective Romano, can I ever get them back?"

"After you hear that all the other guys are arrested and you pay for the car damage, hire a lawyer to help you with that. I don't know the answer and I have to get the real problem guys. Do you know which one put the M-80s on the windows?"

"If I tell you, do you think it will help me and maybe I can still become a cop someday?"

This guy is an idiot, "Maybe, if you testify against them. I'll put a good word in for you," was Mike's quick reply.

"Okay, it was my cousin Eddie. He said that he did it."

After returning to the squad office and before he vouchered Clark's personal property, Romano quickly telephoned Lugo, catching him at his office in Seawall.

"Chief, I just took Clark's long guns and his permit. PD records show that all your men have long guns too. I

215

spoke to a Sergeant in the license division about pulling their firearms because of an open investigation. I was told that legally it could be questionable without proof. It was up to me, if I wanted to chance it. I already have Clark's long guns.

"Have you seen any of them? I'd like you to take their permits when they come in."

"Not a single one. Two of them, Laquin and Harry Goldblum were scheduled to work and called in with family emergencies."

"That was a slick move on their part. Jerk them around to keep them there and call me."

"Yeah, I'm sure they heard about Danny Clark. I phoned the other two to come in and work fill in but got the their answering machines. It looks like they're all in the wind."

Mike, frustrated said, "Damn them. I guess they're not as stupid as Danny Clark."

Pete continued, "It leaves two men and me to cover all tours. It's gonna be tough. I have to start looking for replacements soon but don't want to do it until this case is closed. I'd like to give these guys the option to think that they just might slide on all this."

"Good idea. In the meantime, I'll contact our Legal Division and find out how to get their permits before an actual arrest. I'll ask Legal if you can take them on my orders. Maybe I can be there and collar them at the same time. They might be stupid enough to show up. By the way, who owns the handguns, Seawall or them?"

"The old chief set it up that the village owns them, the Chief being the Gun Custodian. Why?"

"If legal agrees, you might be able to take them. I'll also try to convince a DA to indict them and get a bench warrant."

"Great, let me know as soon as you have more information on how to handle this. I'm ready to help anyway I can."

Romano spent the next few hours t ping up follow DD-5s and vouchering Clark's property. He made several phone calls in an effort to speak with an ADA and discuss his plans. Finally reaching someone, he was told to visit in person the following day.

***

When Mike returned to his office the next day, Charlie Wilson handed him a message.

"Hey Mike, this guy called and said to call him ASAP. He sounded upset."

Looking at the note, Romano saw the name "Danny with a phone number. *"Shit, Danny Clark. What does he want?*

He waited in the break room for the shift change and made a fresh pot of coffee. When Frank Pigro vacated the desk they shared, he picked up the telephone, sitting down as he dialed.

"Hello Danny? Detective Romano here, are you okay. Is there a problem?"

An agitated man spoke rapidly, "I got two calls last night, one early and one very late. Somebody's voice that I didn't know said that I'd better not to cooperate with you anymore. I'll take my chances in court without your help. I'm not going to testify against anybody." The line then went dead.

Frustrated, Mike explained what he was just told to his partner.

Sam asked, "What are you going to do? Remember, you're a bulldog."

Mike telephoned John Mahoney, Chief of the Investigation Bureau at the Brooklyn District Attorney's Office. After hearing about the entire case to date, Mahoney advised Mike as to his options.

"Detective, you have probable cause as required by law to arrest all the Seawall men. However, without the testimony of Mr. Clark your case is rather weak. It could be dismissed during the court process with a good defense attorney."

"That's what I thought sir. Is there any other way?"

"Yes Detective, your complainant, Chief Lugo is certain that the voice he heard was that of Ed Laquin?"

"Yes sir, he worked many hours with the man and knew the voice."

"Then you're in luck, you have Lugo's positive recognition of the voice. It's reasonable that Laquin is either the man who set off the bombs or at least a co-conspirator. You can arrest him with my complements. Please keep in touch."

"Thank you, sir!"

Mike quickly typed out a DD-5 recording the conversation with the bureau chief and brought it into Fitz to sign off on it. Romano's less than cordial interaction with the spineless Sergeant Fitzpatrick started at that time.

"I don't care what the DA told you. You work for me and I say gather more evidence. Got it Romano?"

"But Sarge, Chief Lugo is certain the voice on the phone was Laquin. It's like an admission, almost bragging."

"I'll acknowledge this "5" with no arrest authorized. Get more evidence. I have already received three calls from political figures that are pissed and told me, let me quote,

'Your detective is out for our cops. He single handedly decimated out entire police force.' I will not be the brunt of your bulldog ways. This is not narcotics."

"But Sarge," Mike began as Fitz held up his hand.

"Dismissed, Romano, back to work and gather some real evidence, then come back to get approval for a collar."

Mike, feeling humiliated, spun on his heel and left the room thinking, *fat half-drunk Irish bastard. Now its war just like with Dennis Bryan.*

When Romano returned to his desk, Sam asked, "Hey partner, you look like you want to hurt someone. Want to go across the street and get some coffee?"

Romano didn't answer, *that spineless jerk is wrong. I've got legal cause*; instead, he signaled Sam to wait a minute and picked up his telephone.

Sam just nodded and waited.

After phoning The Puzzle Palace, and conferring with an attorney in the Department's Legal Bureau, Mike fought to remain calm. He was more even more agitated after having secured clearance that any arrest was legal.

He turned to Sam, "Okay partner let's grab some 61s and work on some open cases, but first we get breakfast. I need some time to think."

Ten minutes later, they were sitting in a diner on 86th Street and eating a late breakfast.

Mike began, "Sam, I don't know what to do now. Fitz is pissing me off. He's upset about getting some calls from Seawall Village or somewhere about his Detective that's single handedly hurting their Police Department. It's got to be politically motivated by the old Chief. I don't give a rat's ass about him, but I don't think he was involved with or condones the bombing and damage to Lugo's car. I'm betting that he has enough pull to eventually get his job back. Good for him, but those half-assed cops are a different matter. They're dangerous, especially Laquin."

"You still haven't told me what Fitz or the geniuses at One PP said."

"Legal at One PP and the District Attorney's office told me to make the collar. They said that even without Danny Clark, I can take Laquin on ugo's voice identification. Maybe I can sweat him to implicate the rest. The CO of the license Division told me I can pull all their guns with or without a collar until everything is finalized through the courts. You know Fitz for years; will he try to screw me if I buck him?"

"Well, all I can say is that the man can be treacherous and always covers his ass. If you feel strongly about what you want to do, keep it to youself, do what you must, but cover your ass and go by the book. Above all, make sure you have every DD-5 completed on time and signed by him or Scala."

"Thanks, I'll take all that under advisement. Let's eat."

As they entered their office, Detective Romano had made a decision regarding the Seawall Village case.

I'll back off on this because I'm not in the mood to battle Fitz right now.

He spoke with Chief Lugo and filled him in as to what the Police Department's Legal Division, License Division, and the District Attorney's Office told him. By mutual agreement, Lugo would grab everyone's guns if he saw them. The License Division was to have their own enforcement personnel attempt to locate the missing men and confiscate their weapons.

For the time being, Romano was done with the investigation. He would figure out how to close the case at a later date.

He sat at his desk and began looking over the new cases in his in box.

CHAPTER SEVENTEEN

Several weeks had passed and Romano took particular interest in one of his newly assigned cases. It was unusual in nature, and involved the complaint of an immigrant, Valdas Karaluis. The complainant claimed that a male, Lukas Saveikis, struck him with his pickup truck in an attempt to kill him. He claims no known reason for the assault. His only physical damage claimed to his body is a bruise on his leg.

The complainant further stated that he knows his assailant from his old town, Veliuona, in Lithuania.

Great another foreign mystery, thought Mike as he reached for the telephone on his desk.

"Hello, Mister Karaluis, this is Detective Romano of the Six Four Squad. I am the officer assigned to investigate your case. Tell me something about it please."

"What do you want to know Detective? All you have to know is that I want the man that tried to run me over and kill me arrested. You have his name, Lukas Saveikis. He is Lithuanian like me. There is no reason for what he tried to do. Are you going to arrest him?"

"Sir, there is more to it than that. I would like you to come in and give me a detailed statement. Can you do that?"

"I can come to see you whenever you wish. How is it if I come now?"

This is good, just what I need to get me off my thoughts of how to screw with Fitz.

"Yes that will be excellent. Do you know where the police station is?"

"Yes. I leave now."

"Ask for the Detectives. We're on the second floor."

Twenty minutes later, a man walked in and with a Slavic accent asked Charlie Wilson for, "Detective Michael Romano, please."

Mike looked up from his desk and gave the man a once over. His hair was wavy and not very neat. The man was dressed like what would be termed working man plain. He was wearing dark cuffed pants, blue button down shirt and a rumpled wind breaker jacket.

He gave the impression of a seedy European character in an old black and white Humphrey Bogart movie. What caught Romano's attention were his eyes, they were dark with a hint of deceit in them.

The voices inside the detective's head cautioned, *careful with this guy, nothing is cut and dry. He will lie to you.*

Indicating the empty chair next to his desk, Mike said, "I'm Detective Romano, we spoke on the phone. Please sit."

"Thank you. What do you need to know to arrest that man, Lukas? He tried to kill me with his truck. Your police came and made report, then did nothing. You will arrest him, yes?"

"If I can prove the case, I'll arrest him. But first tell me what happened in detail, and why you think he wanted to run you over with his truck."

"Truth to God this is what happened…"

Karaluis related to Romano how they knew each other from their small town back in Lithuania. The town was small and "everyone knew everyone", adding that he had been childhood friends with Lukas and his wife Edita. He also added that he once had a boyhood crush on Edita but she was involved with Lukas and finally married him.

An odd statement. The man is a snake, shouted the voice in Romano's head.

"Okay, so you all knew each other in your home town. If you were friends, why did he attack you? What did you do to him?"

"Nothing, he accuses me of wanting to steal his wife. He is crazy."

After obtaining some further details, Mike assured the complainant that he would be in contact soon. The man left.

Trusting the celestial voice in his head, Romano notified the Bureau of Criminal Investigation in One PP and requested that they forward any known information they had on Valdas Karaluis.

Two hours later, BCI responded.

They faxed the following information; Karaluis was collared a year before in Secaucus, New Jersey by the State Police. The charges were for rape and kidnapping. He was currently free under $150,000 bail awaiting trial. Having no valid visa, if convicted, he would probably be deported.

Not satisfied, Mike called and asked if they knew who posted his bail.

"His attorney, is listed as Nikolai Kruzhkov from Brooklyn."

Suspicions confirmed, have to interview the Saveikis couple.

***

The following day, Mr. and Mrs. Saveikis were sitting in the break room with Mike, they were about to be interviewed.

The woman, Edita, sat staring at her hands that she kept folded in her lap through most of the interview. The few times she did look up, it was only for a quick glance at Mike, as if to gauge his reaction. Lukas did most of the talking.

"Detective Romano, this animal, Valdas Karaluis has had, how do you say, a thing for my Edita since childhood. Unlike him, I have worked hard since coming to America. I have a good job as a door man at a hotel in Manhattan, and when not there, work in our deli store with my brother, we are partners. Our deli is, how what you call, top shelf in America. Valdas is a bum that does not work and maybe makes money as a criminal."

"Go on," *with that attorney, he must be involved with the Russian mob in some manner.*

"About a year ago, because I work long hours and do not spend much time socializing, he started hanging out with my sister-in-law, my wife and some friends. That is when trouble first started."

"What kind of trouble?"

"Sometimes, when the women would drink too much, he would always ask Edita if he could drive her home. One time he did not take her home; he took her to New Jersey. He began touching her while crossing Washington Bridge. When she resisted him, he drew a knife and said he would cut her."

At that point, Edita locked eyes with Mike and acknowledged the statement with a small nod.

Lukas touched his wife's hand and continued.

"He took her to a motel where he made her drink

more and raped her. Early the next morning while he slept, she went to the hotel office and telephoned for the police. He was arrested in the room."

"New Jersey informed me that he is awaiting trial. Did you know that he filed a complaint against you, claiming that you tried to run him over with your truck? Is the claim valid?"

"Sir?"

"Did you attempt to hit him with your truck because of that incident?"

"No sir, I want to beat him and break his bones. Since the trial is coming soon, he has been harassing my wife, her sister and us, about four months now. Detective, I tell you, he is evil."

"Harassing how?"

"My wife sometimes works in her sister's beauty shop. He would go there when it is crowded and threaten the women. If they say to get out, he claims he will come in the night and kill them with a knife. The police took the big knife he used against my wife when they arrested him. I'm sure he has another one now."

"Did anyone file a police report?"

"Yes, we have been to court several times but they do nothing. In New Jersey, we have court orders say he may not come near my wife or family members. In New Jersey, the court said that they are good in New York automatically. We call police here and when we go to court he comes with a lawyer and he leaves."

This guy needs an ass kicking. "Tell me about the truck incident."

"One night, after closing the store, I forgot something and drove back to the store and he was there putting pictures on the windows. We have a pull gate in front the glass and he put pictures on the glass by reaching between folding parts. I was very angry thinking he was doing damage and I went onto sidewalk. Maybe I tried to hit him, maybe accident, I don't remember."

"Did you hit him?"

"He ran away. I left my truck and looked. He put photos of my wife in the New Jersey motel. She was exposed and looked to be sleeping. I pulled them down and went to look for him. Maybe if I found him, he would be dead now."

"Where are the pictures?"

"I burned them."

"I'll ask you again; did you try to hit him with your truck?"

"What would you have done Detective?"

"I don't know. Right now, I need an answer, and please think before you answer me."

Lukas nodded his head.

While waiting for an answer, Mike looked directly at Edita, "Do you wish to add anything?"

In a childlike manner, she answered, "No sir."

Lukas finally answered, "Detective, I was anxious to get to him. I tried to close the distance to him. I did not want to strike him with my truck; I wanted to jump out and beat him to death, very much, maybe too much. Now, I am thinking about the incident, I did not want to hit him with my truck, I wanted to use my hands!"

"That's fine." Handing him a blank piece of paper and a pen, Mike continued, "Please write down what you just told me and sign it. Thank you."

Romano excused himself and went down to the 124 room (complaint room). He officially requested copies of any complaint filed by Lukas Saveikis or his wife, Edita.

When he returned to his desk, Lukas had finished his written statement and handed it to him.

"Thank you Mr. and Mrs. Saveikis, we're finished for now. I'll check out all the information and I'll get back to you as quickly as I can."

Mike was anxious to dig into the situation in its entirety. To do so required the couple to leave. He handed a business card to each of them.

"Please call if you have any questions or remember something else. Thank you for coming in."

With the couple gone, Romano sat at his desk and began typing his follow up reports, the DD-5s.

Mike was deep into his paperwork regarding the Karaluis/Saveikis case when Sergeant Fitzpatrick bellowed, "Romano, get in here at once; now!"

Mike quickly rose from his chair.

Sam commented, "Oh boy, sounds like the shit just hit the fan. What have you done now?"

Romano shrugged his shoulders.

Fitz was red with rage as he spoke, "Detective Romano, I have just returned from an interview with Captain Sommers of Internal Affairs and I was asked about your actions regarding the Seawall Village fiasco. You have given me great personal pain over that case. You are to report to the Poplar Street office at 0800 tomorrow morning."

Mike opened his mouth to speak.

Fitz held up his hand to silence him.

"Your kind are all hard headed, don't say a word. Call in here when you arrive. Be there on time and get the hell out of my sight."

Romano turned on his heel and left the office grinning. *Bigoted bastard! He is pissed!*

Back in the outer office, Sam said, "I heard the words IAD and Seawall. What did you do?"

"I haven't touched it since we talked about it. Guess I should have closed it out but I don't know how. I'll figure something out after my interview with IAD."

"Do you want Richie to go with you after all he's our union rep?"

"No, I did nothing wrong. I'll be okay."

"It's your choice."

The telephone on Mike's desk rang. Grateful for the interruption he picked it up.

It was the desk officer. "Detective you have several faxes down here. Do you want me to send them up?"

"It's all good. Thank you lieutenant, I'll come right down and get them."

When he returned with the faxes, Mike sat at his desk and carefully reviewed each one.

The information included vouchers for a knife, a blue dress, a pair of panties and lab reports. Also included were statements by the complainant and the perpetrator. Valdas Karaluis claimed consensual sex, Edita claimed rape, stating that she was held against her will and was incapacitated, incapable of fighting back because she was highly intoxicated. Included in the paperwork was a copy of an Order of Protection from New Jersey with a note stating as required by Federal Law, it was enforceable in New York also.

Typical a he said she said case, thought Mike. His desk phone rang again interrupting his thoughts.

"Detective Romano here, how can I help you?"

It was Edita Saveikis. In a little girl voice she asked, "Detective Mike, I must see you alone without my husband. Can I come in tomorrow?"

"Sure Mrs. Saveikis, but it will have to be in the afternoon. I have an appointment at Police Headquarters in the morning. Please give me a phone number to reach you. I'll call when I'm ready to leave there and give you a time to be at the office. Is that alright?"

"Yes please. I will be at my sister's beauty shop." She gave him the number and said goodbye.

***

Before he left the office, Romano opened his locker and removed his personal copies of his entire case file on Seaview Village. He checked to see that he had copies of everything in the official case folder, then returned the paperwork to his locker, and double checked that it was secured.

One can never be too sure that official files get lost.

Detective Romano arrived at Internal Affairs precisely at 0800 hrs. He telephoned his squad office as procedure dictated.

Frank Pigro took the call, "Hey Romano, got your ass in a jam did you? Be careful, they love hurting cops, especially Italian ones. Have fun."

After waiting for several minutes, he was directed to a small windowless room. Inside, sitting at a table were "two suits". He recognized one of the men at once, Inspector Rothwell. Mike had dealings with the man when he nailed the gangster cop, Henry Capelli, back on Staten Island. The second man was unknown to him. Rothwell indicated the empty chair across from them. On the table was a tape recorder.

Mike's mind raced, *this might not be so bad. I wonder if Chief Stranire sent Rothwell to sit in. Saint*

Michael, once again, I thank you.

Rothwell nodded at Romano as the other man spoke. "Detective Romano, please sit down. We'll try to make this painless as possible."

Romano sat down and tried to smile, but was too nervous, "Sir."

The unknown man, reached for the recorder, clicked it on and slid a microphone toward Mike.

"My name is Captain John Racine and this man is Inspector Rothwell. He is here primarily as an observer. I will be conducting the interview."

"Good morning," was all Mike could think of to say.

The Captain began, "This is an official investigation regarding a case that you have been involved in that has come to the attention of Internal Affairs. Before we continue, do you wish to wait for a union delegate?"

"No, I'm good, I did nothing wrong."

Racine continued, "Fine then. We'll inform you of the allegations against you. Before we continued, allow me to remind you that G.O. 15, a cop's Miranda warnings, is in effect and this panel may recommend that this case goes to the trial room where you can be severely disciplined such as loss of The Shield and even dismissed."

"Yes," *heaven help me.*

It is alleged by four men, formerly employed by Seawall Village, a private community within your command, that you are a friend of the acting Chief of the Seawall Village Police Department. They have also stated that you have caused the loss of their employment by removing all their firearms without cause or arrest and have done so because of your personal relationship with Chief Peter Lugo. Do you understand?"

"They can say anything they want to. I acted

correctly after checking all facts and getting clearance from the License Division and Legal Bureau. I even spoke with the DA's Office before taking any action."

"You are aware, I'm sure that we previously have spoken with your supervisor, Sergeant Fitzpatrick?"

"Yes."

"It is his claim that he ordered you not to make any arrests and to close the case. Is that true Detective?"

"No Sir, not entirely."

"Please explain."

"Well, as you know, the Chief's residence was bombed twice. I arrested a civilian who trashed the Chief's private auto. During questioning, he implicated the four cops who lost their guns. According to the District Attorney's Office, based on voice recognition of one of the cops and the civilian's statement, I was authorized to arrest all involved."

Mike paused, took a deep breath, and then continued.

"I prepared all my DD-5s after each phase of the case. Each one was signed off by one of my supervisors, sometimes both of them."

"That's a partial answer, Detective. Did Sergeant Fitzpatrick order you not to make any arrests and to close the cased?"

"He ordered me not to arrest the cops. He told me that he had received complaints from the Village Board. I don't know what that meant, he didn't explain, then he said I should not arrest the men."

"Have you closed the case? To our knowledge, there is not a closing DD-5.

"Not yet, I'm kind of busy. I just caught a kidnapping assault case and a companion case listing that perp as my complainant. As you wish, I'll get right on it, Sir."

Racine turned to Rothwell and asked, "Inspector, do you have any questions?"

Not wanting to give up his prior association with Romano. The inspector was vague as he answered, "No Captain. I feel that Detective Romano answered everything truthfully. It was interesting to meet the man after reading his file."

Mike thought, *wow, good answer Inspector. I hope you have my back.*

Racine picked it up for one more question, "Detective, are you aware that you may have gone beyond the required number of days to file a DD-5 in the case?"

"As I have said, it might be possible. I'll have to go back to my squad and check. I'll complete one at once, Sir." The two bosses looked at each other without speaking. Then Racine said, "Detective, thank you for being so candid. You may go back to your command. You will be notified through proper channels as to our decision.

"Thank you," chirped Mike as he left"

From the lobby of One PP, Mike telephoned Edita at her sister's shop, "Mrs. Saveikis, I'm on my way back to my office and should be there in an hour. If you still want to meet, I can see you then.

"Yes Detective, it's important. I'll be there. Thank you."

***

Just before noon, Mike's complainant stood in the office doorway. She swayed from side to side ever so slightly, indicating impatience, anxiety, or both. Her face, as Mike had noticed when they first met, projected an understated natural beauty and a hint of embarrassment. She wore simple clothing in muted colors.

Mike immediately rose from his desk and walked to meet her. *She looks embarrassed and frightened. I hope that I can help her.*

As he drew closer to her, she extended her right hand.

"Good morning." He shook her hand and then in an attempt to get a smile he asked, "Is it still morning. Thank you for coming."

"Detective Mike, where can we go for some privacy? This is difficult for me. I have need to keep what I will tell to you to stay between us."

"Please, come into the break room. I'll close the door if you like."

Once inside, Romano indicated a chair next to the empty desk in the room. He pulled a second chair alongside of her, but not too close. After a few awkward seconds, Edita reached into her purse and withdrew an envelope.

"Detective, you must promise me that you will make every effort to keep the contents of this envelope from my husband."

"You have my word."

"Lukas is a good man and I owe him to be a dutiful wife. I have been less than honorable."

Turning her head and staring at the wall beside her, she continued, "You may look at them so you understand."

Romano slowly examined the nine photos. Two of them showed Edita and Karaluis, obviously naked, devoid of pubic hair, and dripping wet as if coming out of a shower or bath.

Another was of Edita, alone, sitting on a bed and

smiling clutching her legs against her chest. She was naked in that one too.

The balance of the photos were more of the same, but not as explicit. Lukas explained that they were similar to what he had removed from his shop windows. Mike replaced the photos and put down the envelope.

"When were these pictures taken? These pictures show two lovers, not a rape."

"The pictures of us together were in a happier time. When we used to drink and have sex. The more we dated he became too demanding and sometime physically abusive. I put a stop to it after a few months. The other pictures are like the ones he put on our store. He threw them at me in my sister's beauty shop. If Lukas sees these, he will kill him. Please do something."

"Did all this happen before you were kidnapped to New Jersey?"

Edita looked at Mike and turned an even shade of crimson.

"Mr. Mike, after he threw the photos at me, he telephoned to meet me for one last date. I thought that it would be safe and quiet him down. Maybe he would leave us alone, so I agreed. That is when we went to Jersey."

"What happened next?"

"We drove thru the Brooklyn Battery Tunnel and on to the Expressway. Once on the Expressway, he asked her to accompany him to his apartment. I said no, take me home now."

Edita began to shake. Mike patiently waited.

"At that time Valdas, pulled a knife and told me we would have sex, like it or not. I was terrified and made a plan. I would get him drunk, wait for him to pass out and I could escape from having sex with him. There were man y times he would fall asleep drunk during our affair. This time it did not work. It only got worse. This time he got violent and insistent. He cut me on my thigh with his knife to prove himself." She began crying softly.

"He climbed on top of me and hit me several times. I think I blacked out because I remember opening my eyes and he was inside me. He put a picture of the cut on our store window. I don't remember seeing him take it. That is why I think I was not conscious.

"How did you get away from him?"

"The truth is I never went to the office to phone the police. I convinced him to let me use the room phone to call my family to say goodbye."

"I thought you wanted no part of him."

"I phoned my sister-in-law, Giovana, married to my brother. She is Italian and I speak it some. She knew about my affair. In American, so the pig could understand, I told her that I was running away with Valdas. Quickly in Italian, I told her I was prisoner and to come and get me."

"Could he speak Italian?"

"I do not think so. Again, in American, I asked that she bring me some things to motel. He was so drunk and happy to hear what I said and went to sleep. I prayed. Finally, they came with the police and they took him. The rest you know."

"What about what you two told me about him harassing you at your sister's shop. Is that true or was that in the past?"

"The first time was when he threw the pictures you have seen at me. They were before he took me. What he brings to shop and store is from New Jersey night. He is threatening to bring more of them."

Saint Michael, please help me punish this animal.

"Okay Edita, based on what you are telling me, I believe that I can arrest him for Witness Tampering because you have an open case in New Jersey.'

Edita smiled. "Thank you."

"That will get him off the street until the trial comes up. I must say that I don't know if I can disregard the incident that Valdas reported about your husband and his truck, but I'll try. In addition, I'll need to keep these photos as proof of harassment and threats to substantiate the witness tampering."

"Will other people see them? I will be greatly embarrassed."

"If it goes to trial, yes, but for now only the police."

"I must endure the shame. I was wrong to have ever get involved with that animal. I want my life back to normal. You will hurry, yes?"

"Please try to be patient and trust me. I'll work hard to bring him in. However, it may take some time, at least several days. I do have other cases too. You'll hear from me soon as I have him in handcuffs."

Still trying to hide her embarrassment, Edita thanked Romano and quickly left the office.

CHAPTER EIGHTEEN

The day following his interview with Edita Saveikis, Romano, was to do a four to midnight tour. He arrived at the squad office almost an hour early and signed in. The voices in his head told him that catching Valdas Karaluis would not be easy and he wanted to get some old paperwork out of the way.

He especially wanted to complete the closing DD-5 for the Seawall Village case before any Trial Room findings reached Sergeant Fitzpatrick.

Only two squad members were still present from the day tour, Charlie Wilson and Danny Reyes leaving the desk he shared with Frank Pigro empty. He sat down and set to work.

It was just before 1600 hrs. when Richie Levy and Sam Battle walked in. The day men rose from their desks. Pleasantries were exchange all around when Fitzpatrick bellowed, "Romano, I hear you. Get your ass in here at once and close the damn door!"

All heads turned toward Mike. Richie, being the union rep for the office spoke.

"Mike if you need me for anything, I'm here. Okay?"

"Thanks Richie, I got this."

***

Mike guessed what it was about and wanted to have

some fun with it. He entered and smiled before speaking.

"What has you so upset Sarge? I hope it's not the closing DD-5 on the Seawall case. I'm typing it now. Sorry to be late but I've been busy as you know."

Fitzpatrick's ruddy complexion was glowing as he stood rigidly, almost nose to nose with Romano. *Has he been drinking? This should be fun. Let's go, you pompous ass.*

"First get that smile off your face. You damn Italian guys are all alike."

Romano took advantage of the pause, as Fitz opened his mouth to continue and countered.

"Careful Irish, you're in our neighborhood here, calm down."

Fitz's eyes widened at the remark. "Watch your tone with me Detective." Spittle was begining to form as he spoke.

This is gonna be more fun than I thought.

"Sorry Boss," Mike answered quickly. What did I do that's got you so upset?"

His blood pressure must have risen at least twenty points Beads of sweat began to form on Fitz's brow.

"The hearing officers decided that I was negligent as a supervisor because your DD-5s were late regarding the Seawall case. My reputation has been tarnished by YOU !"

"Sorry."

"You are extremely lucky that I only got a 'Warned and Admonished,' from them. They also recommended that you receive a five to ten day rip for not obeying orders to close the case based on my testimony in addition to being late with your reports. Inspector Rothwell himself told me to decide on your punishment."

"Oh, wow. He must be pissed."

"He told me that I must decide your punishment and he would personally sign off on it."

Mike smiled and off handedly commented, "I've met him before when I worked on Staten Island."

Fitz appeared to ignore the remark. "You're a good detective and an asset to the squad, but a pain in the ass. You not only walk to a different drummer, you have your own band."

Romano's Saint Michael gene kicked in. The voice inside his head cautioned, *careful Michael, he's still your boss.*

Mike raised his voice in anger, "Listen Sarge, first of all, I did them all but the last DD-5 on time."

"Watch your tone Detective."

"Second, you signed off on every one of my 5's and third I don't like your Italian comments. I respect the fact that you're my supervisor, but you'd be better off if I also respected the man. Think about it."

Fitz had spittle on the corner of his mouth as he answered, "Just who the hell do you think you are Romano. I'm your supervisor and the commander of this squad. You are my subordinate. You can't talk to a Boss like that. That's so typical of Italian machismo. I can write you up for your comments take your shield and transfer you. What do you have to say now?"

Outside, the other squad members listened with interest.

Dan Reyes said, "I have ten dollars that says Fitz is gonna bury him, any takers?"

Charlie Wilson answered, "Mikey is the man and I'll take the bet.

Sam quickly added, He's my partner and I'll double that."

The men outside could only listen and could not see

Romano's next response. "Sorry Sarge, you're right. I apologize."

The detective turned completely around to face Fitz again and spoke, "Hey Tim, let me ask you a question man to man, do you know my boss, Sergeant Fitzpatrick?"

Fitz was speechless with his mouth wide open.

Mike continued his harassment.

"Well, Fitz is an alright guy, but a crappy, picayune, sometimes is a no balls boss. He also lied in the trial room and I can prove it. Please tell him that if he fucks with me and takes any time from me, I'll demand a full Department Trial. Thanks." He then turned full circle again and faced Fitz.

"Hey Sarge, did you get the message from Tim?"

Fitzpatrick's face showed disbelief and fascination at once. "Detective you are crazy. Are you on something?"

"No Sarge, I don't take drugs, I'm just pissed off. Oh yeah, I don't drink excessively or at work like some cops do."

"Are you threatening me?"

"Not at all Sarge, I'm just stating the facts. I always cover my ass and I respect your Masters in Literature Degree. I know basically, you are a good guy but I also like a good scrap. If you're so inclined to start one, have at it and let the best man win. Can I go back to my desk now?"

"Get out of my office, I have to decide what to do. Go back to work and I want the closing '5' on Seawall within an hour. Got it?"

"Yes Sir." Mike then returned to the squad room.

The men in the room were acting as if they had just been to a party. There were comments and high fives all over the place.

Richie said, "You are nuts Mike and you know that as delegate, he'll confer with me on this one. I'll do my best."

"Not to worry Richie, if you can't get him away from taking time or transferring me, I'll go back to the trial room and win there. Thanks for caring."

As he left, Charlie slapped Mike's back and said, "Great show."

Sam just said, "Mikey," and erupted with his patented chuckle as he waved a thumbs up gesture.

An hour later, Mike knocked on Fitz's office door and went in to hand him the closing Seawall DD-5, and then he turned and left. Not a single word was exchanged.

Sam grabbed his partner's arm and guided him outside into the hallway. "Mikey, that was the craziest thing I ever heard. You called him out. Maybe you're really crazy. The guys bet that you're gonna get screwed. I have twenty on a win for you. Do you think I'm a winner?"

"Yes. I have copies of all my DD-5's on the case with his signature on them, documentation regarding my conversations with One PP and the DA's office and a Polaroid of the bottle in his desk drawer. I'm ready to roll."

"Holy shit, how did you get the picture?"

"I've been practicing my lock picking skills. I'm sure you understand and I used our camera. He's not the first bigoted Irish boss I went up against. The last one was Dennis Bryan. Do you know him?"

"Yeah, he's Chief of Detectives. You battled him?"

"Sure did. Let's get some cases, especially my new one and go out. I'll tell you about it."

"Good, I just love Eyetalian stories."

Mike turned to his partner and said, "You drive. How about we stop and eat some Chinese food? Do you know a good place?"

"Yeah, there's a good one on 86th Street, Sum Luk,

and it shouldn't be crowded now. I'll be able to hear your entire story about the Chief of D."

The two men signed out to the field.

As soon as they entered the restaurant, a waiter hurried over to greet the two detectives.

"Wecome, Detective Sam, I no see you in many months. Come, follow me prease. I see you have new partner."

Once seated, the waiter brought the partners a pot of tea and two cups. "You know what want gentamen?"

Sam said to Mike, "It's all good here and I eat it all, so you order. Pick three things and we'll share."

"Like spicy food?"

"I'll eat anything that won't kill me. If it tries, I'll kill it and then eat it."

Turning the waiter, Mike ordered, Shrimp with Black Bean Sauce, Pork Angel Hair Chow Fun and Spicy Kung Pao Chicken.

When the server left, Sam leaned forward.

"Okay Mikey, let's hear the Dennis Bryan tale, I'm all ears."

Mike had only shared the story with two others on the job, his old narcotics partner, Alex Veranos and the warrant detective, Sophie Kiminski.

"Well, it started this way...."

Ninety minutes later, as they put down their forks, Sam, totally without comment, finally spoke.

"And you're not afraid of him being the Chief of Detectives?"

"Not at all; I still have my memo book regarding the entire incident in my gun safe at home, and I still have my connections downtown and with some other people. If he starts any shit, he wouldn't stand a chance."

Sam chuckled, "So it's true, all you Eyetalians are all connected."

Mike smiled before answering.

"Every person in this world is connected with each other. That's all you have to know."

"Aw shit. Tell me more."

"Let's get back to the office and hope nothing new comes up tonight. We're scheduled for a turnaround tour in the morning and I have paperwork."

Sam was disappointed.

The following day, before noon, Mike and Sam visited Lukas Saveikis at the fancy apartment building on Central Park West in Manhattan where he was employed as a doorman.

"So Mr. Saveikis, Lukas, can you tell us where we might find Karaluis when he's not stalking your wife?"

"Detective Romano, he goes to an Armenian social club in Coney Island. I don't know the address but it is a block long, low building near where Cropsey Avenue and Coney Island Avenue meet. It looks almost white in color."

"Is it a front for criminal activity?"

"I don't think so. There, men drink coffee, play dominoes, cards and get to know other immigrants. The owner of the club, Karolis Kristupas is a very good man. He gives construction jobs to new people to this country. It's said that he helps all people from former Soviet Union countries."

"We'll check it out. What kind of car does Valdas drive?"

Just as he was about to answer, a Mercedes pulled up.

"Please excuse me, work is work."

Lukas rushed forward to open the rear door and assisted a well-dressed couple onto the sidewalk.

"Good afternoon, Mr. and Mrs. Clavets. How are you today?" he cheerfully asked before he hustled ahead to hold the lobby door open and closed it behind them.

Sam was curious and asked, "Tenants or visitors?"

"They're full time tenants. Nice people, they gave me $500.00 last Christmas."

Battle chuckled, "Got any job openings?"

Lukas went back to the question he had not answered before the Merc pulled up.

"The last car I saw him in was a dark red Ford, four door model, it's the same car he took Edita away in. Are you going to arrest him?"

"Yes, as soon as I find him. Right now, he's facing multiple charges including witness tampering. Once I have him, you and your wife will be notified to speak with an Assistant District Attorney before actually going before a judge."

"What about the truck incident? Will he get deported?"

"I've closed the truck case pending new information. If he pushes it, and wants you arrested, he'll have to come to see me, and then I won't have to look for him."

"Can he be deported?"

"As for deportation, once he's convicted of a from the old case or the new one, by law, he can be deported as an undesirable alien if he is in violation of his visa."

"I hope you get him soon," the doorman answered as he opened the door to allow a family to leave the building.

The conversation resumed when the tenants were out of earshot.

"Edita's uncle is a big general or something like that in the Lithuanian State Police. Maybe if he is deported, he can be met at the airport and real justice served up."

Mike was ready to leave.

"You never know what can happen. We'll call you soon Lukas," Their conversation had been concluded.

As the men walked back to their car, Mike turned to his partner, "Hey Sam, if you have nothing pressing, I'd like to stop by that social club before we go back to the office. Are you good for that?"

"Sure, I see that the old bulldog is on the scent. Maybe we'll get lucky and find him there. You drive."

On the north east corner of Cropsey and Coney Island Avenues was a tire repair shop. Next to it was a single story old,faded tan, brick building about 100 feet long There were three distinct entrance doorways, indicating that it might have three separate addresses.

Attached to it, on the far end, constructed of similar brick was a two-story building. It's sidewalk level had a large double garage type door opening in addition to a ttypical entrance door. The second level appeared as if it was a residence.

"Hey Mike, look at the sign above the first doorway, "Armenian Christian's Social Club."

"Yeah, I see it. Does it look open?"

"I can't tell. The windows are too dirty to see anything inside from here. Stop the car and we can go check."

"I intend to," he answered, as he pulled to the curb in front of the place. "Let's see if Kristupas is in."

The door was unlocked and the two detectives cautiously entered.

Once inside, the detectives closed the door and remained alongside the entrance to allow their eyes to get accustomed to the different light level.

As their eyes adjusted, they could see that they were standing on an entrance platform, two steps above a large room. There were several people inside.

Below the entrance platform, approximately a dozen tables were scattered about, in no apparent pattern, yet they defined a rough empty square in the center. On the far wall was a serving counter, unoccupied, with several bar type backless stools were strewn about in front of it.

The men at the tables had stopped all conversation and whatever else they were doing to look over at the interlopers in business suits.

"Mike said, "I already counted eleven men in the place Sam. What's your take?"

"First, they know we're cops, but I don't get a hostile feeling, next I wonder which one of them is our man. It's your show. I have your back if it gets shitty."

Mike took the helm, waving his arm toward Sam as they both stepped down into the room.

"Good afternoon everyone, my name is Detective Romano and this man is Detective Battle. There is no problem with anybody here, but we need to speak with Karolis Kristupas. We are told that he could help us."

The partners began walking to the center of the room, carefully watching the all the occupants with each step they took.

At a table on the far side of the room, two men stood and advanced toward them, both were smiling in a friendly manner.

The larger man spoke almost accent free, "Yes, good afternoon Detectives. I am Arif, the brother of Karolis. I am sure that you already know our family name. We welcome you both. Please come."

He raised his hand pointing toward the rear counter.

"There we will be able to speak quietly."

The second man turned and walked away. Table activity resumed as the three of them advanced to the counter area.

"How can my brother and I help you officers?"

Mike began, "We are told that your brother runs a legitimate social club here and helps get new immigrants work. What kind of work?"

"We operate a construction company that does a lot of renovation work and some new projects from time to time. We have been in business almost since coming to this country twelve years ago. K, as my brother is called and I are citizens of the United States. Our wives are also."

Sam asked, "And the social club. Is this where you get your workers from?"

"It is and we also help to settle new immigrants from old Iron Curtain Countries and guide them as to the customs and laws of this country."

"Do you personally know all the members of your club?"

"Between K and myself, I hope that we do. Not here, but we have a list of membership and our workers too. Are you looking for somebody special?"

Romano replied, "Yes we are. We are told that a man who calls himself, Valdas Karaluis sometimes comes here. Do you know him?"

"The name is not familiar, maybe K knows him."

"Where is your brother? Can you reach out to him and have him come in to speak with us now?"

Arif excused himself and moved behind the counter.

As he reached down for something, he noticed that both officers put their hands under their jackets and quickly announced, "I will get the telephone we keep here and call to ask him if he could come now."

Both detectives relaxed when the phone was placed on the counter. Arif lifted the handset and dialed.

After a quick conversation in both Albanian and English, their host said, "My brother is at home. It is the larger portion of this same building on the next corner. He will be here in a minute. Can I get you men something while you wait?"

Sam replied, "No thanks, but I see some men smoking. Do you mind if I light a cigarette?" before getting an answer, he looked at Mike and added, "My partner is by now must be ready for a cigar. Do you mind if he lights one too?"

K reached under the counter again.

"Not at all I will get you an old coffee can for ashes."

Mike had smoked half a stogie and Sam was on his second cigarette when Arif introduced his brother.

"Gentlemen, this is my brother K."

Cordial handshakes and introductions quickly followed. K got to business first.

"My brother has told me that you wish to find Valdas Karaluis. Is that correct?"

"Yes, we want to talk with him."

"I know the man and even sponsored him into this country. He used to work for me. Is he in trouble again?"

The two detectives exchanged glances; they were surprised at the question and the unusual level of cooperation.

Mike responded, "Still is more like it. It pertains to an old case, something that he was arrested for some time ago."

"You mean the New Jersey thing with a woman?"

"Yes, we are now involved with it. Do you know where he lives or does he come here and when?"

I don't know where he lives now and yes, he

usually comes here in the night hours."

"What can you tell us about him?"

"He no longer works for me because I fired him before the New Jersey thing. He is not reliable because he is a drunk. He comes here to see some friends and play dominoes for money but I should not be telling police that."

"We don't care about friendly gambling, but we would like to know that we can count on you to call us if he shows up. Are you comfortable with that?"

"Yes, I will do it. Perhaps you will be able to stop his visits. Sometimes he is a problem here, but we still try to help everyone and he has friends here. It is what my brother and I do. You have a business card to leave with us, yes? I will call. "

Both Sam and Mike each handed him their business cards as they shook hands before leaving.

***

When the partners got back to the office, Richie Levy took Mike out into the hallway.

"Mike, Fitz is about to call you into the office. There's been a decision made regarding your punishment over the Seawall Village case."

Romano, trying not to show his anxiety at the prospect of possibly going to war with his Squad Commanding Officer quipped, "Are you guys betting about the outcome or is there some faith in me left in this office?"

"Mike, please just keep your mouth shut and listen. Don't say anything out of the way."

"He sure took his time about it."

Half a minute later Fitz yelled, "Romano get in here and bring Detective Levy with you."

"Romano, just stand there and don't say a word." The words were almost visible as they came out of Sergeant Timothy Fitzpatrick's mouth.

"You are a good detective, almost as good as Richie here, but one royal pain in the ass. You have put a blemish on my record because of your obstinate Italian personality. Yet Detective Levy, as your union delegate, spent a lot of time with me articulating what discipline he thought was appropriate."

"Thank you Richie."

"I said to be quiet. It also seems that you had a friend on the IA panel. I received a personal call from Inspector Rothwell. He wanted to know if I had reached a decision as to punishment."

"Mike smiled to further piss off his boss.

"Detective Levy made a point that he thought the call was a gentle recommendation from the Inspector. After some very lengthy consideration, Detective Levy ultimately convinced me that an official *Warned and Admonished* disposition should be the final result."

Mike tried not to smile.

"I recommend that you accept this decision and sign the acknowledgement form. It will be a permanent addition to your personnel file. What do you have to say?"

"Yes Sir, I will accept and sign it."

Looking as if he was displeased with himself, in an effort to maintain his position of authority, Fitz added, "And remember, just because of the very light outcome, an unheard of one for disobeying a direct order, don't get cocky. Step out of line and I'll pull your rank, and send you back to uniform, with or without Rothwell's approval. Do you understand?"

Mike wanted to say, *Kiss my ass you spineless bigot. You were not responsible for my promotion. I'm*

252

appointed my rank by the PC after a recommendation. You'll have to tell some tale to get me busted down and transferred. I'm ready to rock with you. Ask Dennis Bryan. You obviously lied to the board and you still drink on duty in your office. Inspector Rothwell is only one of the people that I can use to stop you in your tracks if necessary and if you screw with me, I'll bury you.

Instead, he implied what he was thinking with, "Yes Sergeant, I fully understand and I hope that you fully understand what I asked my friend Tim to tell you a few weeks ago."

Fitz pushed the signature form in front of Mike saying, "Shut up, sign it, and get out of my fuck'n office."

Mike grinned, signed where required, gave a salute, and then snapped an about face, closing the door as he left the office.

As far as Mike was concerned, the Seawall Village case was closed. *Screw him and his DD-5.*

CHAPTER NINETEEN

The day after his latest round with Sergeant Fitzpatrick , Romano signed in at his office by 0745 hrs. It was to be his last tour before his regular two days off swing. He was feeling good and was looking forward to a productive day's work.

The first thing he did after exchanging greetings with Sam and Richie was to poke his head into the supervisors' office. Tony Scala was present.

"Good morning Mike. I see the Seawall Village problem is over with. Congratulations. I'm happy that you're still with us. Of course, there wasn't a doubt in my mind. Now get to work."

Romano sat at his desk and began typing his DD-5 reports on his currently most active investigation, the Saveikis case. Levy and Battle were busy with their own work.

An hour had passed and Mike had poured himself a cup of java in the breakroom. Just as he walked into squad's work area, he almost collided with a short Oriental couple.

The man spoke in a slightly accented, agitated voice, "Excuse me please, I must speak with a Detective. I have a serious problem."

Mike stopped in his tracks and tried to get a reading on the diminutive couple. *Young, not more than thirty years old, clean moderate, casual business clothing. Concerned look on both their faces with a hint of annoyance at someone or something.*

As if responding to his thoughts, the guiding voice in his head said, *don't let this one get away Michael. You can help these people. They need you and they need to be taken serious.*

Michael quickly responded to the disembodied voice in his head by addressing the couple.

"Hello, I'm Detective Romano. Please join me at my desk sit and explain what you need."

Being chivalrous, he offered the single, visitors chair alongside his desk to the woman.

The woman sat and the man stood next to her, his left hand resting on her shoulder.

The detective stood, excused himself, and went to check the assignment sheet on the rear wall; he was next in the catching order.

Quickly, he returned and asked, "Please tell me your names and why you are here. Sir, do you want a chair?"

"No thank you. Is Detective Pigro in? We have spoken to him before."

"No, he isn't in. I'll do my best to try to help you. Please tell me what brings you here today."

"I am William Tao and this is my wife Ming. We are here to see what has happened to our past reports. Today we made a new one and want to know if Detective Pigro is going to investigate it."

"Well, he isn't working today. Please tell me what happened today. I can look up the old reports if necessary."

The couple exchanged glances, and then nodded to each other in agreement to explain their plight to this new detective.

William spoke, "Detective, last night, actually this morning, just before the sun came up, we heard what we believe was two gunshots very close to our home and the sound of breaking glass. I jumped out of bed and ran to where I thought the sound came from. In the room next to our bedroom, I found broken glass. One window section was broken and another had a bullet hole in it. Our baby son was crying in his crib. We checked him for injuries and could not find any. Our daughter, Chun, came in at that time. All bedrooms are in the back of our house."

When the complainant paused, Mike quickly asked, "Did you see anyone."

"I looked out of the window and saw a dark figure running away and jumping over our fence. I could not see who it was, but could tell that it was a man. He appeared to be same body size of someone we have trouble with for months. He moved like the same man and I heard laughing. It sounded like him."

"Are you sure?" asked the detective.

"Yes. After much thought about it, we dressed and called the police to file a report. The responding officers said that and a detective would call and someone would come and look for evidence. We have heard nothing since they left and that is why we are here."

Mike called down to the 124 room to see if there was a new complaint, a UF-61, filed in Tao's name.

The responding civilian aide informed him that there was a report for possible shots fired. It was printed, and a copy of it was in the squad's basket.

The clerk apologized that the day's referrals were still in the complaint room. She assured him that someone would immediately bring everything up that was not marked as closed by patrol services.

"The report is being brought up to me, Mr. Tao. While we are waiting, please tell me who you have been having trouble with and what has been going on."

"His name is Zen Quo Quan and he was employed

by me to do construction work in my home some time ago. He was a tenant in my basement while he worked in my home. When his work was finished, I paid him in full and asked him to leave. He refused. Finally we called the police and we were told to file a report in landlord tenant court to evict him."

"Does he still stay in your house?"

"No. I do not know of such matters so I contacted my business attorney and he handled it all for me. I am a businessperson and run an import business. When he was given the notice to be in court, he damaged some of the work he did and left our home."

"How long ago was that?"

"Two months ago."

"You mentioned that he has been a problem in the past. Did you make other reports?"

"Yes, one of your fellow detectives in this office, Detective Pigro, has spoken to us and has not solved our problem. We are disappointed."

One of the aides walked in at that moment carrying several pink complaint reports.

"Detective Romano, here is the 61 you asked about and today's referrals," she said while handing them to Mike.

"Thank you."

After pulling the one he wanted, Romano dropped the balance into the intake basket.

Levy went over to retrieve them, "I'll log the one you have on the sheet for you Mike. What's the 61 number?"

"064-11346, thanks."

Romano then resumed the interview of his complainants.

They explained that two years earlier, they had gone to a Chinatown lumberyard to purchase what they needed to renovate their home.They also requested the likable owner to recommend a contractor. The owner, Bai Wu, introduced them to Quan saying that he was very capable to do whatever work was required in the home.

In addition to Quan doing the work, he acted as the go between with the lumberyard, ordering and reportedly paying for all supplies with cash given to him by William.

They began getting bills for unpaid supplies, so they went to see Wu with their delivery receipts. He allegedly informed them that Quan never gave him payment and there was over $60,000.00 in arrears. He would not deliver unless they paid.

Tao gave all he had on him at that time, $4000.00 against the alleged debt, and promised to pay the back money. If all went well, he promised to use his lumberyard to supply material for expansion on his Brooklyn warehouse. William was given a contact phone number for Quan, but never used it because the man was either at the yard or in their house.

Tao and Ming, even though they were recently naturalized citizens of the United States, operated in old world style. They used cash for everything except their import business and that was only because their accountant and attorney insisted on checks.

"Are you still using the lumberyard for supplies?"

"No, our new contractor has found another supplier."

William went on to explain that when their new contractor began buying supplies from the new lumberyard, Quan began to contact William by telephone and threaten him. William pushed him off; at that point is when the harassment got serious; including, tar on the front of his home on two separate occasions and verbal threats. After each incident, Quan would telephone and ask, "Are you having a peaceful existence?"

Besides the phone calls, they began getting attorney letters regarding the outstanding invoices owed to the original supplier from past purchases.

William gave Mike copies to look at. He was surprised to see that the notices were from a Chinese attorney in the firm of Nikolai Kruzhkov Associates, the Russian attorney.

"Have you been contacted since last night?"

"No Detective, but we expect it."

While the couple explained the entire story concerning their interaction with Quan, Romano had been observing them. Mr. Tao did most of the talking with an occasional comment to wife in Chinese.

They seem sincere and truthful.

Tao explained that he firmly believed that Quan had fired the shots as to frighten him into paying more money.

Mike remembered the reluctance of the Chinese complainant when he worked on 42nd Street and the resulting investigation; he was fascinated as his complainant spoke. It must have showed on his face.

Ming spoke rapidly to her husband in their native tongue. His response was quick and in English.

"Detective Romano, you appear to have caring and understanding about Chinese people. It is a feeling that we both have. We want you to take all our cases and combine them for you to handle. Will you do this please?"

"Sir, I'm honored by your request and will work this current complaint, but protocol requires that I must speak with the other detective before I take his cases too. I hope that you understand."

"Yes, but we wish to work only with you."

"I'll talk with Detective Pigro. First, right now I would like to go and see the window and room in your home."

"Please and thank you," was William's quick reply.

Mike turned to his partner, "Sam, want to come along? I have to look for bullet holes"

Always ready to get away from his desk, Sam asked, "Who driving?"

After examining the bedroom windows at the Tao home, both detectives agreed that the hole in one of the two bedroom windows was probably the result of a gunshot.

The entire glass in the upper glass of the second window was shattered and most of it was no longer in the frame. They were unable to find evidence of a projectile or bullet anywhere in the room across from either window.

Both detectives agreed that the glass was shattered from the outside, yet there was no evidence to support the use of a firearm. The partners also agreed that since they could find no visible bullet holes inside the room, they would not call for the Crime Scene Unit.

After canvasing the adjacent houses for any witness that may have heard gunshots with negative results, the detectives drove back to their command.

When they entered the station house, Mike went directly to the 124 Room to get a copy of any earlier reports with William Tao as the complainant. There were three.

Romano spent the rest of his tour attempting to gather up any information available on Zen Quo Quan.

He learned that the man had two priors, both were for Assault; no convictions. He used an address in Chinatown near the lumberyard where Tao used to buy building supplies. Quan also listed the yard as his employer.

Mike thought *another Chinese mystery.*

Detective Pigro signed in and in his irritating way said to Mike, "Hey Romano, give up the desk and let a real detective have it. Oh yeah, I guess you have connections and a good hook, because you're still here."

Mike laughed and responded, "Listen before you give Italians a bad name, I need a favor from you. I want to take over all these 61's," dropping copies of the complaints in front of Frank as he spoke.

"What is it; do you have thing for Chinese food? Did something else happened and you were up to catch it?"

In dismissive tone, Mike answered, "Kinda something like that."

Undaunted, Pigro continued, "Those people are a pain in the ass, and slightly off. Sure, you can take them over."

"Thanks. I'm swinging out and would like to work them when I get back, so do a DD-5 and officially refer them to me. I'll tell Tony Scala."

Richie Levy, hearing Romano getting irritated during the exchange, commented, "Boys, play nice, I don't want to mediate another compliant against one of our squad members again. The last one wore me out."

Before he left, Romano told his supervisor to expect a DD-5 from Pigro referring a few companion cases over to him. The complainants were all the same.

Scala's response was, "I don't care who does them, as long as they get worked on. I'm sure because of your work ethic that you'll do them justice Mike. Enjoy your swing."

CHAPTER TWENTY

Detective Romano returned to his office from his 74-hour swing to the squad office at 3:30 p.m. Two messages were waiting for him. The first was from Edita Sever and the other one from William Tao.

In her message, Edita stated that she had been notified to appear in court to give witness against her tormentor, Valadas Karaluis, regarding the old order of protection. It was for the following day, May 15th at 10 a.m.

*That's tomorrow, have to request a tour change it's a chance to lock arrest if he shows. I **must** get that tour change. If he shows up, I can nail him.*

Quickly he read the second message; it was from William checking in to see if there was any progress made on his cases.

As Mike signed in, he was relieved to see that Tony Scala was the supervisor on duty and had signed in minutes before him.

The Supervisor's door was closed.

Mike knocked. "Sarge, it's Romano, can I come in?"
"Come on in Mike. Let's chat."

"Good afternoon Sarge. You have a few minutes?"

"Sounds like you need a favor, what is it?"

"Come on Sarge, I don't always need a favor. How did you know?"

"It's easy; I wrote both of the telephone messages that were in your box. Are you going to collar your Armenian tomorrow?"

"He's Lithuanian. Yeah, I'd like to if I can change my tour. Can you do it or do I have to ask Fitz?"

Scala smiled. "Well, for one thing I have read all your DD-5s on the case and even signed off on a few of them. Second, whenever Sergeant Fitzpatrick isn't here, I'm in charge of the squad. Do a '5' regarding the message about his court appearance and I'll authorize the tour change. Go get him."

Elated, Mike quickly answered, "Consider it done. It'll be the first '5' I do today. Excuse me, I want to call my complainant and thank you."

Finding Frank Pigro lurking behind the door as he left Scala, Mike was more than pissed off, his patience with the man was at an end. The bulldog wanted to adjust "Fat Frankie's" attitude. Instead, he decided to keep peace in the squad while waiting for the day tour men to leave, and retreated to the breakroom.

Mike used that phone to call Edita; first trying her residence with negative results and then called her sister's beauty shop.

"This is Detective Romano, can I speak with Edita Saveikis please?"

The voice on the other end shouted, "Edita, your detective wants to speak with you."

Edita was excited as she asked, "Detective, is this call to tell me that you will be in court tomorrow? Yes?"

"Yes Edita, I'll be there. Let me ask you if Valdas has always been in the courtroom when required?"

"Yes, always, so he can smile at me and sneak obscene motions in my direction followed with phone calls."

"Not to worry, if he shows up, I'll arrest him right on the spot. See you tomorrow."

After a phone call to the court's docket room at 120 Schemerhorn Street, Mike obtained the courtroom number and was not surprised to learn that the dubious, Nikolai Kruzhkov, was still his attorney of record.

Romano was looking forward to the possible volatile situation a courthouse arrest might bring.

Returning to the squad room, Mike was pleased to see that Pigro had left for the day. He sat down to type out the notification that Sergeant Scala requested.

After handing the sheet to Scala, he returned to his desk and focused his attention on the Tao case.

The voices in Mike's head kept whispering, *Zen Quo Quan is involved with major gangsters.*

In response to the almost audible warning in his mind, Mike reached out to the Chinatown detective, William Lee. He had worked with him after stumbling on an extortion ring while on foot patrol back in Midtown South. During that time, he learned much about the gangs of Chinatown, both large and small. He phoned the Fifth Precinct.

On the third ring, the very detective he was reaching out for answered.

"Detective Lee. How can I help you?"

After some rehash of their time together, they got down to business.

Lee chuckled and finally stated, "Okay Romano, now tell me why you really called."

"Lee, I could use your help in finding out if the guy that I hope to arrest in court tomorrow is involved with mobsters."

"The Tongs?" Lee asked.

"Maybe, there's a lumber yard, naturally a Chinese guy owns it, where my subject buys lumber, and I smell a connection to the Russians in Brighton Beach."

"My curiosity is aroused. Tell me all about it."

Mike began with, "My two subjects share the same attorney. One is reportedly an illegal immigrant whose visa expired; the lunberyard owner originally sponsored him. The other piece of crap is a rapist and God knows what else. The voice in my head told me, 'if they share the same attorney, they're connected."

It took the better part of fifteen minutes for Romano to give Lee an accurate background on both cases.

After listening quietly, the Chinese detective smiled to himself as he spoke, "Mike, I never heard of Quan, but it's been rumored that the owner of the lumberyard, Bai Wu, is a key figure with the Tongs. We have never been able to make any headway to proving or disproving the story."

"Any information as to what activity Wu is into?"

"Down here the Tongs cover it all, protection, drugs, extortion, kidnapping, drugs and murder. Old Wu always comes out clean."

Mike couldn't resist a little teasing, "What about gambling. I heard your people love to gamble. Is it true?"

Lee laughed as he answered, "For sure. The old world people down here will see two cockroaches cross the floor and wager on which one will get to the other side faster."

After a chuckle, Romano spoke again.

"It's been nice talking with you again, even if it's only on the telephone; working with you last time helped me get the shield. I thank you because it showed me another side of police work. When I got back to my command, I knew that I had to achieve the rank of Detective. It felt natural, almost genetic."

"You took to the work like you were born to it. It

was all you Mike, I had nothing to do with it."

Mike felt his face redden, "Thanks. Listen, I gotta go. Please reach out for me when you have any information that I might be able to use."

"Glad to help. I'll call as soon as I can."

***

The following morning, Romano signed into the Squad's log at 0800 hrs. Detectives Louis Nieves and Alice Sanchez, the only female member of the squad, signed in before him. Due to work schedules, he hardly interacted with either of them. There was no supervisor present.

Sanchez asked, "Wow, the infamous Mike Romano. To what do we owe the pleasure ?"

Mike retorted, "Is my reputation so tarnished that I earned the infamous part?"

Nieves picked up the question. "Rumor has it that Fitz is looking to move you out because you got him his first bad marks. Is it true?"

"If he received bad marks, then he deserved it. I doubt he wants me to leave. I'll be here until I retire."

It was Alice's turn again, "You still didn't answer the question. Why are you here now?"

"I have a date with a perp. I'm going to pick him up in court and close a case with an arrest. You see, a good detective doesn't have to chase his perps, they make appointments to arrest them. Anyway, I'm taking one of our cars. It's been cleared by Sergeant Scala."

With more than a hint of sarcasm in his voice, Nieves answered, "Well, excuse me, seems we're in the presence of greatness."

Cops are like little kids that never grew up. Detectives are worse; they sometimes include jealously of anotherman's expertise and connections in their emotional immaturity.

Romano signed out a portable radio and keys for one of the Chevy Sedans and left without another word.

***

At 9:05 a.m., Mike walked into Part 5A in the Brooklyn Criminal Court on Schemerhorn Street.

After double-checking the court calendar, he slid his shield case into the breast pocket of his suit jacket leaving the shiny gold symbol of his authority exposed. He then elected to sit in the empty jury box to avail him the opportunity to view the entire room and all entrances. Valdas Karaluis' name was fifth on the docket list.

At 9:30 a.m., the Court Clerk approached him.

"Detective, do you have business in the court and if so, how can I help?"

"Yes, I do, I'm here to arrest Valdas Karaluis on charges not related to this case. Can you please inform the judge for me? I'll be happy to meet with him or her if necessary."

"Please wait here. I'll return shortly."

"Thank you."

While he waited for the Clerk's return, Romano scanned the courtroom as the public began to filter in. He spotted Edita Saveikis and her sister selecting seats reasonably close to the action. They chose the fourth row behind the DA's table.

Edita spotted him too and gave a weak wave. He nodded in her direction and held up his hand to indicate that she should sit quietly and wait patiently.

From his position, Mike saw Valdas Karaluis and

his attorney, Nikolai Kruzhov enter the courtroom. The defendant sat close to the front of the room as his mouthpiece advanced and announced his presence to the court clerk.

Promptly at 10:00 a.m. the Clerk shouted, "All rise, court is now in session; Honorable Judge Ruth Ravitz presiding."

After what seems like hours, the Clerk finally called Saveikis' case.

"The court will now hear the case against Valdas Karaluis, regarding a Violation of an Order of Protection on the complaint of Edita Saveikis."

Romano stood and walked quietly toward the ADA's table.

He leaned in and quietly said, "I'm sure you know by now that I'm here to arrest this defendant on other charges."

The DA responded with, "Yes, but please step back to the rail, and do it quietly. Thank you.

"Sure thing, take your time," Mike answered as he backed away.

The Russian attorney was quick to try convincing the judge that there was no violation of the order of protection. He pushed to state that the alleged violations were just in the imagination of the original complainant.

The attorney attempted to convince the court that Edita Saveikis was indeed trying to renew their relationship and was filing false charges because of rejection.

As part of his diatribe, the Russian slimeball even had the nerve to request that a Protection Order issued against Edita Saveikis.

Frowning in disgust, the Judge quickly denied the request as she slammed her gavel down and shouted,

"Order continued. You and your client may leave my presence; next case."

The slimy advocate began to speak, "But Judge, you haven't fin…"

From the bench, the Judge smiled and gave a nod toward Romano.

Mike quickly slid behind Karaluis as he turned to leave the gated area. Kruzhov attempted to get between the detective and his client.

As Romano reached for his quarry, he growled softly, "Stand aside counselor and don't interfere or I'll arrest you too."

The attorney froze.

"Valdas Karaluis, you're under arrest for Witness Tampering. Come quietly or I'll add resisting arrest after I kick your ass."

After applying handcuffs to his prisoner, Romano turned to his lawyer and stated, "Thank you counselor, you can meet him in court later tonight at his arraignment."

He thanked the bench and turned to leave with his man.

In keeping with the fact that he was in court, Romano chose to be official as he passed his complainant, Edita, with his prisoner; stopping for a few seconds, he said, "Ms. Saveikis, I'll call you tomorrow."

Then he shoved his man toward the courtroom door and into the corridor.

***

Mike knew that it would take almost five minutes to move his prisoner down into the bowels of the courthouse where he could lodge his man and arrange to transport him to Central Booking as procedure dictated.

Karaluis was running his mouth big time. "You mister big detective, you could not even make a real arrest. You wait until Valdas in court with that hungry bitch. She is hungry for Valdas. Is she giving you something? Yes?"

At once, Romano wanted to bestow some instant justice yet never condoned hitting a handcuffed prisoner. He certainly wasn't about to break any of his cardinal rules. However, the avenging angel side of his personality needed to be satisfied.

Silently, he spoke to his celestial mentor, Saint Michael, I'm sorry, but I have to do this. Please temper my actions.

With that thought, Mike released the grip he had on the handcuffs, took a step forward and stealthfully put his right foot in between the unsuspecting prisoner's feet, causing him to stumble as he shouldered him into the corridor wall. Valdas' head bounced with a thud.

Several people turned to witness the incident as the detective was assisting Valdas to regain his balance.

"Good Lord man! Didn't I tell you to be careful and walk slowly, because I realize that it's hard to walk while handcuffed with your hands behind your back?"

Valdas quieted down instantly. The booking process continued without further incident. Mike returned to his office as his regular team was arriving.

Richard Levy asked, "How did it go with your court collar?"

"It worked out, thanks. He should be seeing the judge sometime tonight. The guy has a private attorney; he'll probably make bail again."

Sam Battle asked, "Hey Michael, what did you charge him with?"

"Witness tampering was all I could get him on. I discussed the entire case with a writing ADA who wouldn't add any other charges. I guess I'll have to wait until he does something stupid again and I'm sure he will; anyway Fitz will be happy, case closed with an arrest."

Sanchez and Nieves were signing off duty and couldn't help but jump into the conversation.

Nieves commented, "Cheap collar. Better luck next time Stud."

Sanchez added, "Hey Mike, next time you get a chance, charge him with something good. Your little Albanian complainant deserves better than that weak effort to get him off the street." She ended her statement with a giggle.

Mike took the teasing in stride. It was just the usual nut cracking cops do, and answered appropriately with, "Lithuanian and kiss my fuzzy Italian ass. I'm going home to someone who appreciates my expertise."

Sam shouted out as Mike left the office, "Hey Mike, don't stay up all night, we swing to days in the morning."

Romano waved as he left the office.

CHAPTER TWENTY-ONE

The *Dinosaurs* had been in the squad office about 45 minutes when Detective Romano received a phone call from the Brooklyn ADA's office. It was the writing ADA from the previous night's arrest.

"Detective Romano, this is Assistance District Attorney Janice Carter. We met last night when I wrote up the affidavit for your collar, Valdas Karaluis. Once again I'm sorry that I was unable to add any further charges."

"Thank you. No apology is necessary. I'm surprised that you called. Is there something I should know?"

"I'm calling to inform you that your defendant made bail. His attorney, Nikolai Kruzhkov posted it. Last night you seemed very upset that he might have been released."

"I suspected as much. Tell me Ms. Carter, do you have any knowledge of that slime bucket attorney? Do you feel comfortable sharing anyy information you might have with me?"

ADA Carter drew a deep breath as if deciding if she wanted to back away from the question.

Finally, she answered, "Detective, yesterday, after our conversation, I now must assume that you are aware that Mr. Kruzhkov often represents clients that some call *The Russian Mafia.*"

"Yes ma'am, I am aware of the type of clients he represents."

Carter continued, "Why he would have a common

criminal for a client and post his bail, I have no idea. For whatever reason he had, the sitting judge put quite a sum on him, $50,000 dollars, cash, or bond. The attorney paid cash and I doubt that he used his own money."

"Thank you for your time Ms. Carter."

"Good luck in finding out that relationship Detective."

Mike smiled to himself, *Suspicions confirmed. Now to find some way to really nail Valdas.*

The detective spent slightly less than two hours working on some minor cases and typing reports, the telephone on his desk rang.

He reached for it out of habit, "Six Four squad, Detective Romano."

"Romano, William Lee here. Guess who I have sitting in our cage, Zen Quo Quan. He's ready for pickup."

Mike was elated, "Holy crap. How did you get him? Recover any weapon?"

"We got lucky. I have a connection, a friend who works undercover in Chinatown chasing illegals. I'm sure you remember John Eng, he's now assigned to a joint task force with INS. We shared a few beers and I told him about Quan. Two days later, he called and gave me his location. You are not gonna believe where we picked him up."

"Try me."

"Fong Hot Soup, on Pell, do you remember that place?"

"Holy shit, I sure do. The three of us almost bought it that night."

Lee chuckled and said, "That was a righteous gun battle and the good guys won."

"Yeah, too bad Quan wasn't there that night. But,

thanks to you and yourr friend, I can pick him up. Give me half an hour."

"I'll be waiting."

After putting his telephone receiver down, Mike turned to his partner, "Sam, I need you to go with me to pick up Zen Quo Quan, my Chinese bad guy. Detective Lee, an old friend is holding him in the Fifth."

"Wow, another good collar for you and we didn't have to chase him. You're getting good at this. Let's go get him."

Three hours later, Quan was processed at Central Booking and Romano was sitting with a writing ADA.

After hearing the entire story regarding the Tao's interaction with Quan, the ADA would only write up several counts of Felony Criminal Mischief of damage to property in excess of $2000.00 and Aggravated Harassment for the threats and phone calls.

Mike knew that at arraignment, his perpetrator would probably have an attorney, probably the Russian, and be released pending his next court date.

***

The following day was routine for Mike and his team. The three detectives worked on old, still unresolved cases, and other complaints that were sent up to the squad office before they would swing out for two days. They were all routine minor offenses and took no more than a telephone interview to close or note for a second call or face-to-face interview.

The entire day was uneventful. He signed out and went home to his family.

For the first day of his swing Mike was alone the entire day. Lillian and the kids went to work leaving him alone that morning. Mike, obsessed with trying to determine any possible link between the Russian and Chinese gangsters, went to the Queens Public Library. His research didn't produce much information.

He was able to find out that in Far-Eastern Russia, near the Chinese border, the Chinese triads and Russian gangsters were trading Russian women for narcotics. He also read about unproven rumors that the Russians were supplying women to Chinese illegal gambling dens controlled by the triads in Macau and Hong Kong. Those unfortunate women were often referred to as *"Natashas."* and were forced to service high roller patrons.

He could not find any tangible proof about an alliance of the two groups within the United States. *Damn, no luck here, but two dirt bags use the same attorney.*

The detective was stumped. Whenever he tried to discuss it with Lillian, she would caution him to leave the Russian mob to the Russian mob. She would express her fear for his safety and then would reinforce her feelings with "conversations." He always paid close attention.

***

When Mike returned from his swing, he was handed two messages from William Tao. He returned the calls as soon as possible.

"Mr. Tao, William if I may, it's Mike Romano returning your call. What can I do for you?"

"Detective, I am sorry that I was unable to get you, so I did what I thought was best. Now I must tell you what it was. Can you please come to my home tonight?"

"Yes. What happened?"

Tao hesitated before responding, "I am embarrassed

and will explain tonight."

"That's fine. What time?"

"Is eight o'clock good?"

"See you then."

Sam asked, "Where are we going today?"

"That was William Tao and I think he did something stupid. He requested a visit at 8:00 tonight."

"It's fine with me."

The two detectives rang the doorbell of the Tao residence slightly before 8:00 p.m. William opened the door and greeted the men, his wife Ming stood behind him.

"Good evening Detectives, thank you for coming. Please come in."

After leading the investigators to his dining room, he indicated that they should sit at the dining table. Then he spoke to his wife in Chinese.

Turning to the detectives, William apologetically, looked straight at Romano.

"Detective Romano, I must apologize to you and your partner for possibly doing something very stupid."

Mike smiled and made an effort to reassure his complainant with, "Mister Tao, you are a smart business man who has been taken advantage of. In addition, you have been under stress. Please tell me what happened or what you did. I assure you that whatever it was, it was a result of your situation and not stupidity."

Sam nodded his head in agreement in an effort to help is partner relax the nervous man.

There was silence as William furrowed his brow as if deep in thought. Finally he spoke.

"Detectives, yesterday that *Feitu,* excuse me that means gangster in my home country, telephoned me demanding a meeting about how I could make him stop bothering me."

Tao lowered his eyes and continued, "I am sorry I did not contact you first."

"That's okay, we're here now. Please tell Sam and I what happened and what you did do."

Before he could answer, Ming approached them with a large ornate tray laden with an obvious teapot, small ceramic cups, a pitcher of water stacked with ice cubes and two water glasses. As she placed the tray down on the table, a small bowl of what appeared to be some kind of cookies were now in view as well as some napkins.

Ming smiled and quietly retreated.

William picked up the teapot and a cup, "Tea, gentlemen?"

Not wanting to offend him, both cops declined but asked for water. He filled two glasses and placed them on napkins before each cop. He took tea.

Mike was getting impatient and asked, "Will you please tell us what happened?"

"Yes. After he called me at work, I agreed to meet with him in a restaurant near my business. When we were still friendly, we shared some meals there," he paused as if trying to find the right words.

"Quan then told me that he would leave me alone on two conditions; one was that I paid the entire balance at the lumberyard and number two, he wanted $60,000."

Sam whistled and Mike asked, "Did you?"

"I told him that I would pay the old balance at the yard but I would have to give him only half of what he wanted. I did not have enough available."

"Did you give him any money yet?"

"Yes, I met him the same night and paid $30,000."

"So, you still owe him the rest?"

"Yes, but I don't know what to do. If I know for

sure that he would go away, I would pay, but how do I know he will stop? Will he ask for more again?"

"You have given him money, that wasn't the right thing to do. It tells him that you are an easy mark. You should have called me first. We could have been there and arrested him. The harassment case is still open. We could have added witness tampering. It was not in your best interest to pay that kind of man."

William took on a sullen expression making his almond shaped eyes even smaller. He looked down at the tabletop.

"I am truly sorry. What can I do? What can you do as the police. Please, I do not wish to return to a courtroom but I do not want further trouble from him."

Mike and Sam glanced at each other. Sam shrugged his shoulders and Mike indicated with a small movement of his head that they should leave.

Sam nodded.

Mike spoke as he rose from his chair, "Mr. Tao, thank you for your time and don't worry. We will work out a plan of action to help you, but do not meet with Quan again. If he calls, call my office at once. I'll instruct them to find me if I'm not in. Agreed?"

Sam was standing now and shook Tao's hand, "Thank you for your time."

Mike then took William's, shook it and patted him on the shoulder.

In a familiar manner of assurance, he spoke, "Don't worry William. I'll call you when we have a plan of action. Remember, do not meet him again, you have us."

***

Back in their car, Mike asked, "Sam, how tight are you with the owner of that Chinese restaurant on 86th street?"

"You mean Sum Luk?"

"Yeah, is that the place where we ate that terrific meal?"

"Yup, I've known him for several years and had countless meals there. Why."

I want to have Tao meet Quan there with the excuse to pay him the rest of the money. Then we have a talk with the guy, maybe in the men's room. It could get noisy and I don't want the owner to dial 911.

"Why the men's room, are we gonna give Quan a personality adjustment?"

"There's that possibly."

"Sounds like fun. I'm in."

Half an hour after the detectives left Tao's residence, Mike phoned the complainant and told him to offer the balance of the money to Quan at a meal in Sum Luck, the following night at 7:00 p.m.

Tao wanted to know what was going to happen. Romano told him that they were going to have a strong conversation with Quan.

"Detective, you want me to bring the money too."

"No, William and you are not going to pay him."

"Then how will he stop?"

The voices in Romano's head were telling him to be careful and not to step over the invisible line.

Silently he answered them, *don't worry, I got this.*

"William, just trust us. He will understand to go away after we speak with him. Now here's what I want you to do…"

The following day Mike reached out for Detective

William Lee. His first call was from home because he wanted any information that he could gather before the meeting with his target, Zen Quo Quan that night. The man answering the call said that Lee was scheduled to work a four-by that afternoon.

Romano signed in at the office by 3:30 p.pm. and immediately phoned the Fifth Squad office. Thankfully, Lee picked up the call.

"Romano here, Lee. How's it hanging?"

After thirty seconds of small talk, Lee asked, "Okay Mike, what is it this time?"

"Well, remember Quan, the guy I picked up from you last week?'

"What about him?"

"He's been extorting some money and harassing my complainant and I was wondering if I could reach out to John Eng. Do you think he would have any info about my perp? I'm meeting him and my complainant tonight."

"What could he have that you don't already know?"

"I have no idea. Maybe he can tell me just how deep he is into the Chinese mob; and do the Chinese and Russian gangsters in New York have dealings together, or anything at all along those lines?"

"I can probably reach him in a couple of hours. What time are you meeting Quan?"

"We're set up for 7:00 p.m. I would like any info sooner if possible so I can digest it. Oh yeah, if I collar him, can we get him deported?"

"I'll see what I can do and call you when I have something."

"Thanks."

The detective then hung up and turned his attention to his partner.

"Sam, I don't believe Quan will recognize you unless he hears you speak."

"Why is that?" asked Battle.

Mike had just set him up for light racial humor to lighten the mood as good friends and partners often did.

"It's because to non-blacks, especially Orientals, y'all look alike."

"Sam gave him the one finger salute and laughed.

The Italian detective continued, "Sam, if you can be sitting inside when Quan enters the place, it would be good. Tao will be seated and Quan will go to him and hopefully take a seat opposite our victim."

"Yeah, I can do that. What's next? Do you want me to jack him?"

"It would be appropriate, but no. You will have a portable with you and click it twice when Quan sits. At that time, I come in and sit next to our complainant. You walk over and slide in next to Quan. I want you to rattle him, so sit close."

"What if he pushes me away?"

"Then we arrest him for assault on a police officer."

Sam erupted with his deep laughter and added, "After a personality adjustment."

"Not unless we have to. I want to intimidate him if possible."

"What are you planning?"

Romano smiled and said, "Verbal threats that he can understand."

Sam was ready for some *entertainment*, "This is gonna be fun."

"Tao should be inside well before 7:00. Can you alert the owner of the restaurant that we will be meeting two Chinese men later today? Tell him whatever you want to as to the nature of our visit, but make sure to impress on him not to be alarmed regarding what he may see or hear. Assure him there is no danger to him or his place. Thanks."

"I can take care of that Mike, no problem", Sam answered as he rose from his chair.

***

At 6:45 p.m., the partners parked their Chevy almost directly across the street from Sum Luk and switched their portable radios to unused tactical channel.

After adjusting the volume to a barely audible level and checking the radios, Sam exited the vehicle and slid his handset into his pants belt under his jacket. Mike remained in the car.

The team agreed earlier that Sam would only key the radio when the subject sat with Tao. Romano was pleased to hear nothing and spent a few minutes running his tactics through his mind.

Several minutes passed and Romano was getting nervous with anticipation. He reached inside his jacket and withdrew a cigar, planning to light it to calm his anxiety. As he looked down to unwrap it, he heard two static laden clicks on his radio.

He dropped the stogie onto the dashboard and almost jumped out of the car. *Game on.*

When he entered the premises, he almost bumped into the owner who acknowledged his presence with a nod. The restaurateur then moved his head once again in the direction to indicate where Sam was sitting and never said a word.

Mike continued into the interior of the dining area. There was a scattering of diners throughout the large room. After a few seconds, he located Tao seated and facing him at a booth close to the restrooms. Sitting opposite him was Zen Quo Quan, who was unable to see the detective approach.

William however was facing the detective and saw Mike approach.

Without getting up he cheerfully said, "Ah, Detective Romano, please come and join us for a meal. Mister Quan and I are just finishing some business."

The illegal's eyes lost their almond shape as Tao spoke. Zen Quo's head snapped around in shock. Mike shook Tao's extended hand and slid into the booth next to him.

His eyes focused on Quan as Mike spoke, "Some coincidence isn't it, William? Please tell me what's going on here."

Quan, looking nervous as a cat in a dog pound responded, "Nothing Detective. We are just finishing some old business. Did you come here to harass me again? Are you going to arrest me again? Once again, I tell you that I have done nothing. The proof is that I sit here with my friend Tao and are about to enjoy a meal together."

Before Mike could reply, Sam slid into the booth beside Quan and jostled against him.

Quan registered shock on his face and quickly retreated further into the booth.

Mike began, "Mr. Quan, please don't be alarmed. My partner and I are here to have a quiet conversation and resolve the problem you had with Mr. Tao."

Gesturing toward William, he continued, "William and I are friends. We have shared meals together and our families have become friends. That makes the problems you have with him, my problems too. Do you understand?"

"You are not able to speak like this to me. You are an American Policeman, but you speak like a gangster."

Quan's eyes jumped from William to Mike to Sam.

"How do you know that I'm not?"

Sam moved closer to Quan and smiled, "Yeah, how could you possibly know?"

Romano continued, "You Chinese have your Tongs, Italianss have our Tongs too, but we call them Families. Do you understand?"

"What are you saying?" Perspiration rolled down his forehead.

"I'm saying that if you bother Mr. Tao or his family or his business again, I will act like Hong Kong."

There was a hint of fear visible in Quan's eyes.

Mike then turned to William. "William, please give me what you brought for Quan tonight. It is no longer his."

William Tao smiled and pulled a large red envelope out from inside his suit jacket. It was quite thick.

Quan shuddered as William handed the package to the detective.

"You see Quan, even here in this country, we know about the use of *red envelopes* for law enforcement in your country."

The detective acted to further invaded Quan's space by leaning across the table before he continued.

"We also know how a Hong Kong policeman would deal with a criminal like you when he shows disrespect to a cop by harming or stealing from his friends or family. The bad guy disappears without a trace. Are you getting the picture?"

The criminal's eyes widened as he asked, "Wha,,, what connecton?" He was beginning to see the light.

"William Tao now has connections that are better than yourss are. We know about that shady lumberyard and your crooked Russian lawyer, Nikolai Kruzhkov."

"You already sound like a Hong Kong poriceman

and I wish no furter invovement with you."

Holding the red envelope in his left hand, Romano again leaned over the table and locked eyes with Quan.

"Listen, to show you that I'm not heartless, let's go into the men's room and privately talk about this."

"Oh no, I will not be arone with you."

Smiling broadly, Mike responded with, "We will not be alone, Sam will be with us."

As Romano spoke, Sam began to tug at the Asian's shirt collar, "Come on. We want to have a conversation away from the other diners."

Quan began to mumble in his native tongue.

Mike hissed like a Spitting Cobra, "Come with us or I promise you will want to return to China at once."

The foreign mumbling stopped.

Mike waved the red envelope in Quan's direction and said, "We would like to share something with you as a sign of good faith. Please don't become a problem."

The detective's innuendos were working. Quan followed Sam as he exited the booth. Mike followed them both.

Sam headed for the men's room and pushed the door open. Romano shoved their confused subject inside.

Sam locked the door and put his hand on the criminal's shoulder. He could feel Quan's body shaking.

Quan began pleading, "Detectives, please do not hurt me. You may keep all the money. I will even give you what I have taken from William in the past. I mean him no harm. I only want to get some of his money. He is so easy. I did not know he was under your protection. Prease."

"Keep the money you piece of shit."

Romano put his large right hand on the man's other shoulder, digging his thumb into a soft spot between his neck and collarbone and began closing his hand.

Quan tried to wiggle away but Sam held him in place.

"Don't say a word or shout because if you do, I'll break something."

The Chinaman nodded his head.

"Understand this, your association with William Tao is over and you will not speak about our meeting to anyone. If you do, I'll know and you'll be lucky if you get deported. Now, smile when you leave and I never want to see or hear about you again. If I do, you will disappear. Understand?"

The two detectives released their hold on him.

Quan bowed ever so slightly and looked down at the floor before the three men returned to the dining area.

Romano smiled and spoke to William Tao. "Mr. Quan is leaving. He expresses his deepest regrets for ever having inconvenienced you. Isn't that correct Quan?"

Quan smiled than gave a poor excuse of a respectful bow in William's direction. He turned quickly and rapidly walked out of the restaurant.

Sam had a need to say, "Fascinating, we'll talk later partner."

Romano handed the red envelope back to Tao and said, "William, I don't think he will bother you again. Call me at once if he ever does. When your case comes up in court, you can drop the charges if you wish. Explain that he paid you for the old damages. That should end the entire matter."

"Detective, what if he begins again?"

"I don't believe he will, but when you are in the court, you can explain that you wish an order of protection just in case he returns. Call me if you have a problem with the court or anything else."

Tao placed a smaller crimson envelope on the table and slid it toward the detectives.

"You gentlemen have saved me many problems. Ming and I are grateful. Please accept our thanks."

"We accept your appreciation and must now return to our office, we have other work. Call if you need us again."

Both envelopes remained on the table as the two cops left the restaurant.

***

Once outside on the sidewalk, Sam was unable to contain himself.

"Holy shit! Michael, you have a dark side, don't you. Could you really do all those things you threatened? Are you that well connected?"

"Not at all; the important thing is that Quan believed everything. Wasn't that the object of the whole exercise? I like to call it human chess. You move the pieces around and try to outthink your opponent."

"Come on Mike, you haven't answered my question. I'm your partner, what are you hiding?"

"Well, I have a great imagination and a formidable delivery. Yes, I can be very dark if necessary, but not to worry, there are little voices in my head that help to keep that side of me under control."

"I can see that I'm not gonna get an answer from my Eyetalian partner, but maybe someday."

"Come on Sam; let's get back to the office. I want to figure out how to close all the 61's on this case without getting jammed up. I guess I'll close the complaint with a white lie stating that Tao received remuneration. As to the alleged shots, I'll have to close that as unsubstantiated."

"Partner, you must have some hook and be well connected too, besides having brass balls. Some day you have to tell me all about."

Romano liked and respected his partner and felt a need to answer but his celestial guide whispered to him, *careful Michael, don't be foolish, you have a family to protect.*

"You remember my Dennis Bryan story, and you know that Stranire is now the Deputy PC, he's my rabbi, my hook. As to anything else, maybe a little of my darker side got the best of me. Let's stop at Antonio's for a slice before we go back. I'm buying."

Sam erupted with his deep-throated chuckle before saying, "I know when I'm being stroked. I'm having two slices, maybe even a whole dinner."

When they got back to the office, only Richie was present as acting supervisor. As the ranking detective, he was more or less in charge.

"You guys do any good out there?"

Mike answered for the team. "Yeah, we interviewed my Chinese complainant again and he's going to drop all charges against the bad guy. He got some money for the old damage to his house. I'm gonna spend the rest of the tour closing out all the cases as best as I can. Which boss is scheduled to be in tomorrow when we swing back in to day tours?"

"Scala is on the board but you know Fitz, he just may show up, why the interest?"

These cases will be closed without a collar and if Tony signs off on it, Fitz won't pick it apart and bitch. I just wanna cover my ass. You know Fitz and I have been tense since the Seawall case and ever since he's not one of my fans, nor do I like him."

Richie smiled and answered, "Just do a good job and there'll be no problems."

Mike sat down at his desk, pulled his files closer and got to work.

CHAPTER TWENTY-TWO

All three of the *Dinosaurs* happened to arrive at the Six Four together the following morning for the first of back-to-back day tours before they would swing out again.

Richie turned to Mike before he got through the door.

"Hey, how nice, we're all here. Since you have the least seniority in this team, go across to Suzie's and get us some doughnuts. I'll put a pot of coffee on. Oh, bring a small Half-and-Half too; I'm tired of that powdered stuff. We have to get a collection going for a mini-fridge. Thanks. I'll sign you in."

Sam chuckled, Mike grumbled and spun around and crossed the street.

After securing one dozen mixed doughnuts for the office, Mike returned to the squad room.

"Hey Richie, I'm sure that I don't have to ask, but did you guys pick up the referral 61's for our office?"

Sam quickly quipped, "To hell with the referrals, where's the bag of goodies?"

The senior cop answered, "Of course I did, that's why I get the big bucks."

"Hey Romano", Sam shouted, " the coffee should be ready by now. Bring a cup, naturally, black like me, when you bring the bag over."

"I'm putting the bag in here, next to the coffee machine", Mike retorted from the brake room.

"Come on Buddy, it's for a friend."

"I'm pouring my cup now. Better hurry before I eat all the doughnuts."

The silliness went on for several minutes before they were interrupted by the presence of Sergeant Tony Scala.

"Good morning children. You had better save me a doughnut and some coffee."

"Morning Sarge," they responded like a grade school chorus.

The sergeant poured himself a cup of java, and remarked, "Wow, real Half-and-Half. Is it a holiday or somebody's birthday?"

Sam chuckled, "Neither, its just Richie's time of the month is all. We gotta work on getting a mini- fridge."

"Okay guys, what do you have for me? Is there anything out of the ordinary?"

Each man in turn, more or less answered that there was nothing special.

As he turned to go into his office, Scala continued, "Romano, you have that look in your eye. Bring whatever case you're thinking about to my office and let's discuss it."

Mike sat in the chair Tony indicated and put some DD-5's down on his sergeant's desk before beginning to speak.

"Sarge it's like this; "Even though I closed a bunch of previous 61's with the arrest of my Chinese perp, Zen Quo Quan, I sort of re-opened each of them and closed them out again."

The supervisor leaned back in his chair and stated, "I know you must have had a reason for doing that, let's hear it."

"It's like this Sarge, the perp, Quan, has a court appearance in three weeks. He has been calling the complainant since his arrest. At that time, the ADA refused to write up anything but Criminal Mischief and Aggravated Harassment. I put that on my closing DD-5, closing out all the complaints. Just before our swing, Sam and I, met with the complainant again."

"I'll bite, why?"

"The complainant, William Tao, told us that Quan offered to make reparations for the damages if he would drop all charges. Yesterday, we witnessed the exchange at Tao's request. Here is the follow-up DD-5 regarding the whole thing. The only thing I have to do is notify the writing ADA, to notify the prosecuting attorney. The case remains closed."

Tony had listened quietly and then smiled at his detective.

"I think that it's very unusual Mike, but nobody can say you're not thorough. You have my blessing to call your ADA and make the notification."

"Thank you, Boss."

"Knowing you, I know there is probably more to the story and I don't want to hear it. Now go do some work."

"Sure thing Sarge, I'll get right on it."

Romano had just sat at his desk when a petite black female walked into the squad office. Spotting Sam, she ignored the others and headed directly for him.

Battle looked up from his paperwork, he could see anxiety in her face as she anxiously shuffled her feet in place.

"Yes? Can we help you ma'am?"

"The ladies downstairs gave me this report and told me to see the Detectives. They said to give you this."

She handed the squad's blue copy of a complaint

report to him.

"Just a minute please."

Turning around, Sam asked, "Who's up? We have a lady here who needs assistance."

Romano spun his chair around and pulled the clipboard that held the assignment sheet down. After a brief glance, he said, "According to the sheet, I'm next."

Mike stood and said, "I'm your detective Miss, please come over and sit down."

Noting the look of disappointment in her face, Sam reassured her with, "We are all one team here Miss. Even though one of us is the lead detective, we all share the same information. You're in good hands. We all work together. It's gonna be fine, he's my partner."

Slowly the woman walked over to the last desk and sat in the empty chair indicated by the detective.

"My name is Detective Michael Romano and I will be handling your case," he said as he extended his hand in greeting.

The diminutive woman took it and smiled.

"I am frightened and wish to see that person arrested and jailed, can you help me?"

Mike read her name, Marina Batiste; the complaint stated Aggravated Harassment and attempted extortion.

"Can you please tell me how this all came about?"

Romano enjoyed the pleasant sound of her voice. It sounded like a mixture of British with a Caribbean flair.

"Well you see Detective, my family is all from Barbados. I came here about two years ago. My sister, Giselle, came eight years before me. She is now a correction officer on your city prison called Riker's Island. She and my family put our money together and opened a restaurant within your jurisdiction, on New Utrecht Avenue just off the intersection of Bay 23rd Street. We called it Caribbean Flavor. It is becoming a successful endeavor at this time, through hard work and many smiles. On her time off, my sister sometimes works there also."

She paused, waiting for a response.

"Please explain just what the man in this complaint did."

She put her tiny hand on the blue report before continuing.

"Two weeks ago the man reported in here, entered our restaurant with two other black men to eat. There was nothing out of the ordinary at that time. They ate, paid for the meal and left. He returned alone two times after that and sat at a table for some time after eating both times. He just sat, speaking to nobody, and watched people come and go. When he left for the last time, we felt that he was studying our posted hours of operation."

The narration seemed to escalate in intensity as she continued, "I began to wonder why he would do such a thing and wished my sister, Giselle, was there, but she was not. I told myself that Brooklyn was not laid back like my old home but I was being foolish."

She then paused and took several deep breaths.

"Please continue."

"Yesterday, just before we closed, he returned."

"Was he alone?"

"Yes."

"What did he do to alarm you?"

"He smiled and came up to the counter, near the cash register. He then said, 'You fine ladies need a man here. It is not safe without a man on the premises. I could work here to protect you if you wish."

"Did he show a weapon or claim that he had one?"

"Yes, he lifted his shirt and showed a very large knife. I became very frightened and couldn't speak."

"How did the encounter end?"

The little woman too a minute to compose herself.

"Finally, I shouted to my Auntie in the kitchen in my native tongue, Bajan, calling her out to the front."

"Then, did she come out?"

"Yes, with a large knife in her hand and the eyes of an *obeah priestess;* if you saw her face, it might be called the look of rage. He is not from the Islands or he would have been frightened. He just smiled and looked at me."

"Excuse me what is *obeah*?"

Back home, my Auntie, Ninna was well versed in the art of *obeah.* Here in the US some people call it voodoo. She used to help people and had the title of *Madame Ninna.* The tradition and beliefs go back for generations. It is a mixture of beliefs from Africa, where our people came to the West as slaves. In Barbados, *obeah* is not exactly like the same as practiced by Hattians, but close. She tries only to use her gift for good. Some of our family members here and at home believe that the success of our business comes from *obeah.* Perhaps it does. Now I have two detectives to help."

Looking directly into Mike's eyes, she said, "You did not laugh as most Americans do. Thank you for that."

"I don't laugh at what others believe; we are all entitled to our own."

"He looked at the knife in Auntie's hand first, then smiled and said, "No need for that ladies, please think over my proposition and I will see you again in a few days. He turned and left."

The woman began to breathe rapidly.

Speaking softly, in effort to calm her, Mike said, "Miss Baptiste, we have your case now and it will be handled quickly by myself and my partners. There is no need to worry, I assure you."

"Thank you officer, I'll try not to worry. Auntie Ninna has assured me everything would be okay. Will you find out who he is and catch him?"

"Yes ma'am, we will. Do you have some time to go to another command and look at pictures with me?"

"Yes, if I can first call Auntie Ninna and tell her to ask my cousin, Ariel, to remain there until I get back."

"Was your cousin a witness?"

"No, I called her to take my place before I came here."

Sliding the desk phone in her direction, Romano said, "Please, and tell her you will be with us possibly as long as two to three hours. We will escort you back to your restaurant."

"That would be appreciated Detective, I came here by taxi."

Ten minutes later, Mike and Sam were driving Marina Baptiste to the Brooklyn CATCH unit where they had photos of every person arrested within the Borough of Brooklyn; cross-referenced to make searches easier and catalogued by category, gender, race, and type of crime.

After an hour of looking at a myriad of faces of men fitting the description of the person that had intimated the immigrant restaurateur, they struck oil.

Marina identified the photo of Rodney Wellington. His previous arrests listed assault with a knife, extortion, and armed robbery. He was currently on parole after serving two years against his last sentence.

With a good positive identification, Mike heard his

internal voices; *good work detective. Go slow, and get a high bail on him. You know what to do after that.*

"Sure do", he silently responded.

After securing whatever information was available for their subject, the two detectives chauffeured Baptiste back to her business.

When they entered the restaurant, they looked at each other and sniffed the air. It tickled their noses.

Aunt Ninna, a striking woman, seemed to glide toward them from behind the counter. Tall, she wore a full white apron. Under the apron, she wore loose flowing colorful garments. An enchanting smile and a simple, but complicated hairdo added an exotic enhancement to the tantalizing odors permeating the dining floor.

"Gentlemen, please stay a few minutes and let us celebrate the identification of the man who tried to steal from our labors." It was a gentle command.

The partners looked at each other in amazement.

Mike leaned close to Sam and commented, "Nobody called, how is it possible? She couldn't possibly know we got an I.D? Do you understand this voodoo stuff? You seem to be closer to it than I am."

With a broad grin, Sam answered in typical fashion, "It's a black thing, Eyetalians can't understand."

Mike thought, *holy crap, she's the real thing..*

Marina guided the two men to a corner table where Auntie Ninna, with the air of *Madame Ninna*, indicated that they should sit. They did and she disappeared into the kitchen.

The two detectives were left alone to discuss the possibilities of what would happen next for a few minutes before their hosts emerged from the kitchen.

Placed before them were several dishes. The ladies explained each dish and expressed the Bajan equivalent of Bon Apatite.

The men shared all; Cou-Cou, salted cod fish balls, a little heavy on the grease but delicious nonetheless. Chicken stew, that included chicken with a plethora of mysterious spices. There was also vegetables and curried goat meat that was similar to beef stew.

The two detectives ate with no more than three words exchanged between them. The partners, not wanting to insult the women, especially Ninna, ate everything It was all delicious.

After they finished, they washed everything down with ginger beer. Neither man asked if it actually contained alcohol.

After the table was cleared, Marina bought out the richest chocolate pound cake in the universe and hot tea.

The two detectives expressed their satisfaction and even promised to return when notified that a fresh order of flying fish was on the menu.

The owner refused any payment, saying it would be an insult. As they prepared to leave, they promised to call as soon as they got their man.

Once outside, armed with a photo of their perp, the detectives discussed their next move. They were working days and were not available to watch the establishment that evening. Not wanting to give Wellington a chance to return to the restaurant without their presence, they agreed that it would be best to go visit Wellington's last known residence at 1829 Coney Island Avenue and try to pick him up quickly if possible.

The partners sat in their vehicle across from his apartment for half an hour trying to determine if he was in.

The place looked seedy, possibly only three rooms above a small shop. Of particular note was the open window just above the entrance door. It was crooked and appeared as if it would tumble onto the sidewalk if the street level door was slammed shut.

Unable to determine if their quarry was at home, they left their car and went up to the building entrance. The damaged entrance door lock was useless allowing them to push the door open and enter.

The stairway to the second floor was a mere two feet inside the entrance, exposing them to potential danger if their subject decided to challenge their presence. Both detectives drew their weapons and slowly climbed the stairs.

The landing was narrow and afforded no   room to stand beside the actual apartment entrance. Each lawman plastered his back against the wall in an effort to present the smallest possible target.

Romano cautiously knocked while Sam announced, "Police Officers Mr. Wellington, we need to speak to you." There was no response after three attempts. Mike tried the apartment door. It was locked and they turned to leave.

Just as they were about to exit the building, their subject, Wellington walked in.

Instantly, each detective took hold of one of the subject's arms, and forcibly slammed him, face first against the entrance wall and handcuffing him in one fluid motion.

Detective Romano began, "You have the right to remain…."

Sam chuckled and added, "So you better shut up or my partner and I are gonna kick your ass for scaring those nice restaurant ladies. We'll take turns, it should be fun."

Their collar was frisked for weapons and contraband. They found nothing. They then dragged their catch to their sedan and almost threw him into the rear of their car.

Sam climbed in the rear and took a position behind Mike, keeping the arrestee away from the driver as prescribed by rules and regulations and common sense.

Back at the office, Rodney Wellington was locked in the cage while Mike gathered photos of similar looking men. He used a Department folder designed for just that purpose. It contained eight men including Wellington, to show the complainant. Sam prepared an arrest report in Michael's name. He signed it.

Both detectives went back to Caribbean Flavor to show Marina Baptiste and Ninna the photos. Both women picked the correct man and initialed the rear of the photo array with the time and date of their identification.

Aunt Ninna smiled and spoke in her now heavy island accent, "Detective, the spirits say that you be two good men. They be correct. We thank you."

Marina asked, "What must I do now detectives?"

Mike responded, "Nothing I'll take him downtown, lodge and book him, and write up the paperwork for his court arraignment and bail will be set."

"How much bail will it be? What will happen if he has bail money?"

"I don't know. If he makes bail, he'll be released pending his next court date."

"If he does not make bail, where will he go?"

"He will be sent to jail until the next date; either the Brooklyn House of Detention or Riker's Island."

"I hope it will be the island prison, my sister says it is sometimes called The Rock. Perhaps she will see him there."

Four hours later, Rodney Wellington saw a Judge and was charged with Attempted Robbery, Possession of a Weapon, the unrecovered knife, and Extortion. The court held him in lieu of $25,000 dollar bail.

Not able to make bail, Wellington was remanded to the Brooklyn House, pending transportation to Riker's in the morning due to overcrowded conditions. Mike told the ladies.

Unknown to Mike, while he was in court, Marina had contacted her sister, Giselle. She explained that the man she previously spoke about had been arrested and might be sent to her jail. Marina shared his name and asked her to watch for him. Giselle cheerfully agreed to be diligent.

The last workday of their set was uneventful and thankfully quiet for the *Dinosaurs*. At 4:00 p.m., the senior team swung out for two days.

***

When the senior trio returned to work, there was a telephone message from Marina Baptiste for Michael.

He quickly called her back.

"Detective, I thought that you would be pleased to know that the Wellington person is in the jail where Giselle works. My sister has told me that he is sharing a cell with a big homosexual Haitian man and he is very unhappy."

Mike was smiling as he answered, "I'm sure that it is just a coincidence."

"Auntie Ninna claims that the spirits have helped. Giselle says that dating a Deputy Warden may have helped too. Me, I am just grateful he is unhappy. We thank you. Please visit us again. You and your partner are always welcome."

Before he ended the conversation, Mike thanked her for the update and promised to visit. Then he laughed and turned to his partner.

"Sam, you and Richie are not gonna believe this. My last collar, Wellington got remanded to Rikers."

Together both cops asked, "Why is that unusual; why the celebration?"

"I'm laughing because he's sharing a cell with a giant homosexual Haitian. My complainants' correction connection seems to have arranged it."

To tease his partner, Sam loudly replied, "It seems that *Eyetalians* aren't the only ones who are connected. I'll tell you something, they might be charming and pretty but those Bajan ladies scare the crap out of me."

Mike responded, "Sometimes connections are better than ju-ju."

CHAPTER TWENTY-THREE

Months had passed when, Mike received a telephone call from Karolis Kristupas, the owner of the Albanian club in Coney Island.

"Detective Romano, I have been approached by Valdas Karaluis, the man you seek. He wishes to pay me to allow him to use my club as a place for persons to meet and make arraignments to deal narcotics."

"When was this?"

"Yesterday, about 8:00 p.m., he was alone. I told him to come back tonight and we could speak again at that time. I have a family and do not need this kind of problem. I don't know what to do."

"Give me an hour and call me back. I have an idea."

After ending the telephone conversation, the tenacious detective turned to his partner.

"Sam looks like Mr. Kristupas is about ready to do something stupid again. He asked the Albanian to allow him to deal narcotics in the club."

"How are you gonna handle it?"

"I'm going to reach out for a former boss currently with the DEA Joint Task Force. I know him from my narcotics time; he once offered me a job. Maybe I can set something up. It would be terrific if we could nail Valdas and maybe another dealer at the same time."

After several attempts to reach Captain John West, former OCCB Lieutenant in The Puzzle Palace, Romano finally spoke at length with his connection.

West would send him agent Tabor Kiev, to meet Mike at his office by 3:00 p.m. that afternoon.

Hey guy, with that name you better be fluent in Russian and whatever.

His next call was to reach out for "K", leaving a message for him with his wife Nataly, to be at the squad's office by 3:00 that afternoon to meet himself and another cop.

Knowing that he would have to extend his tour to that day, Mike reluctantly went to request permission from the only supervisor who was present, Sergeant Timothy Fitzpatrick.

"Sarge, I'm officially requesting permission to extend my tour today because I'm working with the DEA on one of my old cases. Can it happen?"

With the attitude of a snake stalking its prey, Fitz hissed, "Just how in the world did you involve the DEA and which of your cases is it?"

"Boss, it's about one of my old collars. The guy I took for witness tampering, the guy with the old New Jersey rape and kidnapping charges."

"I thought you were finished with that. What's going on?"

"He now wants to use the Armenian Social club in Coney Island and the owner, Karolis Kristupas, a good guy, to distribute narcotics. Captain John West is sending a man here to meet with me and introduce him to the club owner and I would like Sam to be with me too."

The big Irishman made a face. Mike could almost hear the gears grinding inside his head as the supervisor shuffled papers on his desk. Fitz was a political being and Mike knew it. With West's rank and position, it was almost a guarantee that Fitz would grant Romano's request.

Several moments later, Fitz looked up from his desk and leered as he spoke, "Request approved but with a stipulation, you guys have too much overtime. Downtown is complaining ; so I strongly recommend that you submit your overtime request for compensatory time off and not cash. Agreed?"

You son of a bitch, you are always looking out for your own ass. Mike responded with, "Sure thing Boss, and thanks."

When Mike returned to his desk, he found a simple message from Nataly, "K will be there."

***

Mike and Sam were having a casual discussion about how they would handle the meeting with "K" and Kristupas, when someone said, "Good afternoon gentlemen, I'm Tobor Kiev. Captain West sent me."

Mike was startled, and thought, *holy shit, this guy looks like the re-incarnation of Girgori Rasputin, the old Russian mystic and advisor to Caz Nicholas II. He should be dead because he was assassinated during the Russian Revolution around 1916.*

The undercover officer looked directly at Romano. Richie and Sam looked in Michael's direction as the apparition continued to speak.

"I'm here to see Detective Mike Romano and as the only obviously Italian looking man in the room, I assume that's you."

Romano stood, walked over to take the man's extended hand. "Yes, I'm Mike Romano, pleased to meet you. Please come into the break room."

Mike turned motioned for Sam to join them as they walked in.

Shortly, after the usual small talk, the three men got down to business, with Mike taking the lead.

"...and that's the whole story. I'm expecting "K" in at any minute."

From the next room, Richie Levy shouted, "Hey Romano, "K" is here to see you."

Mike walked to the break room doorway.

"K", it's nice to see you again. Please come in. You must meet someone who will help us both."

As introductions were made, Kiev impressed the club owner by responding in almost flawless Albanian.

"Detective Tabor, you have no accent to your speaking English and your Albanian is accented as if a Russian native is speaking. I can see why Detective Romano has you here. The man who wants to use my club is a Lithuanian. He speaks Albanian and Russian like an uneducated thug, because that is what he is."

Tabor responded, "Thank you. For this investigation, my name will be Rasputin." He chuckled and continued, "I am told that I resemble the man."

Sam interjected, "No shit my man. I've seen pictures of the guy and his own Momma would believe that you were him. Damn it you're scary looking too. Do you hide an extra gun in that beard?"

With a big grin, the agent answered, "Sometimes."

It was agreed that Rasputin, would enter the club about 6:00 p.m. and get as comfortable as he could before meeting their subject.

Once "K" made contact with Kristupas, he would assure the subject that he was ready to enter an agreement with him as long as he could bring in another man to assist, his "cousin", Rasputin. Everyone involved expected the slimy Karaluis to agree. At that point 'K' would call

Rasputin over to them.

Romano then called and requested TARU to set up video surveillance inside the club. They informed him that that they would have to their magic when the place was closed. Kristupas agreed to allow them to do whatever was necessary at 8:00 a.m. the following morning.

Having no actual game plan for the first meeting, they would wing it and demand to be partnered in.

After K and Rasputin made a business agreement with the Lithuanian, they would ask Lukas to bring some sample product the following night.

After their short meeting 'K' left the office, while the cops fine-tuned their plans.

Rasputin would be inside the club alone and wear a wireless transmitter-recorder allowing Mike and Sam to hear everything. If the meet sounded as if it was going south, the two detectives would rush in and, if at all possible, grab their subject and Rasputin.

***

At seven o'clock that evening, Rasputin had already been inside the club an hour.

Mike and Sam were outside in their auto parked in the shadow of a large semi rig, giving them some cover and yet, still allowing them to be close to the action.

"K", acting as if he was checking out the truck while he smoked, told them that all was well and the agent was engaged in a game of dominoes with three other men.

Then, he quickly spun on his heal as if spooked and returned inside.

The two detectives didn't have to wait long. The receiver inside their car began to crackle as Rasputin activated it.

Mike turned to his partner, "Here we go," and hit the recorder on the seat between them.

The first words they heard came from their quarry, "So K my friend, introduce me to this person sitting next to you and explain why he is here."

"I have thought over your offer and my cousin, Rasputin, is not only family, he is important to my club. There are times when I am not here because of my business and helping people, he will be the person you deal with. Please explain to him what we have agreed to as of this time here and now."

Valdas took some time before answering.

"My friend, if you don't know, I have a problem with a cop, Romano is his name. He is a pain in my ass. I like you, so please tell me that you are not in league with him in any manner."

"Who is this Romano?" K asked indignantly.

Rasputin began to rapidly speak in Russian. A chair was heard scraping the floor and then he continued in English, "If you have police trouble, we are not doing business with you."

Karaluis responded, "You have nothing to worry about. It is about another matter entirely. Some bitch from my village has put him on my ass with false charges. Romano is a fool like all *mussor;* they are garbage. I will deal with him."

Rasputin was next, "Okay, if you are certain, we will try it. Now down to business."

The detective team outside heard and recorded the plan proposed by Valdas. They also heard him give a sample of his product to Rasputin.

Both of the detectives giggled like little children.

The next meeting with the three men was set for the following evening. Valdas promised to bring a substantial amount of product with him.

Mike and Sam sat outside in their car and high fived each other.

"We got him. Now TARU will set up the equipment early tomorrow and we nail his ass tomorrow night."

Later, back in the squad office, DEA Agent, Tabor Kiev vouchered the sample product he had received. He completed the appropriate forms necessary to transport the material for a rapid analysis. The tape recording was also marked and vouchered; copies of both vouchers were retained by Mike for his case folder.

Romano and Battle typed out their DD-5's for the evening.

***

The following day all three members of the *Dinosaur Squad* set up outside the club for the "business meeting."

By 9:00 p.m. the meeting had gone bust. It never happened and due to a malfunction of the transmitter worn by Rasputin, the outside team never knew until it was too late.

Mike turned towards Sam and pointed, "Holy shit, there's Rasputin, he's walking down the block. We never heard anything. What the fuck happened? Sam, please cruise the block."

Mike keyed his portable and called the third team member who was watching Valdas' car, "Richie, Rasputin is outside walking. Do you see the subject?"

"Negative. What's going on?"

"Don't know yet. We're driving around the block. If he shows up and gets near his car, yell and we'll come quick. Maybe we can nail him before he leaves the scene."

"Ten-four, will do."

Halfway around the corner, the two men pulled alongside Rasputin as he walked. Slowing the car down to keep abreast of him, Mike rolled down the window and whispered, "What happened?"

In a barely audible voice the answer was, "He got spooked, see 'ya later at the office. Go."

Sam accelerated and continued around to where Richie was.

"Hey Richie, Rasputin said Valdas got spooked. Did he show?"

Pointing he said, "Nope, but there's his car."

"Hold on Sam," Mike ordered. "There's something I gotta do."

Romano walked over to the big old Ford and reached into the grillwork. There was a loud metallic, "Pop", as the hood lock released.

Mike dove under the hood and came out with a complete set of ignition wires, holding them proudly in his now filthy hands.

"He won't be able to drive away. Maybe we can find him."

Then, referring to the local command he added, "Maybe I can get Coney Island to have patrol watch the car and grab his ass if he comes back."

Richie, ever the correct, by the book detective said, "Mike, I didn't see a thing and just what are you going to do with that crap now?"

Mike responded by tying the bundle into a knot and walking over to the sewer opening on the corner, where he leaned down and said, "Night Deposit."

Sam quickly added, "Alright partner, let's get out of here now."

They all laughed and left the area.

Back in the squad office, Fitz was waiting for them.

"Romano, get in here."

Richie, as the elected union delegate for the office detectives, heard the tone of the request and followed Mike into the Sergeant's office.

"Alright, Romano, just what the hell happened out there tonight? I don't see any arrest."

"Sarge, it looks like the meet didn't go down. The DEA cop, Kiev, left the scene and told us to meet him here. I guess he's on his way."

"When he gets here, you will do a DD-5 about tonight's situation and close the case with a referral to Narcotics; that's a direct order. Do you have any questions?"

Before Mike could answer, Richie put his hand on Mike's arm and said, "Sarge, Mike understands and I give you my word as senior man and Union Delegate, that he will follows orders. Right, Mike?"

"Yes. I'll get it done."

"Now get the hell out of my office. Richie, you stay. Romano be sure to closed the damn door."

It was only ten minutes later when Tabor Kiev walked into the office.

"Hey, sorry guys for the cryptic exit at the club, but the subject got spooked and I'm not sure that I know why."

Quickly Mike asked, "How's "K". Was he there with you at the table?"

"No, he wasn't even in the building as far as I know."

"So what do you think spooked him? Did you

recover anything?"

"Nothing, and maybe he was spooked because two suits were there."

"Cops? Ours or yours?"

"Don't know. They sat alone and drank tea. Maybe they were immigration. I have no idea. Anyway, when I asked about what he brought with him tonight, he and two other guys from another table got up and walked away, heading for the rear of the building and disappeared behind the bar. I waited a few minutes and then followed their path. There was a rear door. I guess they used it. The suits never moved."

"Shit," was all Michael could get out.

Kiev asked, "What's your next move?"

"My boss, the illustrious Sergeant Fitzpatrick, ordered me to close the case as referred to narcotics. I would rather close it as referred to the DEA and you as the responding agent. Do you want to keep it?"

"I'm sure that Captain West would appreciate it. I'll call him and let him know to expect it."

"Thanks. Keep me informed will you?"

"He spoke highly of you. It was fun while it lasted. I'll personally keep you in the loop."

"Thanks. Let me do the closing DD-5, replied the very disgruntled Detective."

The team spent the balance of their tour on the mundane task of paperwork. They were about to swing out for two days and return to a day tour.

The heat in Romano's blood had been turned up by his last conversation with the bigoted supervisor, and he almost once again, went back inside to tell him what he thought.

With only a few months to go before he would be

eligible retire Mike had not given it any serious thought up until that moment; subsequently he chose to hold his tongue before he shot himself in the foot.

The end of his work day set had finally worked out to be on a weekend. He would be home like normal folks and he was looking forward to spending some time with his best friend and confident, his wife Lilly.

CHAPTER TWENTY FOUR

Lilly was waiting up for Michael when he got home. He found her propped up in bed watching a movie on TV.

Attempting a poor imitation of a Cuban accent, he tried to mimic the male lead in a popular sitcom; he stopped at their bedroom door and said, "Hi honey, I'm home."

With an impish smile, his flame haired wife answered, "Well, thank God for that."

Mike smiled broadly, as he removed his suit and answered, "Honey, I'm so happy to be home tonight, we have to have a 'conversation'. Then we can talk about something important tomorrow."

Lilly smiled in response and turned off the television.

His voice must have been too loud because from their daughter's bedroom he thought he heard, "Oh, there they go again."

Saturday, over their morning coffee, Mike shared his thoughts about possible retirement with his wife.

"Lil, remember when we were down in Florida and I spoke with your uncle Armand. He explained that disregarding overtime, I could retire with a check that was net, only a few hundred dollars less than my current monthly earnings after deductions?"

"Yes, Michael, but you love your job. What brought this on? Did anything bad happen?"

"No, nothing in particular, I'm just tired of Fitz's

bullshit. He doesn't like Italians in general and it's obvious to me that I'm the personification of that feeling. I'm about to blow!"

"That's not a very smart move. How can you be my Saint Michael if you lose your job?"

"He's not a thief like the Great Pumpkin, but just as bigoted. Last night he ordered me to give away a case I've worked on for months. I almost told him to go shit in his hat and pull it down over his ears.

Lilly tried to look concerned as she visualized what that would look like. It didn't work at all. "My, that's quite a descriptive term. You're really upset."

"Yes, I am. He's taken vacation days from me and written me up for petty bullshit. I think when I finish my Russian connection case; I'm going to put my papers in. Do you have any opinion?"

His crimson haired lover reached across the breakfast counter, took his hand and said, I only want you to be happy Michael. If you retired, what would you do?"

"Maybe start a private investigation firm. I think that would be good for me. I still could help people as usual and even get paid for it. I should be able to at least make enough to cover the few hundred dollars monthly difference that your uncle spoke about. Anything above that would be gravy. The best part is that I could only take the cases I wanted and no Fitz."

"Well, think about it and while you're still with The City, please be careful. That case you're working with the Russian mob involved is dangerous. You can get hurt. You're really no Saint Michael you know."

"Not to worry, I think I have it covered. I can always go talk with Rocco if it gets too messy."

"Whatever you want to do, I support your decision, but I think you should get Rocco's opinion on it first."

"I will. Maybe I'll call him and we could all go to dinner tonight. Now let's enjoy the week end. We don't get weekends off together too often."

***

Normally, Mike never brought his wife to meetings with Rocco. That evening, it was a celebration of sorts and the Romanos met Rocco Banducci at the renowned Peter Luger's Steakhouse in Brooklyn. Rocco, as usual, managed to impress Michael by securing last minute reservation on a busy Friday night.

What the hell, he's connected.

As they all dined on T-Bone steak with all the trimmings and excellent wine, Michael informed his friend of his decision to leave The Job.

They kept business out of their conversation until it was time for an after dinner drink. The men ordered Scotch and Lilly, her favorite, Chambord on the rocks. When the drinks arrived, Lilly excused herself.

"It's probably not safe leaving two such fine men alone here, but I must leave for a few minutes. Please excuse me."

With Lillian one, Mike finally asked Rocco for an opinion about his retirement.

"Well, Michael, you have your pension intact, and your health, along with a fantastic wife, why not retire and enjoy the many years ahead of you?"

"I'm thinking about getting a private investigator's license. What do you think?"

There is plenty of work out there for a sharp, righteous detective with balls like you. I'm sure you'll have fun. If business is slow, let me know and I'll attempt to send some business your way. You won't ever have to deal with the likes of Dennis Bryan again either. I recommend that you do it. There is also the fact that if we are ever seen together, you don't have to worry about getting fired. How good is that?"

"Rocco, it sounds like a plan, thanks."

"Oh, here comes Lilly."

CHAPTER TWENTY FIVE

That Monday morning, Mike was looking out of the window next to his desk and daydreaming. At 9:30, the telephone on his desk rang. The shrill sound brought him back to reality. On the line was a frantic Nataly Kristupas.

"Detective Mike, I need help. That crazy Lithuanian, Valdas Karaluis attacked my husband Saturday night and K shot him."

Romano was taken aback, "What did you say?"

"He came to the club and got in an argument with my husband. They argued, it got bad and they went outside to the sidewalk. They fought and "K" shot him, then ran away."

"Nataly tell me everything you can remember, slowly."

"Detective Mike, he came in about 9:00 p.m. and I think he was drunk. He yelled across the floor that K pulled the wires off his car and set him up. My husband didn't know what he was talking about. He grabbed K and that's when some men from the club grabbed both of them and were trying to separate them."

"How did they get on the sidewalk?"

She was in a such an agitated state that she answered in what Mike assumed was Albanian.

In an effort to calm her down, Romano tried to make a joke.

"Easy Nataly, take a breath and slowly tell me in English, I'm Italian and my Albanian is kind of rusty."

"Excuse me Detective Mike, but I'm so worried."

"I understand. Were there any witnesses? Where is Valdas? Did he go the hospital? Most importantly, where is the gun?"

"Yes, that crazy man was taken away by medics in an ambulance. K has the gun, he took it with him. Police came and people on the sidewalk said they do not how Valdas was shot."

The voice inside his head began speaking, *You have to help these people Michael, they're good people. Valdas is a bad person and a criminal, but think first. Do what is necessary to get justice and remember you want to retire soon.*

Mike was silent long enough for Nataly to ask, "Detective Mike, are you still there?"

Without realizing it he answered his inner voice aloud, "Yes. I will and I understand."

"What did you say Detective?"

"Nataly's question brought him back to the real the real world.

"Okay, now do exactly what I'm going to tell you. First, find your husband; next ask if he still has the gun. If he does, get me the names of the witnesses and then call me back as soon as you can. Can you do that?"

"Yes. I will call back soon. Please help my husband and thank you." The line went dead.

Romano phoned the Six Oh Squad in Coney Island.

He spoke to a Detective Schmidt, who was the case officer assigned to the incident. Schmidt informed him that the complaint was recorded as First Degree Assault with a firearm, Karolis Kristupas was designated as the perpetrator.

According to Schmidt, patrol conducted a search of the scene for a weapon with negative results. The complainant, Karaluis, was currently in Coney Island Hospital with a gunshot wound in his left leg. He would be there awhile with a chipped femur.

"Have you interviewed the complainant or any other witnesses yet," Mike asked.

"Yeah, the complainant claims that the shooter just walked up to him with the gun and shot him. Why are you interested?"

"I have a long and convoluted history with your complainant. There is bad blood between the reported perpetrator and your complainant. Your complainant is currently out on bail and the subject of one of my investigations and one with the DEA. You should run his sheet. He has an open case of rape in New Jersey too. I might have some further information for you later today. I'll call you back and thanks for your help."

The other cop was elated. "I'm swamped lately guy. I thank you in advance if you help me close this thing quickly."

Mike felt good about the conversation.

He knocked on the supervisor's door and walked in. Luckily, Fitz wasn't in, Sergeant Scala was.

"Hey Sarge, I got something going on a shooting in Coney Island over the weekend and need to re-open the case on my Lithuanian guy. He's involved and to avoid any Fitz problems, I wanted to let oyu know first."

"You know, Bulldog is a great nickname for you and fits your personality. Go ahead and I'm not even going to ask what's going on now. Just don't step on your dick. Fitz is always waiting to nail you again. Have fun."

Just as Mike finished filling in his teammates, Nataly called again.

"Detective Mike, I have the gun and witness names."

"Great, I want you to now bring me the gun and your husband as soon as you can. Can you do that?"

"Why, what will happen?"

Instead of answering her question, Mike spoke to her carefully and slowly.

Please correct me here. I'm going to repeat the facts of Saturday night as I understand them. Are you ready?"

"Yes, please begin."

"Saturday night, Valdas came to your club, drunk and started an argument with K. It ended up with a fight on the sidewalk."

"Correct?"

"Yes, that is what happened."

"Then Valdas pulled a weapon and pointed it at your husband, shouting that he was going to kill him. K jumped him and tried to get the gun when it went off. In his panic, K grabbed the gun and ran. Is that correct?"

There was dead silence for several seconds before she answered. "Yes, the gun went off while they fought. That is all true."

"Did your husband ever own a gun?"

"Yes, Back in Albania many years ago."

"Here, in this country, did you ever see him with a gun in this country?"

"No."

"Then, Valdas brought the gun, after all, several witnesses saw him point it at K. Is that correct?"

"Yes, Detective there are witnesses."

"Do you trust me Nataly?"

"Yes"

"Then bring the gun that Valdas brought with him and your husband, and any witnesses. Come quickly. I now have some things that I must do before Valdas is arrested for trying to kill your husband."

"You are going to arrest Karaluis for trying to kill my husband?"

"Yes, because that is exactly what he did."

" Thank you Detective, we will be there soon."

Romano phoned Detective Schmidt. "Hey, Romano here. Can you be at my office by noon. I'll have the gun and at least one witness to the shooting we spoke about. Your subject is bringing it in."

At 10:00 a.m. Karolis and Nataly sheepishly walked into the squad room. Nataly carried a brown bag. Inside, wrapped in a rag was a .38 snub nosed Colt revolver. They were followed by another man, a witness.

Mike brought them all into the break room and took their statements well before the noon hour.

Sam returned from the desk officer with a voucher and a request for lab analysis for the weapon. Mike vouchered it as the recovering officer with Scala signing off on it and a chain of evidence was established.

Five minutes before noon, Schmidt and Calaway, his partner arrived. Mike introduced everyone and handed copies of the gun paperwork to Schmidt. He also included copies of all his DD-5's regarding his involvement with Karaluis. He made special note regarding the New Jersey kidnaping and his constant harassing of the complainant in that case.

By 1:30 that afternoon, K shook hands with Mike and Nataly hugged him. They and their witness went home.

Detectives Schmidt, Calaway, and Romano went to Coney Island Hospital.

Valdas was found flat on his back in a snall ward, looking very uncomfortable, when he spotted Mike.

"Detective Romano, you are here to tell me that you are going to arrest "K". He tried to kill me. Who are those other Detectives?"

"No scumbag, I'm here to witness your arrest for the attempted murder of Karolis Kristupas. Detective Schmidt will inform you of your rights. Your bail will be revoked and you're going to jail where you belong. Have a nice day."

***

The following morning, Mike walked into the Sergeant's Office. Both supervisors were present.

"Gentleman, here is a request for time off, I'm going downtown to submit my retirement papers. I'll see you tomorrow night and let you know when I'm actually leaving. Thank you."

Tony gave him a man hug, and wished him luck.
Fitz muttered, thank God.

Three weeks later most of the Six Four Squad members were attending a retirement dinner in Dowd's Steak House in Bay Ridge for Detective Mike Romano. Tony Scala and Tim Fitzpatrick were also present.

As usual, all the detectives promised to keep in touch and were tipsy when they left.

Mike had arranged to take his terminal leave combined with all his vacation days. The effective date of his retirement would be July 4th, 1993.

The Detective and Lillian would celebrate America's Independence Day and his too.

Mike could hardly wait to get home and begin the celebration.

Joe DeCicco is a decorated retired New York City Detective and licensed private investigator. Originally, he attended college to practice electrical engineering.

Life circumstances decreed that he join the New York City Police Department.

Joe's writings reflect on his life personal experiences in a well-defined attempt to show that, "The Job", is not a vocation but an avocation that spans all the nuances of the human spirit.

His works show the complex personalities of those who choose to be the daily guardians of our society.

Joe has been a featured guest on American Heroes Talk Radio, San Dimas, California and Blue Line Radio, Wilmington North Carolina.

DeCicco now resides in the coastal area of Wilmington North Carolina with his wife Judy and still continues as a licensed private investigator.

If you enjoyed this novel, please comment on
www.amazon.com/Joe-DeCicco/e/B001K8EV4M

Thank you

The real Mike and Lillian shortly after their marriage
(Joe and Judy DeCicco}